LEAVINGS

A GAY MYSTERY

RIPLEY HAYES

D1522416

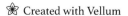 Created with Vellum

PROLOGUE

The man stood in Harriet Marston's kitchen and admired the new sunroom with its pretty rattan furniture. A little dog looked up at them from a blanket on the floor.

"Can I make you a coffee?" Harriet asked, and the man said yes.

Harriet used two of the brand new Wedgwood mugs she'd bought the day before in a smart Chester store. She hadn't had time to unwrap the rest of the china, and she was looking forward to it, and looking forward to taking her old stuff to the charity shop.

"You're thinking of a cruise?" the man asked, as she brought their coffee into the sunroom. He was looking at the brochures on the glass-topped table. He stood up to take the tray with the coffee from her and put it on the table.

Harriet's face reddened a little.

"I saw the brochures yesterday in Chester, and I thought there was no harm in looking."

They smiled at each other.

. . .

LATER, as the man carefully washed and dried the mugs, and put them away in the cupboard, he thought that Harriet had good taste. He almost felt sorry that she wouldn't be going on a cruise. He pushed the little dog out of the way with his foot, ignoring its growl, stepped over the body, and left the house.

1: FORTY IDENTICAL SUITS

Daniel Owen sat on his living room floor, comparing the relative sizes of the pile of torn cardboard, polythene, and plastic bags, to the pile of unopened boxes. He thought that the unopened boxes might still have the edge. To be fair, their contents had to furnish a spare room as well as providing enough wardrobe and shelf space for Daniel's boyfriend, Maldwyn, to move into Daniel's half-finished house. Daniel had counted the bedroom as one of the finished rooms until he saw the number of shoe boxes, suitcases, garment bags, and crates of books piling up downstairs as Mal emptied his rented home. They had bitten the bullet and made the trip to IKEA, returning with the Land Rover full of heavy cardboard boxes, and for Daniel at least, warm, fuzzy, couple-y feelings.

It turned out that although Mal could iron a shirt in less than a minute, cut his own hair, and keep his car looking pristine whatever the weather, he was completely incapable of assembling flatpack furniture. Daniel had the opposite skill set and had put together an enormous wardrobe in the big bedroom and was ready to start on the spare room. Mal's contribution had been restricted to carrying cardboard boxes full of furniture components up the stairs and making tea.

The house was a labour of love, and sanity, for Daniel. He'd rebuilt it piece by piece, learning as he went. It had been almost derelict when he bought it. No one had lived there for years, roof tiles had blown off, windows were broken, and it hadn't been that well built to start with. But Daniel had fallen for the view over the river valley, the thirteen acres of overgrown land, and the chance to get away from the horrors of his job and come home to something completely different. He told his sister Megan that it would take him the rest of his life to finish, and he was OK with that. The house was in the village of Bryn Carreg, a few minutes' drive from the market town of Melin Tywyll, where the police station sat like an alien amongst the old stone buildings.

Daniel heard the front door open, and he put the bag of screws and Allen keys on top of the boxes and stood up. Mal was, as always, dressed in black, tight jeans, even tighter T-shirt, and leather jacket. It was raining outside, and Mal brushed the raindrops from his black hair. Daniel's heart turned over.

"That's it," said Mal. "I dropped the Melin house key off on my way here. You are now officially stuck with me."

Daniel smiled. "You, and the entire menswear collection at Liberty."

"Love me, love my clothes," said Mal.

"I think the wardrobe's done, so come and see." He took Mal's hand. "There might even be enough space for all your stuff."

Mal growled and followed Daniel upstairs to view the empty and pristine wardrobes on 'his' side of the room.

"I love you, Daniel Owen," he said, and pushed him down onto the bed, wrapping his arms around Daniel's wiry form and laughing as he wriggled free.

"I should hope you do love me," said Daniel. "I've spent two days building enough space for you to hang forty identical black suits, forty pairs of identical black jeans ... don't tickle me ... stop ...." Daniel rolled into Mal's arms, loving the warmth, and the scent of Mal — peppery cologne, rain and clean clothes. He could feel Mal's arousal, and his own, but for the moment what he mostly felt was *happy*.

"MANCHESTER IN THE MORNING," Mal said as they sat in front of the fire with glasses of wine and full stomachs. The dishwasher was rumbling in the background, the clothes were mostly put away, and the other boxes were stacked in a corner.

"Buying drugs again?" Daniel asked. Mal had been on secondment to Manchester Police for several weeks.

"Giving it my best shot. So, the sheep rustling is all yours."

"Six months you've been here, six fucking months. Not one single case of sheep rustling."

"Stolen tractors then."

"Uniform has caught all the stolen farm stuff. As you know perfectly well."

"It's five months, and I've been away for most of it. You might have been keeping the sheep rustling and tractor stealing quiet."

Daniel put his wine down and wriggled along the sofa to put his head in Mal's lap. He pointed to a large cardboard box by the kitchen door. "You know what that is?"

"No."

"It's a polytunnel. A plastic greenhouse. And when you get back from trying to buy drugs in Manchester, you are going to help me put it up, and then you can help me grow things in it, and if you make one more remark about sheep rustling, I will make you come with me to a meeting of the Clwyd Smallholders' Association. Which conducts its business entirely in

Welsh. Which you understand perfectly well, whatever you say."

Mal leaned over and kissed him, and Daniel thought *I don't want to be anywhere but right here, right now.*

LATER, when they were in bed, Mal said, "I meant to tell you, when I dropped off the key to the rented house, the guy in the estate agents was called Connor. Isn't that who Hector's been seeing?"

"Sounds like him. What's he like?"

"Nice looking. But if I was the sort of copper who had *instincts,* I'd be checking up on him. I might do it anyway. You remember the bloke who came to fix my electrics when the water was dripping through the light fitting?"

"You had so many people in trying to fix things in that house ...."

"Well, anyway, the electrics bloke said not to rent anything else from those agents because they were crooks."

"I think it's a given that all estate agents are crooks. Along with journalists and politicians. And you're a senior policeman going off to buy drugs. Why was he working for them if he thought they were crooks?"

"I asked that. He said they owed him money and kept promising to pay, but they always needed one more thing doing first."

"Sounds like he should have cut his losses."

"That's what I said."

"I hope Hector's bloke isn't a crook. Hector really likes him."

"I don't suppose they are crooks. They are just more up to date than all the others, so they must be up to no good."

Daniel laughed, thinking about the contrast between the

bright, modern shopfront Mal was talking about and the dim and dusty agencies favoured by the older residents of the town.

"You should have seen the estate agents who were advertising this place. They were still gluing photographs onto typed paper particulars. None of this modern technology nonsense. The bloke who showed me round was about eighty and could tell you everyone who owned it since Noah was a lad."

Mal sighed. "Melin Tywyll moves into the twentieth century, one estate agent at a time."

2: THEY'VE STOLEN OUR HOUSE

I t was too cold and damp to go for an early morning run, but Daniel got ready anyway. It was probably going to be cold and damp tomorrow, and probably the day after that too, but he would cross those bridges when he came to them. He shivered in his thin running gear as Mal loaded his case into the car. One last kiss and it was time to go, and an hour later it was time to go to work.

The Melin Tywyll police station was a glass box, hidden behind the livestock market, totally out of character amongst the mixture of stone terraces and half-timbered black and white buildings around the town centre. By ten o'clock, Daniel had finished the weekly Domestic Abuse Conference Call and decided he needed a break, some decent coffee, and, if the bakery had any left, a cinnamon bun.

A man and a woman were standing at the reception desk when he came back in. The woman was in tears, and the man was shouting, "But they've stolen a *house!*" On the bench around the wall, a few people sat waiting their turn. Some looked fascinated, their eyes moving back and forth between the couple and the civilian clerk. Others pretended nothing was happening and stared at their phones instead. Daniel raised his eyebrows to the clerk, and mouthed, "Need help?" She nodded and Daniel stepped forward.

"I'm Detective Inspector Owen. Can I help you?"

"Thank God," said the man. "Someone has stolen our father's house, well *our* house now, and there doesn't seem to be anything we can do about it."

Daniel looked up at the big clock behind the desk. He needed to meet the new uniformed inspector in half an hour. But a stolen house? He wanted to know, even if it meant waiting for his cinnamon bun.

He asked the clerk to buzz them through the door and led the couple through to the least intimidating of the interview rooms. When they were seated, Daniel said, "Perhaps you could tell me who you are, and why you think we can help."

The woman wiped her eyes and blew her nose, and the man said, "I'm Mike Price, and this is my sister, Katherine Rees. Our father was Iolo Price. Who died in the flood."

"I remember," said Daniel. "I'm sorry for your loss." Iolo had been the only casualty of the devastating floods of the year before, his body discovered in his home, after the waters receded.

"It was a shock," said Mike, "but Dad was almost ninety, and too stubborn to move in with one of us."

Katherine added, "But it was horrible that he was on his own. I was on my way round there to see if he was OK, when the police came to say he'd been found ...."

Daniel thought about people's reluctance to say the word 'dead'.

"What about the house?" Daniel asked, because that's why they were there.

The two looked at each other, and Mike spoke.

"Dad said years ago that he'd left us everything. So, we applied for probate, and cleared the house out ... we know it all takes ages, but to be honest, neither of us needs the money."

"We've both got grown up kids," Katherine continued, "so we were just going to split the money between them, when we sold the house. Dad would have approved. Only now this company say they own the house. They've changed the locks and put up a For Sale board."

Mike produced a letter from his inside pocket and pushed it across the table to Daniel. "Our solicitor got this."

The letter was from "Daffodil Equity Release" and asserted that Mr Iolo Price had entered into an agreement (attached) to receive £100,000 in exchange for the house on his death.

"We knew nothing about it," said Katherine. "If he needed money, we'd have given it to him."

"And Dad's place is worth twice that. But our solicitor says it looks legal."

Daniel read the letter again and glanced through the agreement. The legalese might have concealed anything.

"I can see why you're upset," he said, "but why do you think it's police business?"

They both started speaking at once.

"He was an old man, vulnerable—" Katherine started as Mike said, "They've robbed us, and swindled him."

Daniel lifted his hand to slow them down.

"It certainly doesn't look fair," he said, "but I'm not sure that we can do anything about it. Let me have a chat with some of my colleagues, and I'll get back to you. Would that be OK?"

Daniel thought that there was almost nothing the police could do, and that it probably wasn't police business anyway. But it was worth a phone call to his colleagues in financial crime, because this was a small town, and it was always useful to know what was going on. He took phone numbers for both Katherine and Mike, and they left, calmer than when they arrived, Daniel walked up the stairs to the CID office and was about to take the first bite of his cinnamon bun, when the new uniformed inspector knocked at his door.

MAL WALKED out of his new home to the sound of — nothing. Except, when he made himself stand still, he could hear birdsong and the rustling of dry branches, and smell the cold, damp earth. He could see the mist lying in the river valley in front of him. Behind him, Daniel was shivering as he laced up his running shoes. The car was freezing, but it would warm up, so he put his padded jacket on the passenger seat before he kissed Daniel goodbye, and turned the engine on.

In the rear view mirror, the village scrolled out behind him, and Mal breathed out, shoulders dropping, tension easing, as he drove away from Melin Tywyll and his own inadequacies.

Daniel teased him about not speaking Welsh, but the truth was that he was afraid of getting it wrong, so it was easier to pretend. He told Daniel that Welsh wasn't his language and that he hated it. Everyone else in the office flipped effortlessly between the two, and he felt stupid. He was exposed here, in a way he never had been in a big city police force. People knew he was gay, they knew he had moved in with Daniel, and they knew that if he hadn't appeared, Daniel would be DCI, and they'd all be much happier.

Mal thought that there was no one kinder, funnier, more thoughtful, smarter or sexier than Daniel Owen, and he'd thought it from the first moment they met. Daniel had walked into the middle of one of Mal's cases and turned it, and him, upside down. Mal had seen someone tall, slender, and as graceful as a cat. A cat with tousled hair that he kept trying to smooth into place. A policeman with an overactive imagination and no impulse control. Someone who relied on intuition rather than procedure. Someone living happily in the town where he was born, where everyone knew he was gay, and whose best friend was his own sister.

Mal knew himself to be attractive, even handsome, but he also knew that he came across as uptight, inflexible, and short tempered. Someone who did everything by the book, who didn't do spontaneous, except when he was with Daniel. Mal knew that he loved Daniel, would go on loving him whatever happened. But he would never have Daniel's ease with himself, Daniel's inner confidence that he *fitted in.* So Mal was relieved to be getting away, going somewhere where people weren't comparing him to Daniel, where he could do the job and know that he was doing it well.

Only Daniel won't be there. If I miss him it will be miserable, and if I don't miss him, I'll feel guilty.

A HOTEL ROOM at Manchester Airport wasn't where Mal had expected to meet the Assistant Chief Constable, Major Crime, Dexter Harries, and a DI Andy Carter to hear about the operation to catch the boss of one of the most successful organised crime groups in Manchester. Harries stood with his back to the window, oblivious to the relays of planes taking off and landing. Inside, the room was quiet, and still, the airport belonging to another world, beyond the layers of glass, like an oversized TV screen turned to mute. Mal was silent too, as disconnected as a figure in a Hopper painting, sharing the space but nothing else.

Mal had told Daniel that he'd been seconded to work on a drugs sting in Manchester, a not uncommon role, and something he'd done before — an unfamiliar face to the local drug lords. This time was different. A few weeks to get used to working in Manchester, then he was going undercover pretending to a cop willing to change sides and get rich.

"Wade Addison has a vacancy in his organisation. He needs a bent copper, a senior one, and you'll be applying for the job."

Apart from one short stretch, when he was forced to run his business from inside, they described Addison as Teflon man. There was no form of organised criminality that Addison wasn't involved with: prostitution, people smuggling and slavery, drugs, guns, protection, gambling, car theft.

"He does his own dirty work," Andy Carter said. "People who get in his way either behave or get killed. He doesn't mess about; we just find the bodies."

Harries continued," Our problem is his legitimate businesses, and the connections he's making with politicians. He's been buying up derelict buildings and turning them into top end flats. He's buying respectability, and it's working.

"And just so that you know, the last UCO who got anywhere near him is dead."

"Addison rumbled him?" Mal asked.

"Our guy was trying to play both sides," said Harries, "to take Addison's money, and then turn him in. That's why only a very few people know about this. As far as everyone is concerned, you're on secondment to Major Crimes. God knows they need the help. There's a viable suspect for a bunch of armed robberies — nothing to do with Addison by the way — and we need him found ASAP, and I want you working on the strategy to get guns off the streets. You won't be *acting like* a member of Major Crimes, you *will be* a member of Major Crimes.

"Then you bend a few rules when you're dealing with Addison-related business and wait for Addison to try to recruit you. That's how he's worked in the past."

"How will I know if it's something I need to bend the rules on?"

"DI Carter has a list."

Mal asked whether there were any doubts over the honesty

of the rest of the Major Crimes team, the people he'd been working with while he waited for this briefing.

"None," Harries said. "After the last guy, we've made bloody sure of it. It's a good team."

"So, I'll be making myself unpopular," Mal said.

Andy Carter grinned. "If you wanted to be popular, you should have joined the fire brigade."

Harries shut him down. "Popularity is the least of your worries."

Mal was given the password for a restricted network. "Everything we've got is there," Andy Carter said, "official, speculation, and more newspaper cuttings than you've ever seen. Happy reading, and try not to be too jealous."

Why would I be jealous? There's something odd here.

3: AS IF SHE'D NEVER SEEN ONE BEFORE

Inspector Sophie Harrington looked familiar to Daniel, and she looked at him as if she felt the same way. He was sure that they knew each other but not as fellow police officers. She was tall and curvaceous, with dark, wavy hair pulled into a clasp at the back of her neck. Police uniforms weren't designed to show off anyone's figure, but she looked good, and a flowery perfume emphasised her femininity. The papers, files, bags of running gear, empty cups, and spare shirts which filled his office seemed to untidy themselves in her presence, and the computer screens developed a new coat of dust.

Then it came back to him — the LGBT society at university. In those days her hair had been a mass of wild curls, and she dressed in cargo pants and tight T-shirts. The contrast between then and now was striking. Realisation dawned on Sophie a moment later.

"It's a small world," she said, and smiled. Daniel hadn't known her well; they hadn't been close friends, but they'd been out with a big group more than once. They had also both been involved in a couple of welcome events for new gay students.

"Welcome to Clwyd police," Daniel said. "It's good to have you here."

"It's good to be here," Sophie said.

Daniel looked at his cinnamon bun, and Sophie must have seen him. "Eat it," she said. "Who knows when you'll get another chance."

He offered to share, and she shook her head. "I'm making a new start," she said. "Healthy living in a new place. I've spent far too long living off buns and bad coffee."

"That's police work. Even here."

"I can but try," she said, "but I've got to say, it's great to see a familiar face."

"Do people know that you're gay?" Daniel asked. "Because I don't want to cause you any problems. Everyone knows about me. I grew up here, small town, no secrets. And,"—Daniel blushed—"I live with my boss, DCI Mal Kent."

"*Now* I get why everyone was saying I'd get on *so well* with you," Sophie said. "Seriously, every woman in this job is assumed to be a lesbian, as if that's a bad thing, unless she's married, and even that's no guarantee. It stinks, but they still have to call me ma'am and do what I tell them." She grinned.

"Come for a walk round the town," he said, wanting to get out of the office that had become so shabby and unwelcoming. "Let me show you the sights, and I'll buy you a healthy lunch."

THEY HEADED out into the cold and damp. Daniel remembered Sophie as lots of fun and always willing to volunteer, not leave all the work for someone else. The contrast between wild-child student Sophie and ultra-neat, uniformed Sophie must be mirrored by the contrast between camp student Daniel and be-suited policeman Daniel.

"So," asked Daniel, "why the move?"

There was a pause. The chill made Daniel pull the collar up on his coat, and the taste of petrol fumes and woodsmoke, held down by heavy clouds, irritated the back of his throat.

"I guess you'd say I was tired of banging my head on the glass ceiling," Sophie said. Daniel heard hesitation in her voice, as if she expected him to deny the misogyny of the police service. He sighed and touched her elbow lightly. "Work twice as hard, get half as far?" he asked.

"Something like that. I thought that if I couldn't move upwards, at least I could try somewhere new. I was in Derbyshire before."

"You passed the Welsh test?"

"By the skin of my teeth. I started out online, but now I'm here, I've signed up for classes. I like learning languages, though I think Welsh is going to be a challenge."

Daniel smiled. "You'll be fine."

They wandered around the town square, huddled into their coats like everyone else, and Daniel pointed out the signs of the flooding six months before. Sophie said that there had been floods in Derbyshire whilst she had been there, but nothing on this scale. They stood on the bridge and looked down at the gorge, and Daniel told her about the body they had found there. He told her about the other body, in the wheelie bin at the old station.

"It's not always like that, I hope," said Sophie.

"God no," Daniel said, "busy, but this is a pretty low crime area. Drugs come in from Liverpool and Manchester, there's lots of domestic violence, and since the recession, much too much thieving."

"Crime caused by poverty and misery?"

Daniel nodded. "And made worse by cuts to everything that moves."

"But it looks so pretty."

It did. The houses along the streets they could see from the river were painted in pastel colours, cheerful even on a dull day. The canoe club slalom poles were back up in the gorge, and the worst of the debris from the floods had been cleared. Daniel pointed out snowdrops lighting up a bank beside the river, and as they strolled up from the bridge, a few gardens had their first daffodil leaves. Forested hills lined the river valley, cradling the town where a glacier had once inched its way towards the sea.

"I love walking in the hills," said Sophie, "another reason for coming here. And the sea. I've never lived as close to the sea as this. I know a lot of the coast is resorts, but it's still the seaside."

"Not much of a gay scene though," said Daniel, "or do you have someone already? Sorry, is that too personal?"

"It's fine. There's no one, but it's OK." She smiled, but Daniel thought it probably wasn't OK.

IT WAS Sophie who got the call, just as she and Daniel were finishing their lunch.

"I thought you said it was quiet here. We've got a body, and it's my first day."

This is getting to be a habit, Daniel thought. Mal had started his first day at Clwyd Police with a body too.

"Want me to come?" he asked, and she nodded.

"At least you know where it is — number twenty-five, Clos y Ddraig Goch?"

The street was part of a typical 1980s development, as out of keeping with the rest of the town as the police station. The houses were small, faced with a kind of yellowish stone, with sometimes a bit of red brick or cream-coloured render for variety, and a triangular canopy over every third front door. The McDonald's of house building; not awful, not great, but absolutely consistent. He knew what to expect as they turned into the street. Daniel had never understood why they were so popular, but they were never on the market for long.

PC Morgan stood in the tiny front garden of number twenty-five, his police car parked on the narrow street outside. He was holding a very small Yorkshire Terrier. "Ma'am, Sir," he said.

"What have we got?" asked Daniel.

"Welfare check, sir. Locksmith opened the door. Found the dead lady on the kitchen floor and called it in. A Mrs Harriet Marston, widow."

"And the dog?"

"That's what alerted the neighbours, sir. I didn't want to leave him in the house, and it's a bit cold to lock him outside."

Sophie put her hand out to stroke the tiny head. "Looks like you've made a new friend, constable."

PC Morgan blushed. "PC Morgan, ma'am," he said. "I'll get someone to take it away."

"In good time, Morgan, it's not the dog's fault. Perhaps one of the neighbours?"

"Shall we?" said Daniel to Sophie, indicating the front door, "Assuming PC Morgan has a couple of paper suits in his car."

SUITED UP, they went into the house, which was as small as Daniel had expected. Stairs went up straight out of the living room, and underneath them a shelving unit with photographs and pieces of "collectible" china. A two-seater burgundy sofa and an armchair faced the TV, and a dark wood gateleg table with chairs tucked neatly away, filled the rest of the space. The room was decorated in magnolia-painted textured wallpaper, with a mahogany chair rail and burgundy curtains. Upstairs, Daniel knew that there would be one bedroom just big enough for a double bed and a wardrobe, a separate bathroom, and another minute single room. Everything he could see was spotless. A plug-in air freshener masked the odour of death.

Next to the table, a door opened into the kitchen, and beyond that to a sunroom. And an untidy looking garden. In the middle of the kitchen floor lay a small, very still figure.

"Poor woman," said Sophie.

There was something heartbreaking about the woman, lying so unmoving on the floor, and Daniel understood why PC Morgan had called her a lady. She wore a neat, blue pleated skirt, cream blouse, and a blue cardigan to match her skirt. Daniel knew that he was overburdened with imagination, but he thought she would have hated being stared at like this by strangers. He was glad, for her sake, that her skirt covered her legs.

"I can't see any signs of violence," he said, "but my sergeant will have called the pathologist, and she'll be ringing us anytime now, about organising the house-to-house."

Right on target, the phone rang, and Daniel heard Bethan's voice. He put the call on loudspeaker.

"Hector's on his way, boss," said Bethan, and Daniel mouthed *pathologist* at Sophie, "but do you need forensics?"

"Let Hector have a look first," said Daniel, "and then I'll have a poke round the house and a word with the neighbours."

He glanced at Sophie. Her face had turned pale, and she was staring down at the body as if she had never seen one before.

4: A SMALL BUT INTERESTED CROWD

Hector arrived a few minutes later, and they went outside to meet him. Hector also stopped to pet the little dog. Daniel made the introductions.

"Hector, this is Inspector Sophie Harrington, just started today. Sophie, Dr Hector Lord, our pathologist, and one of the good guys."

Hector held out his hand to Sophie. "A pleasure to meet you. Welcome to Clwyd," he said, in his cut glass accent. Daniel gave him a nudge and looked at Sophie.

"Ignore the way he sounds, it all the fault of his upbringing. Some of his school friends are running the country, some of the others are making millions, and Hector cuts up bodies in Wales. You get used to it after a while."

Sophie smiled, her equilibrium apparently restored.

"Thank you for the endorsement, Daniel," said Hector. "Now, *is there* a dead body you want me to look at? Or shall we stand out here in the cold all day?"

The three of them went back into the house and Hector crouched down by the body, touching it gently.

"Well, I can tell you that she's dead," he said, "and that poor little dog has been on his own for far too long. I think she died sometime yesterday, probably yesterday afternoon. Rigor mortis has come and gone. As to what she died of, that isn't obvious, but I can do the autopsy tomorrow."

"Hector, mate, that doesn't help. Suspicious? Or not?" Daniel needed to know.

Hector stood up. "My gut says suspicious. There are no injuries that I can see, no reason why she should just have collapsed and died. She may have had a massive heart attack, or a stroke, but she looks to have been in good health. No evidence that she was a smoker or a drinker. I can't tell, so for what it's worth, treat it as a crime scene. But I could be wrong. It wouldn't be the first time."

"OK, I'll call the circus," said Daniel, and rang Bethan to start the ball rolling, as Hector called for the mortuary van.

"I need a list and quantities of any prescription drugs, and any over-the-counter drugs too," said Hector, "and ask them to look for a syringe."

They went outside to wait. A small but interested crowd had formed around PC Morgan, who was still holding the terrier, and starting to look cold and beleaguered.

"Give me the dog," said Hector. "I'll wait in my car." PC Morgan handed the dog over, and it nestled into Hector's fleece jacket.

"Names, addresses, witnesses," said Daniel to the constable. "I'll stay here." Sophie stripped off her paper suit and joined PC Morgan in asking the watchers whether any of them had any useful information.

It didn't take long for the crime scene investigators to arrive, along with DC Charlie Rees and two uniformed constables.

"You don't need me," said Sophie, "but before I go, did you see the sunroom?"

Daniel nodded.

"It was brand new, and so was the furniture," Sophie said. "Much more modern than the rest of the house. Better quality too."

Daniel nodded again. He said, "That's why the garden looked a mess. She hadn't had time to clear up after the installation."

"I don't suppose it's significant," Sophie said. "I just noticed. I guess it made me sad that she'd had the new room added on and hadn't had time to enjoy it."

DANIEL TOLD Charlie and the investigation team what Hector had asked for and said that he wanted to look round the house when they'd finished. Then he went and knocked on the window of Hector's car. Hector opened the passenger door, and Daniel got in, thankful to be out of the worst of the cold. The little dog was fast asleep on Hector's lap.

"He's called Bob," said Hector. "Tag on his collar. Let's hope Mrs Marston has a relative who will take him in. He's only young. And very cute."

Bob snuffled in his sleep, and Hector stroked his head.

Daniel rolled his eyes. "That dog has got everyone bewitched," he said. "Never mind poor Mrs Marston, we'll just make a fuss of the dog."

Hector poked Daniel in the ribs.

"Careful, you'll wake sleeping beauty," Daniel said. "Anything to add before the van gets here?"

"No. Healthy women don't usually just drop dead. That's really all I've got, until I can do the autopsy. Sophie seems nice."

"She is. I knew her a bit at uni; she's gay. We should meet up for a drink. Bring Connor."

"Sounds good." *But*, Daniel thought, *you've said that before, and it doesn't happen.*

"Friday? Mal should be back by then."

"Let me talk to Connor. He might have plans."

"Anyone would think you don't want us to meet him."

"I said I'll talk to him." Hector rarely sounded anything but cheerful, but Daniel thought there was a clear No Entry sign. Maybe the relationship wasn't going well. He decided to leave it for now but stick to his plan of asking Sophie to meet up for a drink.

"That's the mortuary van," said Hector, sounding relieved, as if he didn't want to be here, talking to his friend. "Let me go and see if the crime scene investigators have finished."

They had. Daniel found himself standing in the street, holding Bob, as both the mortuary van and Hector drove away, without a word.

What just happened? Why is my friend being weird?

He put the little dog in PC Morgan's patrol car. "I'll take him back with me if no one claims him," he said to Morgan. "Or you can."

Then he went back into the house and asked the CSIs if they had found anything. Not much was the answer: no signs of a struggle, nothing out of place. He was handed a stack of papers.

"Everything related to the house, all her bills and so on, plus her address book. You may as well take it back to the station — there isn't anything else. That is every bit of paper in the house."

"No prescription drugs?"

"Only paracetamol and vitamins, and no syringes. I've bagged them up. We're about done if you want a walk round."

Daniel left the stack of papers on the kitchen table and followed the CSI into the sunroom.

"This is the only place with any fingerprints that aren't from the deceased," he said.

"The guys who built it, I suppose," said Daniel, thinking that the conservatory could only have been finished for a few weeks, if that. The furniture was rattan; a two-seater sofa and matching armchair, plus a glass-topped coffee table. An attractive ceramic bowl sat in the middle of the table, and on the sofa, a library book. A folded blanket on the floor indicated Bob's spot.

"There might have been other prints, but she obviously did a lot of cleaning," the CSI said.

Upstairs, the layout was what Daniel had expected. The main bedroom had a neatly made double bed, a wardrobe, chest of drawers, and a dog basket. The dog basket held a couple of chewed toys. An elderly and much-mended stuffed rabbit was propped up against the pillows, and the chest of drawers held a photograph of a woman Daniel supposed must be Mrs Marston as a young mother, with a baby and a toddler. Two other frames also held wedding pictures, presumably the same children grown up, Daniel thought. He noticed that the late Mr Marston didn't feature.

The wardrobe held well-cared-for clothes and a small selection of shoes. A box held a pair of brand new Clark's boots. A new dark blue wool coat — still with its Marks and Spencer tags attached — hung on the rail.

The small bedroom had a single bed with a crocheted blanket as its only cover. On top were brand new toys, still in their boxes — a Barbie doll with extra outfits, some Lego models, a compendium of board games, and several children's books.

"Her papers were all in a box under the bed," said the CSI.

"And these toys? Where were they?"

"Right where they are now. Grandchildren, I suppose. Looks like she'd been splashing out a bit. You wouldn't believe the cost of those Lego sets. Ask me how I know." Daniel did know. He had a nephew and niece, and he was startled anew every time he went shopping for them. The CSI went on, "There's a couple of holiday brochures in that pile of papers — cruises. Poor lady never got to go."

"Or to wear her new boots and coat," said Daniel. They stood and looked at the toys and books for a moment. Things left behind.

"One thing that's a bit odd. She'd bought a set of china, good stuff, Wedgwood. Plates, bowls, even a teapot. It's all still in boxes in the kitchen cupboards. But there are two mugs unwrapped. They look like they've been used and washed up."

"As if she'd had a visitor and wanted to use the new things?"

"That's what I was thinking."

Then there was a shout of "Boss?" from downstairs, and Daniel turned away and went down to talk to Charlie.

5: I HATE THESE PEOPLE ALREADY

"We've talked to everyone in the street who isn't at work," Charlie said, "and one of the PCs is coming back this evening to catch the rest. Consensus is nice woman, friendly. Out walking her dog a couple of times a day."

"What about her children and grandchildren?" asked Daniel.

"Nothing much. A couple of mentions of a young man, so that could have been a son, but ..." Charlie looked through his notebook, "he was assumed to be a salesman for the conservatory."

"So, who knew her best do you think? If we have to go back and ask anything else?"

Charlie thought for a moment. "Probably the woman from that house." He pointed, then ruffled through his notebook. "Mrs Angharad Jones. Number ten. Another widow. They met up for coffee and cake every week."

Daniel heard the front door to Mrs Marston's house being closed and the rustle of a paper evidence bag. PC Morgan held out the bag. "It's all the papers, sir. They say we're done here.

Um, sir, what about the dog? We brought his basket, and his food, but where is he going?"

There was a bin bag by the front door with part of a dog basket sticking out.

"Give us a lift back to the station, Morgan, and bring the dog. Someone must be able to look after the little mutt."

"All the best mysteries have a dog, boss, though usually they don't bark. We need a dog whisperer, because little Bob is the only one ..." Charlie dropped his voice to a husky whisper, "... *who knows the truth about what happened.*"

"For that, you're in charge of finding him somewhere to stay," said Daniel, "and I might make you come and do the next of kin visits too."

CONTACTING the next of kin was urgent, thought Daniel. *We need to find out who they are and where they are.* He assumed that they were the people in the younger wedding pictures, parents of the intended recipients of the books and toys. As soon as he was in his office, he turned the bag of papers out onto his desk and looked for an address book. It was there, a National Trust gift book, with names, addresses, and telephone numbers written in a neat handwriting. Only three names didn't have surnames. One was Angharad, with a local phone number, the other two had multiple crossed out addresses and numbers. Bingo, he thought, grown up kids.

Daniel went out into the CID office with his find. Neither address was far away, so he could do one with Abby Price, and Bethan and Charlie the other.

"Find out everything you can," he said to Bethan and Charlie, "but remember that we don't know how she died yet."

Roderick Marston lived about twenty minutes' drive from Melin Tywyll, in a converted barn. By the time he and Abby arrived, the sun had started to sink, painting the clouds in shades of red and purple. They parked Abby's Ford Focus next to a dark blue Tesla. They both looked at the car and sighed. "I hate these people already," said Abby. "I fantasise about these cars."

"I bet they're rubbish in snow," said Daniel, "but you know what? I'd put up with that."

"Just keep the Land Rover for snow days," said Abby.

"Yep, all that stands between me and a Tesla is a big chunk of cash I haven't got. Come on, we're not here to dribble over a car."

He rang the doorbell on a huge, solid oak barn door, and after a moment, it opened smoothly. A man in his forties stood in front of them, and Daniel had no doubt that firstly, the Tesla was his, and secondly, he didn't deserve it. He was trying for the same look that Mal pulled off effortlessly: hair shaved at the sides and thick on top, only this man's hair was thin, and starting to slide backwards off the top of his head. He was also dressed in all black, but the tightness of his clothes emphasised his soft stomach. None of it would have mattered if he had made any attempt to look welcoming or even just not hostile.

"Yes?" he said. "We don't buy at the door."

Daniel produced his warrant card. "Mr Roderick Marston?"

The man nodded.

"May we come in?" Daniel asked.

"What's it about?"

"It really would be better if we talked inside," said Daniel, and watched as the man's instinct to refuse battled with his curiosity. In the end curiosity won, and he opened the door.

"Shoes off," he said pointing to a line of outdoor shoes.

A voice floated into the hall. "Who is it, darling?"

"Come on," Marston said, and led the way into an enor-

mous room. A barn-sized room. Daniel was sure that the archi-
tect would have talked about *volumes* and *zones*, but the single
most notable thing about the room was its size. At one end was
a kitchen big enough to serve a medium-sized restaurant, with
a breakfast bar backing onto a dining table with seating for
twelve, an acre or so of empty space, and then a gigantic sofa
curved around a vast stainless steel and glass wood burner.
They were not invited into any of these spaces. Instead,
Marston stood just inside the door. He was joined by a woman
whose expression was as dissatisfied and unpleasant as
Marston's own. Daniel hoped she was his wife, remembering
his mother's comment that *either one of them would spoil another
good couple.*

"You might want to sit down," said Daniel. He saw that the
woman looked worried, and liked her a bit more, but Marston
said, "Get on with it."

Daniel looked at Marston and said, "I'm sorry to have to tell
you that we found the body of a woman in your mother's house
earlier today. We are provisionally identifying her as Mrs
Harriet Marston, your mother."

"Provisionally? What does that even mean?"

Well at least he's consistently nasty.

"We are sure that the body is that of your mother, but until
we have a formal identification, ideally from you or your sister,
we can't be one hundred percent certain. Would it be possible
for one or both of you to come to the hospital in Wrexham
tomorrow?"

"What did she die of?"

"We don't yet know, sir. We are hoping that a post-mortem
examination will tell us more. May I ask when you last saw
your mother, Mr Marston?"

Marston looked as if he didn't want to answer, but the
woman said, "It would have been before Christmas wouldn't it,
darling? For our meal?"

Daniel could feel Abby beginning to smoulder beside him. "You didn't see her at Christmas?" she asked.

"Oh no," the woman answered, "we always go skiing over Christmas and New Year. We see all the parentals before we go. Take them out for a meal. We went to Bistro Castro in Melin. Lovely place."

Daniel had been there. Once. The music was loud enough to prevent conversation and the food had been cold. But the chips arrived in trendy buckets, and the entrées sat marooned in the centre of enormous and heavy "platters". He didn't think it would last long.

"What time in Wrexham?" asked Marston. "I've got work to do."

"What sort of work do you do, sir?" Daniel asked in his mildest voice.

"Sales. What time?"

Daniel decided that he'd had enough for one day, suggested nine am and prepared to leave.

"We need the house key," Marston said. "When can we get it?"

"We can discuss it tomorrow. I'll see you at nine." He pulled the hall door open and held it for Abby. As they left, Daniel said, "Thank you for your time, sir," but the door had already closed leaving them standing back in front of the Tesla.

"I want to run my keys down his paintwork," said Abby. "I guess you won't be asking them if they want the dog."

"I wouldn't inflict them on the poor creature. Let's hope the sister is more pleasant."

She wasn't. At least not according to Bethan.

6: VICTORIAN IDEALS

Mal looked at himself in the hotel mirror as he tied the bow tie. *Not a hair out of place,* he thought. He'd told Daniel that this dinner, an awards event for 'Designing out Crime', was about bonding with the rest of the drugs team. The reality was that Wade Addison would be there. He wondered at his own ability to lie to Daniel, to not tell him about the potential for the job to go wrong, for it to go on for longer than the few weeks he'd told Daniel he'd be gone.

Daniel had said it would give him time to finish the bookcases. Mal had put his arms round Daniel at that, looking into his soft blue eyes, feeling the wiry muscles covering long limbs, imagining the tattoos of trees, birds, and squirrels around Daniel's biceps, Daniel in his running clothes, hot and sweaty .... Daniel had laughed at Mal's made to measure dinner jacket, and in turn Mal had pointed out that Daniel had a custommade wetsuit. We laugh a lot, Mal thought. *I should be able to tell him the truth.*

Mal told himself that he kept things from Daniel to protect him, to stop him from worrying. He hadn't told Daniel the full story of his year-long struggle to bring Ethan Maddocks' rapist to justice, back when he worked for Glamorgan police. Sex worker Ethan had killed himself after being assaulted in a police cell, and Mal refused to let it be covered up, or the officer who did it be let off with a warning. Mal hadn't been able to hide the way his colleagues treated him — with overt hostility and finally violence. But he hadn't told Daniel about the endless harassment from senior officers who wanted the issue to go away, or his efforts to find and help Ethan's friends. It had been a miserable, lonely year, and Mal had made it worse by ending his relationship with Daniel almost before it had started. He had a second chance, and he didn't trust himself not to blow it.

MAL's first impression of the Great Hall in Manchester Town Hall was of polished wood and glittering lights. He ran his fingers over the door frame and found it as smooth as glass. Every table had a candelabra, and chandeliers hung from the painted ceiling. Arched windows reflected light back into the room, off the glasses and silverware on pristine white table-cloths. Everyone around him was dressed up to the nines and holding glasses of champagne. Chattering voices bounced around the huge space. The scents of perfume and cologne filled the air.

He found his place card, on a table amongst a slew of senior officers and their wives. He needed an excuse to meet and talk to Wade Addison, and ideally his Council buddies. But there must have been over 200 people in the room, all the men dressed in dinner jackets, and the women in formal gowns. Mal set off to circulate, pretending to look at the murals painted on the walls. He was in front of *The Trial of Wycliffe* when someone spoke,

"The policeman looks at the trial, eh?"

Mal looked round and hoped the shock didn't show on his face. He'd see pictures of Wade Addison, and this was the man himself. What the pictures didn't show, was that at first glance, Wade Addison looked like Daniel would look if he was wearing a DJ and had neat hair.

"I'll be honest," Mal said, "I'm not a hundred percent sure that I remember who Wycliffe was. Something to do with translating the bible?"

"Spot on. Also said to have inspired the Peasants' Revolt, and an advocate of poverty for the clergy. The murals are supposed to represent Victorian ideals, so it's an odd choice, the Victorians not being big fans of poverty."

Addison smiled and held out his hand, "Wade Addison," he said. "My company is up for an award."

"Maldwyn Kent, here with Manchester Police." Mal said how impressive he thought the Town Hall was, and the floodgates opened. Addison pointed out the columns holding up the vaulted ceiling, and talked enthusiastically about the engineering, and the materials, the acres of leaded glass, the ways the murals were painted, and he was as charming as Mal had been told. It was hard to reconcile this enthusiasm for architecture with someone who killed people and made money from misery. Mal allowed himself to be charmed, a task made much easier by Addison's resemblance to Daniel, the two of them chatting until dinner was announced.

After dinner came the speeches — an interminable flood of self-congratulatory back-patting. Addison didn't win an award but got a special mention. Mal saw one of Addison's tablemates lean over to commiserate, and the officer next to him said, "That's Councillor Terry, the main bloke in the Manchester First group on the Council." Terry was everyone's image of a corrupt councillor. Red faced with droopy jowls, thinning hair, ill-fitting suit, hand superglued to his wine glass. As Mal watched, Terry moved close to one of the women at his table, pressing his thigh into hers. She moved away, too polite to tell him to get stuffed.

All Mal wanted was to get back to the hotel and talk to Daniel, but there were still more speeches to endure. He excused himself and texted Daniel from the gents (marble, dark wood, brass, fluted columns, more leaded glass), staying as long as he dared. By the time the speeches were over, Councillor Terry looked too drunk to remember his own name and all the women on the table had moved somewhere else.

Addison caught Mal's eye across the room and gave a "What can you do?" shrug.

Mal shrugged back. He'd had enough. He'd met Wade Addison and that's why he was there. All around him, people were getting drunk, and he wanted no part of it. He'd spent the day coordinating the search for their armed robbery suspect, Declan Hughes, and trying to get up to speed with everything else on his desk. He went back to his hotel and talked to Daniel, carefully not saying anything about his assignment. Tomorrow, he thought, I'm going home, even if it does make me feel like a loser.

DANIEL LAY on the sofa in front of the wood burner, staring into the orange flames, empty plate on the floor beside him, waiting for the phone to ring. He imagined Mal in a grubby warehouse, or a cold car park, waiting to meet someone who wanted to sell a shipment of cocaine, or heroin. He made a convincing drug dealer Daniel thought, but that wasn't doing much for the ache between his legs. He thought how easy it had been to get used to having lots of good sex.

Mal didn't ring until Daniel was in bed.

"Sorry," he said, "these people are like vampires. Only come out at night."

"How's it going?"

"Slowly. But I'm coming home tomorrow, even if it's just for the night."

Daniel sighed. He didn't mean for Mal to hear it, but of course he did.

"Hey, we agreed this was for the best," Mal said.

"I know. It's just that the bed seems empty and cuddling a pillow doesn't do it for me."

Mal laughed. "If you only knew. I've been listening to people in the next room having sex. One of them was louder than you."

"That isn't helping," said Daniel. He had an all-too-clear picture in his mind of Mal, naked, muscular, and deliciously hairy, next to him in bed, running his hands over Daniel's body. Daniel stroked himself, imagining it was Mal's hand. This time his sigh was more of a moan.

"Are you ...?"

"Yes."

"Then let me get out of my clothes and I'll join you."

Daniel heard rustling and Mal said, "Did you have a good run today?"

"Yes. Why?"

"Jockstrap under your shorts?"

"Too cold. Tights and shorts. Didn't need a jockstrap, my balls were hiding from the weather."

"That skinny running top with the long sleeves?"

"Are you getting off on my running gear, Maldwyn?"

"I love it. When you get back all sweaty, and tired, and peel it off in the bathroom. Especially the jockstrap."

"You like me all sweaty?" Daniel had stopped caring what Mal was saying. He had his eyes closed, stroking himself and listening to Mal talking, knowing Mal was doing the same.

"I want to get in the shower with you and give you a good wash. Behind your ears, between your toes, lots of soap in your hair, so you have to close your eyes ... so you don't know which bit of you I'm going to wash next ...."

Daniel could feel the warm water, could feel Mal's hands, and he shivered with pleasure.

"It's what I think about all the time," said Mal, "you with no clothes on, at my mercy and loving it."

"Fuck yes," said Daniel and felt his orgasm building until it crashed over him and left him vibrating sweetly, listening to the same thing happening to Mal at the other end of the line.

7: SPENDING OUR INHERITANCE

Mal fell asleep after talking to Daniel and them woke unwillingly at three am. Despite everything, he'd enjoyed his brief chat with Wade Addison. Probably because he looked a bit like Daniel, but also because his enthusiasm for Victorian Manchester was infectious. Mal didn't know the city, but he'd noticed the streets of nineteenth century buildings and the Town Hall was the icing on the cake. He woke up his laptop and scrolled through pages of fabulous old warehouses and civic buildings, and then looked again at the information DI Andy Carter had given him. Addison was beginning to make a name for himself as a developer of old Manchester buildings. Mal read newspaper reports about *Bringing the past to life* as well as complaints that the city didn't need more expensive flats. He finally fell asleep over a brochure advertising *City Centre Loft Living*.

DANIEL DROVE over to the hospital in Wrexham to find both Roderick Marston and his sister, Jennifer, waiting to identify their mother. They didn't seem any fonder of each other than they had been of their surviving parent. Roderick simply nodded and said, "Yes, that's her," with no sign of grief at the sight of his mother's body. Daniel asked them to meet him at the station in Melin Tywyll later, and they agreed with the bad grace that he realised was their default setting.

Daniel's own parents lived in Spain, so he didn't see them as much as he would like. His sister was his closest friend. He couldn't help feeling sorry for the Marstons, but it didn't make him like them any more.

He would have told Mal all about the Marstons, their sneering faces, their too-loud voices, and the way they dismissed him by turning away without a word. He would have described the over-large barn with its empty space, and they could have been outraged together that Roderick and Jennifer left their mother in a tiny house with cheap furniture and no car. Daniel loved those conversations, the sharing of the day's events, while they cooked or ate together or cuddled on the sofa in front of the fire, listening to the wind outside.

Except it's only been six months, and I managed perfectly well before.

He gave himself a shake and went in to see Hector to try to find out why Harriet Marston had died.

"Did you find any prescription drugs?" Hector asked, and Daniel shook his head.

"Only paracetamol, some generic vitamins, and no syringes."

Hector nodded. He was the same rather subdued Hector that Daniel had seen yesterday. Under normal circumstances, Hector was bouncy and bright, loving his job and always ready to torment Daniel about Mal, or commiserate with him about work or weather. They met regularly outside work, only not for weeks, Daniel realised. He was about to say something when Hector grunted. "That's it," he said, "that's what I saw yesterday. Come and look."

Daniel moved closer. Harriet Marston's clothes had been removed and bagged up, but Hector was pointing to a tiny red spot on her neck, something he could have seen when she was still dressed. "And here," Hector pointed to another red spot on her upper arm.

"I think they are injection sites," he said. "The one in her upper arm could be anything — flu jab maybe, although it would be very late — or vitamin B12. But this one in her neck is strange. I'll excise them and we'll see."

The rest of the autopsy proceeded without much talk, Hector speaking into the microphone about his findings, but that was all. So, Daniel stood quietly too, watching Hector work and wondering why his friend seemed so subdued.

Autopsies weren't fun, but they bothered Daniel less than they bothered many of his colleagues. What upset Daniel was the thought of people suffering. Once they were dead, they couldn't suffer any more. They never became 'the body', they were always people to Daniel, but his imagination tortured him with the moments before death, the knowledge that death was coming, unwelcomed and terrifying. The day before, Hector had said that Harriet Marston had *collapsed and died* which implied suddenness and no time to suffer. He hoped that was what had happened. Then he started worrying about the little dog, whether Bob had seen his mistress's death and how he'd been affected.

"Stop being ridiculous," he thought. Only Hector looked up, and Daniel realised he'd spoken aloud.

"Me, not you," he said. "I realised that I was worrying about Bob the dog having seen her die."

Hector smiled, and Daniel felt better.

He can still smile, then.

"Come and have a coffee," Hector said, "I'm about done. You can tell me about Bob."

HECTOR HAD a kettle and a coffee pot in his office. He poured Daniel a cup. Hector's coffee was one of his superpowers, rich and strong, the smell enough to give caffeine addicts a buzz.

"I think she was murdered," Hector said, "but it will be hell to prove. In fact, I'd be surprised if you can prove it at all, unless the murderer comes into the police station with a written confession."

"Great," said Daniel. "Tell me more helpful stuff."

"Harriet Marston died of a heart attack. Sudden and massive. She wouldn't have known anything about it."

"But?"

"But I think someone gave her an injection of insulin, probably when she was unconscious."

Daniel's confusion must have showed on his face. Hector picked up a pencil and scribbled as he spoke.

"I know, right? It sounds mad, and maybe it is, but if she'd been given a powerful anaesthetic, and I'm thinking Ketamine," Hector drew a big letter K, and a series of lines and circles, "because my colleagues tell me that there's a lot of it about just now, then that would cause unconsciousness. Ketamine can cause cardiac arrhythmia." He drew a heart shape with the four chambers, veins and arteries. "And in that case, insulin could cause sudden death. But it's vanishingly rare. The blood tests will take forever to come through, and it's quite possible that they won't show anything. The heart attack is as clear as day." Hector drew arrows pointing to the heart. "Most pathologists would say *old woman, heart condition, problem solved.*"

"Only you aren't most pathologists?"

"I saw her house, and her fit young dog, and the contents of her food cupboard. She didn't smoke, she didn't drink, and she was in good shape. No osteoporosis, good muscle tone. She could have had a hereditary heart condition, and I'll need to find that out." Hector drew a question mark next to the heart. "If she did, then game over. If not, I'm sure she was murdered." He drew some more arrows on his pad.

"So, what you're saying is that I should investigate her death as murder, only there's almost no chance of proving it medically."

Hector nodded. "Sorry about that."

There was silence while they both thought about the impossible task.

"At least while Mal's away, I'm in charge," said Daniel, "so I can have a nose around. I'll give it a couple of days and then we'll see."

"Tell me about Bob the dog. Did you find him a new home?"

"I did. And I'll tell you where if you agree to bring Connor out for a drink at the weekend."

Daniel saw Hector's face close down. He reached over for Hector's hand. "You OK, mate?" he asked. Hector pulled his hand away, pretending to need it for his coffee cup.

"I'm fine. Tell me about the dog."

It wasn't fine, but Daniel didn't know what to do about it.

"Sophie," he said. "Sophie's taken the dog. We'll have to ask the awful relatives, but for now, Bob is staying with Sophie. She's looking for doggie daycare. It's really sweet."

Hector smiled, though Daniel thought his heart wasn't in it. But he had to go and start investigating a murder they couldn't prove had happened.

～

DANIEL HAD an hour before his appointment with the younger Marstons and wanted to go through Harriet Marston's papers before they arrived. Harriet had been as ruthless with her paperwork as she had been with dirt; she had kept a year's worth of her utility bills and bank statements, no more, neatly clipped together. They showed someone living frugally, on a small pension. Daniel wondered whether she had been getting everything she was entitled to, because it was a *very* small pension. He made a note to find out. He also wondered where the money had come from for the sunroom, and the new clothes, toys, and dinner service.

The answer was in the latest bank statement. A deposit of £80,000 from Daffodil Equity Release. He ruffled through the rest of the papers and there was the same agreement that he'd seen the day before — a lump sum in exchange for the house on Harriet Marston's death. He quickly googled house prices for places like Harriet's and wasn't surprised to discover that they started at over £160,000. Daffodil Equity Release were going to do well.

The rest of the papers held no more surprises. There was an invoice for the sunroom, and a receipt showing that it had been paid. There were brochures for cruise holidays, and an application form for a special offer store card from Marks and Spencer.

Daniel felt a wave of sadness wash over him. Harriet had been robbed of the chance to enjoy her modest injection of wealth, to wear her new coat and boots, to give her grandchildren some toys, or to have the pleasure of deliberating about which cruise to take. He said as much to Bethan, expecting her to agree. Instead, she rolled her eyes. "You are too soft for this job, boss," she said.

8: IT'LL NEVER STAND UP IN COURT

Daniel felt even sadder for Harriet when he and Bethan met Roderick and Jennifer. Maybe she had been a terrible mother, but surely the woman everyone described as friendly and pleasant didn't deserve these two. Daniel took them to the soft interview room and ordered tea and biscuits. He was hoping to find out more about Harriet, but instead he found out far too much about Roderick and Jennifer. Roderick began by demanding the key to his mother's house.

"Because we need to get it cleared out and sold. No point in hanging about."

"Not that it's worth much," said Jennifer, "but it will help with school fees, and god knows Mum did little enough for her grandchildren."

Daniel thought of the toys and books on the spare bed.

"I'm afraid that the house has been sold already," he said. " Or rather, not sold exactly, but your mother transferred it to an equity release company. I'm sure you will be able to remove your mother's things." He showed them the agreement and waited for the explosion. It didn't take long to arrive.

"This is outrageous. Mother was obviously duped." This from Roderick.

"I thought she was starting to go gaga before Christmas. She'd got Alzheimer's." Jennifer.

"Eighty thousand pounds? It's a joke. This'll never stand up in court."

"Mum wanted us to have the house."

And so on until they had exhausted every possible explanation for why their mother had signed the agreement, except for the simple one that she needed the money. Both Roderick and Jennifer had flushed red in their temper, rendering them even less attractive.

Daniel said, "I don't think your mother had a lot of money. In fact, she was entitled to a bigger pension. I looked it up. She seems to have been living pretty much hand to mouth." He didn't care that he had taken sides. He'd seen Roderick's house, his car, and Christmas skiing holidays didn't come cheap. Nor did school fees.

"She should have consulted us before gambling away our inheritance," said Roderick. Daniel saw Roderick had begun to sweat, and for a moment he smelled the unpleasant odour of stress. He wondered how badly Roderick had needed his mother's money.

"It wasn't hers to give away," said Jennifer.

"Didn't she own the house?" Bethan asked with her blandest expression. They all knew that she did.

"Technically," said Jennifer, "but it was supposed to come to us. We should be getting more than eighty grand. Way more. She had no right."

Daniel knew that it was wrong to *want* to tell them that it wasn't going to be eighty thousand, that some of the money had already been spent. But he did it anyway.

"God," said Jennifer. "I thought it couldn't get any worse."

It was fun to bait them, but Daniel wondered again how

much the siblings were relying on the money from their mother's house. They looked well off on the surface, but perhaps looks were deceptive. If the house had sold for its true value, they would each have inherited a decent sum, enough to give them a motive for wanting Harriet out of the way. He asked them both when they had last seen their mother.

"I told you last night," snapped Roderick, "before Christmas. Jennifer was there too."

"And when did you speak to her last?" Daniel asked.

"Christmas Day, I suppose," said Jennifer. "The duty call."

"So, you were neither of you close to your mother?"

Two pairs of eyes looked at Daniel as if they didn't understand the question. Jennifer answered.

"She had her life, we have ours."

"Your mother had a dog, Bob," he said. "Were either of you planning to take him?"

Their expressions gave him the answer. They had both clearly forgotten all about Bob, and if forced to take responsibility, would dump him at the nearest dog rescue. Sophie would be keeping her new companion.

"You've both been very helpful," he said. "Before you go, could you tell me where you were the day before yesterday? Say from lunchtime until midnight?"

The reactions were predictable. More outrage, this time directed at him. So much anger must be exhausting, he thought. Daniel kept asking until he had some sort of answer. Both siblings claimed to have been at home with their spouses. As alibis they were worthless, but there was nothing to say they were lies either.

They can be vile and still be telling the truth.

"Well, aren't they the delightful pair," said Bethan as they made their way back up the stairs, after escorting Roderick and Jennifer out of the building. "Her husband is actually OK, tried to offer us a drink when we went last night, but she stopped him."

Daniel asked Bethan if she'd wondered about how much Roderick and Jennifer needed money. She nodded. "I'll get Charlie on to it."

He'd already told the team about the inconclusive autopsy. "We can't afford to put too much time in," he said. "It's not like we're short of work."

"Sure, but that Daffodil lot are going to make a mint. Isn't it worth having a look at them, too?"

"If I get some of my paperwork cleared," he said.

"You can always run it past the DCI," said Bethan, knowing full well that Mal would be up to his eyes in Manchester.

"I will ring Hector to see if he knows any more, and I'll make an appointment with Daffodil, but the rest of my day is all reports. You can look at the house-to-house to see if there's anything new, and Charlie can look at Rod and Jen. The DCI is away, *and I'm not bothering him with this.*"

"Boss."

If Daniel was honest, he *did* want to look into Harriet Marston's death. He believed that Hector *had* seen something suspicious, but he also believed Hector when he said his suspicions would be difficult to prove. *A couple of days won't hurt though*, he thought.

HECTOR RANG to say that he'd been in touch with Harriet's doctors. "No history of heart disease," he said, "which doesn't mean she didn't have heart disease, only that she'd never gone to the doctors about it."

"No further forward, then?" Daniel asked.

"The thing is that the combination of drugs is so rare. But

there were two injection sites. Someone must have been there to give those jabs."

"Bethan's looking at the house-to-house. If there's a witness, we'll find them," Daniel said with a confidence he didn't feel. He made a note to check the house-to-house for any sighting of Roderick or Jennifer.

Then he made an appointment with the manager of Daffodil Equity Release. The sun was shining outside, and the sky was a bright blue. He knew from his morning's run that it was an illusion — the temperature was barely above freezing, and there was an evil wind that cut through any garment. He pulled the weather app up on his phone, and noted the "0 degrees, feels like -5" and sent a screenshot to Mal, with the caption *But it looks lovely. Better than Manchester, I bet.*

The answer came back straight away: *perfect sheep rustling weather :)*

DANIEL MISSED Mal but didn't miss having him as a boss. Mal's substantive post was to run Melin Tywyll CID. That had been Daniel's job in all but name, until Glamorgan Police had needed to somewhere to move Mal to before his honesty could cause them any more trouble. Their compromise was that Mal took every secondment on offer, which suited them both. Mal got travel and variety and Daniel stayed at home where he knew everyone, like the spider in the middle of his web, senses attuned to every vibration. It wasn't the first time Mal had acted as an undercover drugs buyer for another force, and he'd also been involved in an anti-corruption investigation. How long they could continue this way, Daniel didn't know, but for now, it was working. Except that he missed Mal.

He sent another text: *Miss you x*

9: WEARING AN AUBURN HAT

W*hat new fuckery is this?* A bright pink sticky note had been left in the middle of Mal's empty desk in the Major Crimes office. It read "HGV theft - see email." An email from the Superintendent apologised for dumping the case on him but hoped that he could get it sorted out ASAP, because the Police and Crime Commissioner was getting pressure from the local Road Haulage Association, who were getting pressure from their members.

Mal read through the files, all of which were reported thefts of commercial vehicles carrying high value goods. In most cases the goods had been removed from the vehicle while the driver had been asleep or absent. But there were a significant number of reports of the vehicle itself being stolen, and of these, Mal noted, building supplies made up the majority. But nothing tied the thefts together. Some were from motorway services, others from depots, yet others where drivers had been duped by fake police officers. In most cases the drivers were unharmed, in others left tied up or drugged. In every case, the vehicle was recovered, without its cargo. Except ....

Mal's policeman's instinct, the instinct he always denied

having, was stirring. He started searching for thefts of building materials. Most were thefts from building sites. But in the last few years, thefts from warehouses and delivery vehicles had increased steadily. *Correlation is not causation,* he told himself. He made a lot of notes, marked up an A-Z of the city and began working on a spreadsheet.

A DCI SHOULDN'T BE SITTING in a comms van staking out a suspected brothel, though Mal thought that it made a change from a sandwich at his desk, reading reports about the continued non-appearance of missing armed robber Declan Hughes. DI Andy Carter told Mal that Councillor Terry used the brothel regularly, and that Mal should let him "escape" in the raid, building up his persona as a copper prepared to bend the rules. Technically, the observation was for the arrival of more trafficked women.

It was an ordinary residential street in a pleasant Manchester suburb. Mal couldn't equate the charming man he'd met the night before with someone who thought it was OK to make money this way. He could see Wade Addison as the owner of the house, but not as the owner of a brothel.

"Here we go," said one of the guys on the cameras. "Incoming from our right."

A car pulled in to the kerb in front of the house. Two men got out, and one of them opened the back door, gesturing to the passengers. Three exhausted-looking young women scrambled onto the pavement, each carrying a small bag. The two men escorted them into the house.

"Let's do it," Mal said.

Because Andy Carter had insisted that this was one of Addison's brothels, Mal authorised the release of all the men, including Councillor Terry, discovered with his trousers round his ankles and far too much pale flab on display. One of the officers commented that he'd seen better looking pork scratchings.

Eyebrows were raised that Mal didn't arrest the clients. He said that the men had been humiliated by uniformed police seeing them naked and afraid, and anyway, who needed the paperwork?

Andy Carter had expected Mal to let the women go too, because they were *property*, *assets*, not free humans with rights. But Mal wasn't returning them to a life of slavery, so he'd been in touch with a charity for trafficked people before the raid, and they were waiting in the wings. The women weren't part of his deal.

That's enough favours for one day.

Mal went back to his spreadsheet and his A-Z. His phone pinged with a text and he picked it up expecting Daniel. Instead, it was the electrician from his old house, the one who'd complained about not being paid. There was something he wanted to talk about. *Later*, he thought. The guy had probably found out he was a policeman and wanted help getting his money. His brain connected the electrician to Hector's new boyfriend, but he told himself to leave it alone. Not all estate agents were crooks.

DAFFODIL EQUITY RELEASE had an office in a building that had once been a bank, on Melin Tywyll High Street. Daniel couldn't remember which bank, so many had closed over the years. The building was one of his favourites; four stories, built of heavy blocks of dressed stone, with big, mullioned windows and a large oak front door in a tall archway. The door was open, leading into a modern hallway and what should have been a grand staircase. Fire regulations meant it had been closed in with cheap panelling, painted an uninspired pale green. A list of the building's tenants showed that Daffodil's office was on the top floor. As he climbed, his phone pinged with a text from Mal: *Miss u too xx*

Daffodil Equity Release's manager had the unlikely name of Barry Kettles. Daniel suspected that he was the only employee, or at least the only one in this office, which appeared to have been converted from a broom cupboard. There was room for a desk, a filing cabinet, and a chair for visitors. All of it had seen better days. The only daylight came from the glazed panel in the office door.

"It's mostly somewhere to get mail," said the man behind the desk, as he saw Daniel's look of bemusement, "and to keep our paperwork."

"You visit your clients at home, then?" Daniel asked, once they'd done the introductions.

"Most of them are elderly. It's better for everybody if I go to them."

Kettles himself was one of the ugliest men Daniel could ever remember having met. His face was compressed, so that it was all horizontal lines; wrinkles across his forehead, then straight dark eyebrows, meeting in the middle, more wrinkles radiating outwards from his nose, and a curiously flattened chin, looking as if it had been pushed upwards into the rest of his face. Kettles' hair was cut very short, grey around his ears and the front of his head, but the rest was the kind of ginger that must have made his life a misery at school. The red and the grey didn't blend in together, instead it was as if Kettles was wearing an auburn hat on his grey hair. Then he stood up and came round the desk to shake Daniel's hand, and Daniel saw that the ugliness didn't matter. When Kettles smiled, his face changed. Somehow, he communicated that he was *interested* in what Daniel had to say, *interested* in Daniel. Daniel had seen Mal transform in the same way with a witness or a suspect, to look and talk as if he *understood. This man would be a good salesman,* Daniel thought, *especially for older people who might be lonely.*

Kettles looked at Daniel. "I'm guessing you're not here because you're looking for equity release," he said.

Daniel smiled, thinking how much was outstanding on his mortgage.

"I think I'd need some equity first," he said, "No, your firm's name has come up a couple of times recently, and I wanted a bit of information about how you work. There's no suggestion that you've done anything wrong."

Kettles made himself comfortable behind the desk, and turned on his sales face, and Daniel prepared to listen.

"Equity release gets a bad press. But we offer a service that people need. There you are stuck in a house you don't want to leave, that you've paid for, but you haven't got enough money to renew the heating or get double glazing. I'm not ashamed of what we do. It makes people happy."

"I'm sure," said Daniel, "but how do you know who might need your services? And are you a national firm, or just in this area?"

"Different ways. Leaflets, advertising. I'm not concerned with that side of it. I just get given a list of leads and follow them up, but only round here."

"And if someone wants your service, do you do the legal work?"

"I organise the valuation, check that the client actually owns the property, work out how much of a lump sum we can offer, and stay in touch with the clients, make sure they know what's happening. The legal agreement is standard, we just fill in the blanks. We tell the clients to show it to their own solicitor."

Kettles leaned back in his chair and spread his hands. *Nothing to hide.*

"So, every case is the same?" Daniel asked. "You give the homeowner a lump sum in exchange for the property when they die?"

Kettles nodded. "Some firms have different offers, but that's all we do here."

"And, not to put too fine a point on it, the sooner your client dies, the better for the firm?"

Kettles nodded again. "That's about it. But at least they will have had some money to spend before they go."

10: FALLING OFF A LADDER

The phone rang as Daniel headed back down the stairs to the street, and Sophie said, "I've got a bit of an odd one, a poor bloke killed himself falling off a ladder." Daniel's mind was processing Barry Kettles and equity release, as well as mentally composing another text to Mal, until the tangle of phone, stairs, and trying to button his coat against the cold brought him to a standstill. He dropped the phone, but somehow managed not to fall over it, *which was a result*, he thought.

"That doesn't sound like anything you can't handle," Daniel told Sophie, when he sorted himself out.

"Except we've been to see his wife, and she says her husband was frightened. Frightened enough to want to leave town and start again somewhere else." Sophie's tone said that there was more.

"Okaaaay. That sounds like something I should know about."

Sophie asked Daniel to meet her at the scene, on River Terrace. He put phone and hands into his pockets and set off, wishing he'd brought a hat. The biting wind gave the lie to the bright sunshine and blue sky. There were —of course—young women wearing leggings or ripped jeans, and young men relying on a hoodie to keep warm, but most people were dressed for the Arctic.

The house Daniel was headed for was in one of the oldest parts of the town, high above the river, one of a short terrace of small houses with no road access. The path in front of the houses still had the original cobbles, with weeds poking through the gaps. The houses must have been rendered and painted at one time, but on several the render was falling off showing the untidy stonework beneath. Each house had a tiny front garden, though no one had done any gardening for years. They could have been lovely, Daniel thought, but without somewhere to park a car, they would be hard to sell.

A police car blocked the end of the terrace, and Daniel could see activity around one of the middle houses. A ladder lay along the path, but the body had gone. Sophie walked up to meet him.

"I'm about to talk to the tenant of number four — where the guy fell. She saw it all, and it's taken her a while to be calm enough to say what happened."

"You want me to come?"

Sophie nodded. "I'm getting the CSI team too, but I think it's all pretty contaminated."

She led the way to the fourth house. It was, if possible, in a worse condition than the rest of the terrace. Render was missing all around the front door, and Daniel was fairly sure that he could see through the gap around the doorframe. The windows were all single glazed, in rotting frames. Upstairs, two panes of glass had been replaced with either wood or cardboard — he couldn't tell underneath the water stains.

"The man who died," Sophie said, "Arwyn Jones, was supposed to be fixing a leak in the roof. But you'll see."

Inside the house was cold and felt damp. The front door

opened straight into the living room, with the kitchen beyond, and probably the bathroom beyond that. Daniel noted black mould around the living room window, spreading onto the thin curtains. The only heating seemed to be an electric fire, and it wasn't switched on. Sophie introduced him to a young woman with very red eyes.

"This is Alis Jenkins, who lives here," she said. "Alis, this is my colleague Detective Inspector Owen." She turned to Daniel. "We don't have long. Alis has to collect her daughter from the after school club."

The signs of poverty were all around them. Cheap, battered furniture, a wood effect laminate floor, which had warped at the window end of the room, the absence of a TV, and Alis herself, who looked as if she hadn't eaten properly in months or had a haircut in years.

"Would you tell DI Owen what you told me, Alis? About what happened earlier?"

Alis pulled her cardigan more tightly round her and sat on the very edge of one of the armchairs. Daniel sat down too, not wanting to loom over her. The chair felt damp through his trousers.

He saw Sophie walk to stand in the kitchen doorway, and fiddle about with something in her pocket.

"He's nice, Arwyn," Alis started. "I always like it when he comes. Some of the others are horrible. But he says he doesn't want to work for them anymore. They take too long to pay, and they always want a bodge job."

"That's your landlords he was talking about?" Daniel asked, hoping he had understood.

Alis nodded. "Primrose, yes."

"Why was Arwyn coming today?"

"There's a leak in the roof. Some slates blew off. We can't use one of the bedrooms because of it, only now the water comes in over the stairs too."

"So, what happened today?" Daniel asked.

Alis looked as if she was trying not to cry.

"Take your time," Daniel said.

Alis took a deep breath. "He wanted me to show him where the leaks were inside, in case he needed to take the ladder round the back. You can see where the slates are missing at the front from the street."

"So, you brought him inside and showed him the leaks?"

Alis nodded. "He said it was probably just the front. So, he went and got the ladder off his van."

"Where did he park?"

"Same as that police car. That's where everyone parks when they make deliveries and stuff. When he'd got his ladder off, and his tools, he moved the van."

"So, he brought the ladder and his tools. Then what?"

"He brought some other stuff from his van — tiles, and some waterproof stuff. Then he put the ladder up. I came back in to wash up, and I could hear him banging about. After a bit I put the kettle on and made us both some tea." There was a pause. "That's when ...."

"That's when he fell? When you went out with the tea?"

Alis nodded, tears back in her eyes. "He sort of wobbled the ladder from side to side" — there was a sob and an indrawn breath —"then it all fell down."

Sophie moved away from the kitchen door to put her arm around Alis. "It must have been horrible," she said. Alis buried her face in Sophie's shoulder and sobbed, as Sophie rubbed her back.

"I don't think you and your daughter should be staying here," Daniel said, when Alis was a bit calmer.

"There's nowhere else," Alis said. "I was lucky to get this. No one wants people on benefits. Or people with kids."

"I don't think you should be here tonight, or until the landlord has done some repairs."

Daniel looked at Sophie. "If it's a crime scene, we need to find somewhere for Alis and her child," he said, "and I think it is." Daniel had no idea whether it was a crime scene or not at this point, but he was sure that no one should be spending the night in a freezing house, where they had witnessed a man they liked fall to his death.

"If we can find her somewhere for the next few days, an AirBNB or something, then I know a social worker who might be able to help," he said.

"I can't afford ...." Alis began.

"Don't worry about that," said Daniel. "If we're telling you that you can't stay here, we'll pick up the tab." It would be stretching the regulations to breaking point, and Sophie's expression showed that she knew it. "I'll get Bethan on it," he said. "Her family have a couple of holiday lets, maybe one of them is free."

Ten minutes later it was fixed. Alis had gone to collect her daughter Tianna from school, and then Sophie had arranged a car to drive them and their things to the holiday cottage. Bethan had a dig at Daniel for being an old softie and then organised the cottage in record time, making sure that it was warm and stocked with basic groceries.

"I'm going to want to talk to Alis again," said Daniel to Sophie. "We need to know more about Arwyn's employers, and we need a formal statement about what happened. But that can wait until we've talked to his wife."

"Is that how you treat all your witnesses?" Sophie asked, and Daniel blushed.

"I couldn't leave them here, not a child, with all this mould and a leaking roof. I could ask you what you were doing in the kitchen."

It was Sophie's turn to blush. "I may or may not have been putting some money in Alis's handbag," she said. "Alis is right about one thing though, she was lucky to get this place, even if it is mouldy. I wanted to rent when I first came, but there's absolutely nothing. Everything I saw was falling down or so overpriced that it was a joke."

Daniel thought about the house Mal had just left. It was a nice enough house, but things went wrong with it constantly. The heating only worked about 50% of the time, taps dripped, light bulbs blew for no reason, and the oven door could only be opened when the kitchen door was closed. He wondered whether Mal had met Arwyn, or whether there were other tradesmen in the town complaining about not being paid.

11: A LOVELY MAN

It being a small town, Daniel should not have been surprised that Arwyn's bereaved wife was one of his sister Megan's school friends. Helena Jones was in shock, and it made her talk, as if by building a wall of words, she could keep the pain out.

She kept saying, "I can't believe it. He was fine." Or she blamed herself for not forcing her husband to give up his job or not listening to his complaints. "I made him go to the doctor, and I made him take the pills, but I should have done it sooner. I didn't take him seriously."

Daniel teased her story out slowly, over several cups of tea made by Helena's mother, who hovered, not knowing what else to do but make drinks. Arwyn had trained as a plumber, Helena said, but "He can turn his hand to anything, ask anyone. Look at this house. It was a wreck, and he did it all." Helena's mother nodded. Arwyn had started taking all sorts of repair work, not just plumbing, and it had generally worked out well. "He was making good money, doing bigger jobs, but he liked working by himself," Helena said. Bigger jobs meant taking on other workers, and Arwyn hated being a boss, so he went back to lots of small repairs.

"Primrose looked like just the thing. Lots of little jobs, all local."

"But it didn't work out?" Daniel asked.

"It was good at first. Then they started taking ages to pay. But there was always some excuse and he kept believing them. Then they started skimping, not letting him do a proper job."

Daniel asked for an example.

"Say it was a boiler," Helena said. "They'd make him keep fixing it rather than buy a new one, even though it would break again in a month, or they'd say a part hadn't arrived, so the poor tenant had no heating."

"So, he didn't want to work for them anymore?"

"Except that he was afraid that if he blew them out altogether, he wouldn't get any of the money they owed. It was making him ill. And then he started talking as if he was scared, like physically scared, of what they'd do if he kept asking."

But Helena didn't know who Arwyn was frightened of, or why. He'd been to the doctor and been prescribed antidepressants.

"But he kept saying we should leave Melin, only all my family is here. I should have listened to him."

Daniel asked how much money Arwyn was owed, but Helena didn't know. "Plenty," she said. "He wouldn't tell me." Daniel asked if he could look through Arwyn's accounts, at his phone and his computer, and Helena agreed. "Take the lot." Daniel was preparing to bundle it all up when the front door opened and his sister came in, wearing her district nurse's uniform. She held her arms out to Helena, and the dam holding back Helena's tears broke.

"I came as soon as I heard," she said. "Arwyn was a lovely man."

Daniel gathered up what he needed and left the women together.

MEGAN RANG as Daniel was getting dressed, after a long and careful shower. He took the phone downstairs, where the dinner was starting to smell very good. He stirred the curry and got a beer out of the fridge. Then he rang his sister back.

"At bloody last," Megan said. "I've been ringing for hours."

"I'm here now," he said, "but I'm in the middle of making a delicious dinner." Then he popped the lid off the beer and took a long drink.

"Well, I'm sorry to disturb your romantic evening with information about my *friend's husband who was killed today.*"

"What information? Do I get to finish my beer? Eat my dinner? Talk to my boyfriend?"

"Like you're interested in anything but getting Mal into bed. Jesus Dan, you're obsessed."

"Hey, wait up, where did that come from?"

"Sorry. Sorry. Forget I said it. I'm being a cow."

"Meg, he's moved in. We're an item. Get used to it. Tell me about Helena?"

Daniel could hear Megan's desire to remind him that Mal had ghosted him after they'd first got together, and it had *hurt*. It was going to take longer than six months for his twin to forgive and forget. Fair play, he thought, it was Megan who had to listen to him being miserable, but her default setting was *he's not good enough for you.*

"OK." Megan took a breath and spoke without the resentment. "Helena said that Arwyn had a work friend who he got on with. A guy called Ian Goldsmith. Mostly an electrician but does other stuff too. She thinks he might know more about

Arwyn's troubles. So, I said I'd pass it on. She's in bits, poor lamb."

Daniel thought the name sounded familiar, that he'd probably seen it on a van around the town.

Then he heard the sound of a car door slamming outside. Daniel said goodbye to his sister, ended the call, and turned the heat down under the curry. Because Megan was right, and dinner could wait.

THEY GOT to the dinner in the end, and a catch up after their time apart. They walked down to the pub in the village and found the settee by the fire was empty. There was a low table for them to put their pints on, and the only other people were sitting by the bar, so no one to notice if they sat close together, or if Daniel had a bad case of stubble rash. The pub had thick walls and small windows, and a ceiling stained yellow by years of smokers. There was a back room with a pool table, a TV, and a dart board, but on a January Tuesday evening, everyone was in the front, with the fire.

"How long have you got?" Daniel asked, "before they want you back in Manchester?"

"Thursday," Mal said, "so I get to come in and be your boss tomorrow."

"Good. I've got lots of reports that you can finish. There's enough paperwork that you can probably take some back to Manchester with you."

"Yeah, no. Tell me about this poor bloke who fell off the ladder."

So, Daniel did, describing the awful house and Alis' distress, then the interview with Helena and finally Megan's phone call about Ian Goldsmith.

"I said I'd try and track him down tomorrow," said Daniel,

"because Helena convinced me that Arwyn was afraid of something, and I'd like to know what."

"Ian Goldsmith was one of the electricians they sent to my old house," said Mal, "the one who complained about not being paid. To add to the coincidences, he tried to ring me yesterday, sent a text. I meant to ring him back."

"So, it's not going to be hard to track him down."

"He didn't say what he wanted, but I guess we'll find out more about Primrose Lettings."

"I wonder if Primrose Lettings is related to Daffodil Equity Release?"

Which brought them on to Harriet Marston and Hector's conviction that her death was suspicious. "Only he says we'll never prove it."

Daniel's phone rang. It was Sophie, asking whether he'd heard if Alis had "settled in". He thought that what she really wanted was someone to talk to.

"Come and meet Maldwyn," he said. "We've got a table by the fire in a lovely pub, and Bob will be welcome too." He described how to get there, and twenty minutes later, Sophie arrived, looking much more like the Sophie he remembered, in jeans and a thick sweater. She had Bob under her arm. Daniel made the introductions and went to get drinks.

"You're sure they don't mind dogs?" she asked.

"If they didn't let dogs in, they'd lose half the customers," Mal told her.

He looked over at little Bob. "Does he want a bigger knee to sit on?"

Daniel laughed, as he put their drinks on the table, and Sophie handed the dog over.

"He's seriously cute," said Mal. "I always wanted a dog, but my Dad wouldn't have one. Though I have to say I'd always thought of something a bit more butch than this guy."

"He might look like a teddy bear," said Sophie, "but he's all dog. The postman said that little dogs can be just as nasty as big ones. He certainly goes in for barking when anyone goes past the window."

Daniel was happy to see Mal playing with Bob and relaxed with Sophie. Sophie said that her Welsh classes would be starting soon and Mal shuddered.

"Don't let's go there," said Daniel. "I want a nice, civilised evening, with no arguments, thank you. You can practice your Welsh on me, Sophie, and I'll just keep on at Mal when he's feeling weak."

Mal laughed, and then sat up and waved.

"It's Hector," he said, "and I guess that's the boyfriend we never get to meet."

It was too late for Hector and the other man to escape. Daniel waved too. Hector didn't look pleased to see them, and the new boyfriend looked positively murderous when he saw Hector wave back. But they couldn't pretend that they didn't know Daniel and Mal.

Mal turned on all the charm. "We met," he said to the boyfriend, "when I dropped my keys off last week. I wondered if you were the guy Hector had been keeping to himself. Connor, isn't it?"

Connor had to smile and shake hands, though Daniel didn't think he wanted to. Nothing he could put his finger on, and Hector didn't seem to be his usual bouncy self.

"Let me get you both a drink," said Daniel, starting to get up.

"Hector will get them," said Connor, and then to Hector, "you're driving, I'll have a pint of whatever's good." It wasn't rude, but it bordered on it, Daniel thought. Instead of a snarky remark, Hector went to the bar. Daniel thought he was moving stiffly and followed. "You OK, mate?" he asked when they were both stood at the bar.

"Sure," said Hector, "it's just that Connor isn't mad keen on big groups."

"Then it's a good job there's only three of us."

"I think he was hoping for just us."

When they got back to the table, the atmosphere was noticeably strained. Hector saw Bob on Mal's lap and smiled. "Hey, little fella, how're you doing? This is the dog I was telling you about, that we found in the old lady's house."

"It's a bit of a silly thing," Connor said.

"But sooo sweet," said Hector, picking the dog up.

"Not as sweet as you," said Connor, ruffling Hector's hair, "so don't get too attached."

The dog growled, very softly, but a growl nonetheless. As Sophie had said, he was a proper dog, just small.

Hector gave the dog back to Mal.

"So," said Daniel, "you're an estate agent, Connor."

"North Wales Estates on the square," he said, with a smile. "I've only been there a few months, but we've got some lovely property. This place is booming, so if you want to sell, just call in."

"And Primrose Lettings? You run that too?" Mal asked.

"Not really," said Connor. He draped his arm over the back of Hector's chair and looked round the pub. "This is a great place."

"I've only just moved to this area from Derbyshire," Sophie said. "What about you two?"

Connor answered for them both. "We're from the Home Counties."

"And do you like it here? I think I'm going to love it."

Connor raised an eyebrow at her enthusiasm, then winked. "I like it a lot," he said, "mostly the people," and squeezed Hector's arm.

"I'm sure that I bought my house from your agency," said

Sophie. "I didn't want to buy straight away, but there was nothing to rent."

Mal chipped in with the problems he'd had in his rented house, and Connor talked about a *booming market.* Daniel couldn't help thinking about Alis, but some instinct said that this wasn't for sharing with Connor.

The barman came for their empty glasses and Connor stood up, Hector following.

"Better get back," Connor said. "Work in the morning."

Daniel stood up too, ready to give Hector his usual hug, but Hector stepped back, with a half-smile. "See you," he said, looking at Bob, asleep on Mal's knee as if he wanted a last pat, and then looking away. Connor put a hand on Hector's back and almost pushed him out of the pub.

"How weird was that?" Daniel said. "There's something wrong there." He looked at Sophie. "Hector is usually like a puppy. Bouncy and forever cheerful."

Mal nodded, and said, "He didn't look well to me."

"I think," said Sophie, "even though I've never met Connor before, that we should listen to what Bob had to say."

Daniel thought she was probably right. Bob had been pleased to see Hector and growled at Connor.

Mal smiled. "Maybe we should get Bob onto all our cases. But seriously, Hector wasn't himself. And it's a half-hour drive from Hector's. A long way for one drink."

Daniel said, "Hector told me that Connor doesn't like big groups, prefers it to be just the two of them."

"That rings alarm bells," said Sophie, and Daniel agreed. He spent too much time listening to stories about how people, mostly women, had been slowly separated from their friends until their only social contact was with the abuser.

"And Connor was borderline rude," Sophie said. "Like, all charm on the surface, but I didn't get a good vibe. Which is weird, because he looks so like you."

"No, he doesn't!" Daniel said.

"Yes, he does," Sophie and Mal said together.

"Hector obviously goes for the tall blond type," said Mal.

Daniel blushed. He'd slept with Hector once, but it had been a one-off when they were both single and were both feeling beaten down by a case.

"Whatever he looked like, something wasn't right," Mal said.

Daniel nodded again. But this was Hector, and surely Hector was smarter than that. He'd looked embarrassed. "I don't like it. I don't like the way Hector was walking, or the way he was making excuses for Connor. He's not like that."

The other two nodded in agreement.

"I've got to go and see him at some stage this week — well, I could talk to him over the phone, but I'll go. Try to find out more, see if he's OK," said Daniel. Because he was worried.

"What I'd like to know," said Mal, "with my work hat on, is why he said he had nothing to do with the letting company. I rented the house from Primrose or whatever they were called, and Connor took the keys when I left."

Sophie went to the bar and when she came back, Mal was persuaded to relinquish Bob.

"I think he's a bit confused about moving house and wondering where his mistress is," Sophie said, "but it turns out that my next door neighbour has a sideline in dog walking. She just says keep him exhausted, and he'll be OK. It's worked so far. But it's only been two days."

At the end of the evening, they walked Sophie back to her car. Mal gave Bob a last hug, and they left.

"You really *did* want a dog," said Daniel. "We always had dogs when I was a kid, and Mum and Dad have a dog in Spain, but I couldn't have one and be a copper. Not with the hours we do. You said your dad wouldn't have one?"

There was no answer from Mal. Daniel saw that Mal's face

had its familiar No Entry sign, but he decided to take a tentative step onto the eggshells.

"He doesn't sound like the easiest man, your dad."

"*Bastard,* sums him up. I don't want to talk about him."

Daniel held Mal's hand as they walked home, because no one could see them in the dark.

12: MORE FRIGHTENED OF THEM THAN US

Daniel rang Ian Goldsmith after breakfast the next day and was surprised to hear a familiar voice say, "Hello."

"Sophie?" said Daniel. "I'm trying to get hold of Ian Goldsmith."

"Then come to Wrexham hospital," she said, "because that's where he is, following a serious assault last night. I'm here because they said he was coming round, but he hasn't."

"We're on our way."

Outside, it was warmer than in recent days, but at the expense of the sunshine. Grey clouds hung over the hills, stripping the colour out of the landscape. Mal pointed towards his own car, which somehow managed to look clean despite its being January. Mal always referred to Daniel's venerable Land Rover as the 'mobile skip,' which didn't stop him loading it up with flat pack furniture, thought Daniel. Still there was no argument that Mal's car was a hundred times warmer and more comfortable, and he settled down into the passenger seat with a sigh of pleasure.

"Harriet Marston's vile son has a Tesla," he said, "but he was furious that he wasn't getting half his mother's house. I've got Charlie trying to find out whether either of them needed the money, or if they were just greedy."

"I've never lost money betting on greed," said Mal, "and Tesla do an all-wheel drive now. Just saying."

"I still think they'd be rubbish in snow. And hopeless for flat pack furniture."

"Just keep telling yourself that."

They grinned at each other. They both knew that Daniel would be keeping the Land Rover until it fell apart, and that Mal would always have a large, shiny, black car that went like the clappers.

"Tell me again what Ian said about not being paid," Daniel said.

"That he couldn't stop working for the company because he was afraid that he'd never get what he was owed. Which is what your guy told his wife. It has to be the same company. Look up Companies House."

It was quiet for a moment, as Daniel looked at the internet on his phone, then, "OK, here we go. Primrose Property Management, Sunflower Lettings, Tulip Gold Management, Jessamine Development. One of the directors is called Flowers. And there are links to more. I'll get Charlie on it when we get back."

Daniel reached for Mal's hand and twined their fingers together. "I love working with you," he said.

"We make a good team," Mal replied.

"When we're not fighting."

"No fighting then," said Mal and ran his fingers over Daniel's palm.

〜

THEY WALKED into the hospital and found the ward. Sophie and a PC were waiting in the corridor.

"He was unconscious when they brought him in, but he's been awake and now he's just asleep," Sophie said.

A nurse came over and spoke to Sophie. "Ian has woken up. You can go and see him, but you can't stay for long."

Mal asked, "What injuries does he have?"

The nurse looked as if she wanted to ignore him, then she looked again and saw him properly. Whether it was Mal's good looks that got her attention, or that she worked out he was in charge, it changed her attitude.

"Broken ribs, dislocated shoulder, a bad concussion, and lots of internal bruising. He's going to be with us until we can be sure about the internal injuries."

"Someone gave him quite a beating, then?" Mal asked.

"Several someones according to the doctors," the nurse replied, "with big boots."

She showed them into a private room, leaving the constable outside. It wasn't big, but Daniel thought that if you were going to feel as ill as Ian Goldsmith looked, you wouldn't want to be bothered with other people.

"Hi Ian," said Mal, to the figure on the bed. His arm was in a sling, and every bit of visible skin was cut or bruised. Daniel tried not to wince openly, but he hoped that Ian had been given some strong painkillers. He saw that Ian moved his eyes and not his head.

"Hi," he said back to Mal.

"This is DI Owen, and Inspector Harrington," Mal said. "You were picked up last night in the street ... Inspector Harrington?"

Sophie filled in the details. Ian had been found unconscious in an alley off the Main Street. The pubs had closed, and a man had gone into the alley for a pee and tripped over Ian. Thankfully, he was sober enough to call an ambulance.

"Did you go to one of the pubs?" asked Mal.

"Yes. Didn't stay. Too busy," said Ian, with difficulty.

"Then what happened?" Mal asked

"Don't remember," said Ian.

Sophie leaned forwards. "Mr Goldsmith, we found your van, with all its tools, parked in the car park at the far end of the alley. Were you planning to drive home?"

They watched as Ian frowned, pulling his eyes together and wincing as he did so. "Only had a pint. OK to drive."

"All your tools were still in your van, Mr Goldsmith, and your keys were on the ground next to you. So, the people who attacked you didn't steal anything. You still had your wallet and your phone."

Ian didn't answer.

Mal said, "You left me a message yesterday. What were you going to talk to me about?"

"Nothing."

Daniel thought that Ian was lying, and that they all thought he was lying, and that Ian knew it. Mal tried again, sitting down on one of the plastic chairs and pulling it closer to the bed.

"Do you remember coming to my old house and fixing the electrics? More than once."

"Sure."

"You told me that the firm you worked for was very bad at paying. You told me not to rent from them again."

"OK," said Ian, neither agreeing nor disagreeing.

"Was that why you rang me? Did you want to tell me more about it?"

"It was nothing."

"Was the attack something to do with your work, Mr Goldsmith?" Mal's voice was gentle, but he wasn't giving up. "Or was it something to do with the reason you rang me?"

"No."

"Do you know an Arwyn Jones, Mr Goldsmith?"

Ian started to nod, but changed his mind, pain turning his cheeks red, and pushing a tear from his eye. "Yes," he croaked.

"And do you know that Arwyn was killed yesterday, falling from a ladder?"

"Yes." The croak was fainter.

Mal said, "I'm sorry for your friend's death. I know he was your friend, because his wife told us. Did Arwyn work for the same people who owed you money?"

This time there was no answer at all.

Mal looked over at Sophie, and she leaned forward. "Helena Jones said that the company, Primrose, owed him a lot of money. She said that he seemed scared of them. Did he talk to you about it?"

Again, no answer.

"So," Mal said, "you were on your way back to your van, and some men attacked you. But you weren't robbed. Why do you think they attacked you?"

"Don't know, don't remember."

One of the machines attached to Ian started bleeping. The door opened and a nurse came and switched the alarm off.

"Sorry, but you need to leave now," she said, holding the door open in a way that brooked no argument.

"We can't do protection, but if Goldsmith does decide to talk ... I'll give the nurses our numbers."

Daniel and Mal waited for her to get back.

"Complete load of crap," said Mal, "like anyone's going to randomly beat him up and not steal his wallet, or the keys to his van."

Daniel had to agree.

The hospital floor was shiny, though the walls were scuffed, and there was the usual detritus of beds, wheelchairs, and trolleys full of notes lining the walls. Daniel wondered, as he often did, whether any of the things had a home, or if they would be moved from corridor to corridor until the end of time.

Sophie came back from the nurses' station.

"I talked briefly to the doctors before you came," she said, looking between the two of them, as if not sure whom to speak to. "They said that Goldsmith was attacked by more than one person, probably with baseball bats or something similar, and that he was kicked once they knocked him over. He was lucky not to have died."

Mal's face didn't give anything away, and Daniel wondered whether he was remembering how it felt to be attacked by men with baseball bats.

Daniel said, "Hopefully when he's feeling a bit better, he'll realise that we're on his side and tell us what happened," but Mal shook his head.

"He knows who beat him up, and he's more frightened of them than us."

13: A WEDNESDAY'S WORTH OF REPORTS

Abby Price was usually confident enough to knock and just walk into Daniel's office. This morning she hovered at the door.

"The thing is," she said, "it's more of a family thing."

"Come in and tell me about the thing that is a family thing," said Daniel.

"It's Harriet Marston, or rather it's Iolo Price. He was my uncle. Or great uncle, not really sure. And my Aunty Karen and Uncle Mike, or cousins ...."

"Abby. What did they want?"

"Sorry, boss. Uncle Mike had heard about Harriet Marston being found dead and that we seemed to be taking it seriously. And that she'd done the same thing with her house as their dad did with his. He wanted to know if there was anything suspicious about Uncle Iolo's death."

"Does he think there is?" Daniel asked.

"I don't know. I can't decide whether he just wants an answer to why his dad died, or whether he thinks there was something odd."

Daniel thought for a moment. It had seemed like a genuine coincidence to him, but maybe it was worth another look.

"Tell you what, Abby, why don't you have a look for similar cases — people who've had equity release and then died. Obviously, we'd know if there was anything really suspicious about the deaths, so I guess you'll be looking for people who died alone, or where there was an inquest."

And if she found anything, he would have another excuse to talk to Hector. Because if there was anything odd about a death, Hector would know. He'd have done the autopsy on Iolo price. But Daniel wanted to talk to Hector about Connor, or rather about the way Connor had behaved the night before.

Abby spoke again. "Uncle Mike said he'd been having a look at Daffodil Equity Release, and it turns out that they only work in this area, mostly just in town."

Daniel thought about his meeting with Barry Kettles, who'd said the same.

"You wouldn't have thought there was enough business round here," he said, "so have a look at that too. It's on my to-do list, only I'm putting it onto yours. Find out about the company — I'm sure you can do better than your Uncle Mike."

"Not sure about that boss, he's an accountant."

"Do your best, and be sure to pick his brain then."

Daniel tipped his chair back and let his mind wander. Was it completely out of the question that Iolo Price's death and Harriet Marston's were connected? On the surface, no connection at all. Elderly people died. They were all individuals and important to their friends and relatives, but statistically, elderly people died and there was nothing special about these two deaths. They had equity release in common, but how many other elderly people had made the same decision? Abby would find out. He was still cogitating when his phone rang.

"Rod Marston here," said an irritated voice.

"Mr Marston, what can I do for you?" Daniel asked, mustering every bit of patience at his disposal.

"I want to know what action you are taking against the criminals who stole from my mother. Those so-called equity release fraudsters."

"Do you have evidence that fraud was committed, Mr Marston?"

Because if you do, thought Daniel, *that would be great, but I bet you don't.* He was right. Roderick Marston was indulging in a spot of magical thinking. If he just kept on saying 'fraud', maybe he'd get his mother's house back

Daniel walked over to Mal's office. Mal had been with Superintendent Hart for most of the morning, but he was back now, and staring miserably at his computer screen. He was interested to see what Mal would make of an equity release connection between Iolo Price and Harriet Marston. Not much, was the answer.

"In a novel, maybe," he said. "In real life, I doubt it."

"I've asked Abby to see what she can find out," Daniel said, "because Hector is confident that Harriet Marston was murdered."

"*If* she was, then start as if you'd never heard the words 'Equity' and 'Release.' Because Daniel, *come on.* Start with the relatives, start with local villains looking for cash. *Yanno?* Regular police work."

Daniel smiled. "It's a bit far-fetched, I admit. But I'm looking anyway."

"Like anything I said would stop you."

Daniel wanted to lean over and kiss him, but the offices were mostly window, and he thought that whilst everyone knew about their relationship, he didn't think public snogging was good workplace behaviour.

"The other thing is, that if I think there's a connection between the two cases, then I can go and ask Hector about it, can't I? And then I can keep asking him about Connor and his behaviour."

Mal nodded. Daniel thought his boyfriend looked more unhappy than a Wednesday's worth of reports would account for.

"Are you OK?" he asked, "Apart from a maybe-murder, I mean."

"Manchester's getting more complicated," Mal said. He looked at Daniel and the misery on his face was heartbreaking.

"I've just agreed to another month's secondment."

Daniel spoke before he had thought about what he was saying. "You didn't think about discussing it with me first?" he said.

"You don't need me here to cramp your style, and they do 'need' me there. They've been onto Hart, and to be honest, I didn't have much of a choice."

"Well, that's OK then. No need to consult me at all."

Daniel stood up.

"Don't go. Hart has also been on my case about the alleged crime scene where Arwyn Jones fell off a ladder. Specifically, about why we're paying for a witness to stay in a holiday let."

"So, you don't want to cramp my style, but you do want to micromanage what I do? How does that work?"

Daniel could keep his temper with everyone except Mal, but Mal pushed all his buttons. Always had. And judging from the look on Mal's face, it worked the other way round.

"It. Was. Hart." he said. "And this isn't the place for this argument."

"Fine," Daniel said. "We can pick it up at home. I'm going to see a social worker about rehousing our witness and her child. Because the alleged crime scene has water coming through the roof and broken windows mended with cardboard."

He realised that he was shaking. He'd made the appointment with Veronica Brown first thing, and asked Sophie to go along too, so she could meet more of the people she'd be working with. But now Daniel wanted to throw things, rather than have a calm and considered meeting about something that he wanted as a person, but was nothing to do with him as a police officer.

HE WALKED DOWN to the bottom of the stairs and back up again to the second floor where Sophie's office was. It helped dissipate a bit of the tension, but not enough. So, he went back up to the top floor, only to run into Mal, who had clearly had the same idea.

"Dan, don't let's argue. I hate it."

Daniel felt tears at the back of his eyes. He looked up and down the stairs. No one.

"I hate it too," he said, and put his arms round Mal and pressed his face into the crook of his shoulder. Mal stroked Daniel's hair and muttered, "l love you Daniel Owen." Then they heard one of the doors opening and sprang apart, Daniel blushing. Mal laughed. "That blush never gets old. Go to your meeting and say hi to Veronica from me."

They had met Veronica the year before, on another case involving young people being recruited by drug dealers. Hart had agreed to not prosecuting the young people for crimes they had committed, in the hope of a better relationship between the police and social services. So far, it was working. Daniel was hoping they still had some credit, and that he could use it for Alis and her daughter.

14: OK IN THE SUMMER

Daniel decided to visit Alis on his way to the Social Services office, and Sophie was happy to come along. After a day in the warm holiday cottage, and with enough to eat, Alis's cheeks were pink, and her hair looked shiny and bouncy. The cottage had central heating, as well as an electric fire with fake coal, which was flickering away and making it seem even warmer and more cosy.

"This place is so nice," Alis said, "Thank you so much for fixing it. We're warm for the first time in weeks."

"No problem," said Daniel.

Daniel had called on Alis because he wanted to know how she had first found the house on River Terrace. She'd told him she'd been lucky to get it, and he'd realised that no one had asked how she'd come to rent it.

"Someone at the Job Centre," she said, "gave me a number and told me that this company had places to let, and that they took people on benefits."

"Someone official, or another claimant?" Daniel asked.

"Oh, the benefits advisor," Alis replied.

"And then what happened?"

"I met this bloke at the house, and he showed me round. I thought you were him actually, when you came round after, you know, Arwyn. I said I'd take it, so he made an appointment to meet again with the paperwork. He said he'd get some of the repairs done, but you know that mostly didn't happen."

"So, you never went to an office?"

She never had, although the man she described sounded a lot like Connor, *who looks nothing like me*, Daniel thought. The Tenancy Agreement she showed him was with Primrose Lettings, at the North Wales Estates address. Alis said that she asked for repairs over the phone, and sometimes someone came, and sometimes they didn't.

She continued, "My friend rents from them too. She said the places weren't great, but as long as the rent was paid, you didn't get any trouble. Some places, the landlords want, you know, *favours*. Or if you make too much fuss, they come and get rough."

Daniel knew that the days of local councils providing decent housing to everyone in need had gone, but surely they had to provide *something*. He asked.

"Yep, we were officially homeless, and they had to house us. We got one room in a bed and breakfast. Me and Tianna, with her about to start school. I was desperate. I could have been there for years before anything came up in Melin. And River Terrace was OK in the summer."

VERONICA SHOWED Daniel and Sophie into what she called "our delightful meeting room". It was even more battered than its equivalent down at the police station. Mismatched tables pushed together, and chrome-framed chairs with bobbled red tweed seats, which must have been donated by a richer department when they got some new ones.

"I'd offer you a coffee," said Veronica, "but I can't inflict it on you. When you've worked here for a while, you can tolerate most things, but even we find the coffee a bit much."

Daniel made the introductions and explained why they'd come. Veronica said that she knew about the terrace of houses where Alis lived. "We do try and keep an eye on the housing down there, because it's awful. But we haven't got anything else to offer them."

"There's water coming through the roof," said Daniel, "and black mould, and windows with cardboard instead of glass."

Veronica looked at him with what appeared to be pity. "You have no idea," she said. "No idea."

"So, tell me."

"I have a friend in Environmental Health. He has been to see people living in garages. And all sorts of illegal outbuildings. We call them *beds in sheds*. And if you're desperate enough, you'll pay rent for the privilege."

"This is a child, though. It's not safe."

Veronica hesitated, and then the words came tumbling out. "Are you going to do something about all this if I tell you what I know? People like Alis living in those awful places?"

"I don't think it's our business," Daniel said, "which doesn't mean it's legal, or right. Just not police business. But Alis said that she was told that the landlord of her house *wouldn't give her any trouble* as long as the rent was paid. We want to know about *trouble*. I want to know about fraud. About sexual harassment or threats of violence. Those are the things that we can make our business."

Veronica nodded slowly. "So, if I told you about someone living in an illegal outbuilding in a garden then you couldn't do anything. But if the owner threatened the tenant with violence, then you could?"

"Or if the owner demanded sexual favours in return for

living there, or if they took money for a deposit and disappeared."

They looked at each other, and Daniel saw the same stubbornness that he recognised in himself. He knew that Veronica was going to keep looking for *beds in sheds* until she could bring him something he could use. She didn't have to tell him that she'd be plugging away at it in her own time, because that's what he'd be doing too.

"I think," he said, deciding to trust her, "that there are people here using the housing shortage to make money illegally. Primrose Lettings is just one part of it. But they might be dangerous."

"I *know* they're dangerous. Have you got half an hour?" Veronica asked.

Daniel nodded, but Sophie said she had to go back to the police station.

Daniel reached for his coat. Veronica's car was outside the main entrance. "Get in," she said, and then she said something Daniel hadn't expected.

"Inspector Harrington, Sophie, is she single?"

"That's what she told me," Daniel replied, and Veronica nodded, but said nothing.

15: TROUBLE

Veronica drove them to a terrace of houses on the outskirts of town. It was close to the river and the old station, but not close enough to be flooded. They got out of the car and Veronica led him to a front door with two doorbells. When she rang the doorbell on the right, they both heard the pounding of feet coming downstairs and the door opened. A young woman with long blonde hair dressed in jeans and a teddy bear fleece stood waiting for them.

"Hi, Veronica," the young woman said. "Come on in." She led them upstairs and into a tiny living room where another young woman, also with long blonde hair and a teddy bear fleece, was waiting. Veronica made the introductions, and Daniel couldn't mistake the look of alarm on their faces when they realised he was a police officer. "I'm not here to cause you any trouble," he said, but it didn't have a lot of effect.

The two young women, Jemima and Casey, were, Veronica explained, care leavers. They both had jobs in the town, Jemima in a pub, and Casey in a couple of shops, and sometimes one of the coffee bars.

"They are two of my success stories," Veronica said, and

both young women blushed. She turned to them. "Tell DI Owen what you told me about those men who came to visit, when you didn't pay the rent, and about how you've got this flat and what's wrong with it."

Daniel looked round. The flat didn't look too bad. It was clean and tidy with pretty throws over the two sofas. The curtains looked clean, but the single glazed windows were streaming with condensation.

"Let me make a cup of tea," said Casey. And when they all nodded, she got up and went into the kitchen, which meant squeezing behind one of the sofas. She looked over at Daniel. "Come and see," she said. "The kitchen is one of our problems. And then I'll show you the bathroom, and you'll understand."

At first glance the kitchen looked okay. Small, very small, but clean. There was a battered stainless steel sink and draining board, a small fridge, and a stove. There wasn't a lot of room for cupboards and the workspace was tiny, just about enough room for a kettle and toaster. Part of the reason was the door leading to the bathroom. Daniel supposed that the bedroom must lead off the tiny hallway. Casey pointed to the cooker. "It looks alright, but only one of the burners works, and the oven is a bit dodgy, so we mostly eat things that only take one pan." She laughed. "We eat a lot of toast." She filled the kettle at the sink and switched it on. "Let me show you the bathroom," she said, "while the kettle boils."

Again, the bathroom looked okay on the surface. Wash basin, toilet, and a shower over the bath. When Daniel looked more closely, he saw the signs of burning around the shower. Casey saw him looking. "They told us it was live," she said. "It could've killed us. We've rung over and over again asking for a new one, but no one ever comes. This guy Ian said we shouldn't use it, but that was three months ago." They heard the kettle switch itself off and went back into the kitchen. Casey made tea and they took it into the living room.

"It's what we can afford," said Jemima, "and if the things were fixed it would be fine. It's cosy, so we can keep it warm, and it means we can stay here, in Melin. Everything else we saw is in Wrexham or on the coast, and we don't want to go to those places."

Veronica had nodded as Jemima was speaking. She said that there were very few places in the town that people on low wages like Jemima and Casey could afford. She said she thought that they were doing really well, they had jobs and a home, and that if she had anything to do with it, they were both going to college.

Daniel told them that they may as well agree to go to college now, because Veronica always got her own way. The two girls smiled, and they all drank their tea.

"Okay then, tell me about these men who came," said Daniel.

The story was a simple one. Both young women had done well in the run-up to Christmas, then afterwards both shifts and tips had dropped away to almost nothing. They were struggling to find enough money to pay January's rent. And they were angry because the repairs to the shower and the cooker still hadn't been done. In desperation, Casey had rung Primrose Lettings and said that they wouldn't pay any more rent until things were fixed. The next day three men came round to the flat, pushed their way in, and threatened to break everything in the place unless the rent was paid. They paid the rent, even though it meant going to the food bank. They had been too frightened to ring the letting company again about the repairs.

Daniel asked them to describe the men who came.

"They were just big," said Jemima.

"Tall like you, but fat and wide, and they wore beanie hats and scarves pulled up like masks. They were scary, got right in our faces, and one of them kept picking things up as if he was going to throw them out of the window. I mean, we've been in care, and some of the places we've lived weren't great. We didn't try and argue with them, there's no point with that sort. We just said we'd pay and hoped they'd go away."

Daniel asked if any of them were the people they dealt with at Primrose Lettings but both young women said no.

"We dealt with a guy called Connor," said Casey. "He was the one who showed us the flat, and he was the one we were supposed to ring if we had a problem."

Veronica said that it sounded as if Connor had called the thugs. Then she said that she wanted Daniel to meet the tenant downstairs. He left his card with Casey and Jemima and extracted a promise to call him if they thought of anything else, or if they saw the men again.

"I've told them that they don't have to put up with this," said Veronica, but they both knew it wasn't that simple.

The man downstairs had even less space than the two young women, essentially one room and a bathroom. Unlike upstairs it was not neat and clean. Empty vodka bottles and full ashtrays littered the floor. The tenant, Dave, was working his way down another bottle of vodka. It wasn't hard to see why he might not always be able to pay the rent. Veronica said that he'd had several visits from the three men, and somehow he managed to pay enough to keep them away. "But," she said, "one day he's not going to be able to, and then he's on the streets."

16: MATCHMAKING

Daniel made a point of calling into Sophie's office on his way up the stairs, with a sandwich to eat at his desk. "I thought you might be interested in what I found," he said, and told her about the three thugs, and the dangerous flats.

"I liked Veronica," Sophie said when he'd finished. "She seems committed."

"I think she liked you too," said Daniel, and was pleased to see that he wasn't the only one who blushed.

"Stop matchmaking," she said, blushing harder.

"Veronica's a nice woman," he said and left, smiling to himself. It wasn't the first time he'd been accused of matchmaking. Mal's brother Huw and their friend Rhiannon were getting married in the summer, and both credited Daniel with bringing them together. He and Mal were planning a weekend in Cardiff so that Mal and Huw could be measured for their wedding clothes.

Daniel had met Rhiannon and her sister Sasha when he'd interviewed them on a case the year before, in the village where Mal had grown up, and where most of his family still lived.

That case had been the first time he'd met Mal, when they'd got together. Sasha was the single mother of a six-year-old and worked as a night cleaner. Rhiannon was her younger sister and worked in the Spar in the village. Much later, Daniel had discovered that between them the sisters ran the local food bank, toy bank, and a children's clothes swap. In their spare time, they campaigned to keep the library and the swimming pool open. Both had known Mal at school, and now Rhiannon was marrying Mal's brother.

Sasha had always maintained that he and Mal were made for each other, and that Mal walking away from their brief affair was no more than a blip. "Get used to it, Daniel," she'd said. "Mal doesn't know when he's well off, but he'll always come to his senses in the end."

"You're saying I should expect him to ghost me again?"

"Probably," she said, as if it wasn't important.

"Sasha! I'm a white picket fence kind of man. Think *settling down*, not emotional rollercoaster."

Sasha had just laughed. "All I can say, Daniel Owen, is that you need to do some work on your self-knowledge. *Settling down* my arse."

IN THE CID OFFICE, Bethan was visibly tamping, her face screwed up, her jaw clenched, and her fingers stabbing at her keyboard.

"Wassup?" Daniel asked, slipping into the seat next to her, and unwrapping his sandwich.

"Roderick Marston is what's up," she said. "He's a liar, and a thief, and he's bullied Daffodil into giving him the full value of his mother's house."

"I understand the individual words, but I need an explanation. Are those agreements illegal after all? How is he a thief?"

Bethan said that she had been to see Marston's former employers. "He'd been stealing for years, no doubt about it. He was taking home a couple of grand a month on top of his salary, untaxed. He only got found out because of a stupid slip up. The auditors didn't notice, which is why the company decided not to prosecute in the end."

"Bad enough to employ a thief, worse to employ an incompetent auditor?"

"You've got it, boss. And even with all that extra money, they are still basically living on credit."

So, the Roderick Marstons needed their mother's house to pay some of the bills. Daniel asked Bethan why Daffodil had torn up what appeared to be a legal agreement.

"I don't know. I went round to ask Roderick about his alibi, to see if he could come up with something better than *I was at home* and he wouldn't let me through the door. Just stood there gloating that the Daffodil lot had offered to buy the house from them at its full value, less the cash they gave to Harriet. So, they don't even need to mess about putting it up for sale. He even boasted that he'd *driven them up on price.*"

That didn't mean Roderick hadn't killed his mother, Daniel thought. He hadn't known about the equity release and expected to inherit the house.

"Did he have an alibi?" he asked Bethan, and she groaned.

"Nothing he hadn't said before. Just at home, working. We could go for computer records and phone calls."

Daniel nodded, but he was thinking that paying off Roderick and Jennifer pointed to Daffodil's having something to hide. Whether that was that the equity release agreement wouldn't stand up in court, or something else, he didn't know.

He looked up to see Abby Price by his shoulder. "You'll never guess what I've just heard, boss," she said.

"Daffodil Equity Release has offered to buy your uncle Iolo's house for its full value," he said, and her eyes widened.

"Ask Bethan," he said. "And those enquiries you were making into the company? Keep making them. In fact, make them a priority. I'm going to see Barry Kettles.

"Finish your sandwich first," said Bethan. "If you get any thinner your trousers will fall down.

17: WHAT WOULD TEMPT YOU?

The door to the Daffodil broom cupboard office looked closed, but when Daniel knocked, it opened, letting out a strong smell of whisky. There was a half-full bottle and an empty glass on the desk. Barry Kettles was leaning back in his chair, no mean feat in the tiny space, and Daniel had opened his mouth to say hello, when he realised that the figure behind the desk was far too still. He took the single step that was all he needed to get around the desk, then reached over, calling, "Mr Kettles! Mr Kettles!" in the hope that the man was asleep. He didn't wake. Daniel felt for a pulse, then pulled out his phone and called for an ambulance,

"He's got a pulse, but only just, and I can't rouse him at all," he told the dispatcher. Then he called Bethan. The office was cold, so Daniel took off his jacket and sweater and tucked them round Kettles. He found a small fan heater and put it on to warm the room as he waited. The ambulance, Bethan, and Mal all arrived at the same time. Daniel and Mal helped carry Kettles down the stairs while Bethan looked quickly round the office and sealed it for the CSIs.

"He's in a bad way, mate," said the paramedic as they loaded Kettles into the ambulance. "But we'll do our best."

"We'll follow you," said Mal.

They walked back to the office to pick up Mal's car via a stop at the bakery, where they snagged donuts and some decent coffee.

"It really doesn't need both of us to go," said Daniel, wondering if he could eat the donut in Mal's car without dropping crumbs, and deciding that he didn't care. They lived together now, and Mal would have to deal with Daniel's imperfections, including dropping crumbs in his always pristine car.

"No, but I want to hear about the whole case, and we can talk in the car. And we can make five minutes to see Hector."

Then, when they got in the car, Mal said, "I've got to go back to Manchester tomorrow. I should go tonight. But it's getting harder to keep leaving since I moved in. Not harder to leave Melin, just harder to leave you. So, the truth is I wanted an extra hour of your company that I'm not really entitled to."

Daniel told him what he'd learned from Veronica, from Alis, and from the two young women.

"The three thugs might be the same as whoever beat up Ian Goldsmith — *if* he was beaten up because of something to do with his repair business. Either way, it's definitely something I can get my teeth into."

"But we don't know for certain why Ian was beaten up," said Mal, "so I vote we have another go at him while we're at the hospital."

Mal put his hand on Daniel's thigh, and Daniel covered it with his own. Mal wanted to tell Daniel about the work he'd been doing. Not about the risks, but about the doubts he was having about DI Andy Carter. He came at it sideways.

"What would tempt you into corruption, Dan? It's a serious question."

"Yeah, but I don't understand it."

"Well, Rob Hughes, last year, it was money. He wanted money, and he lied and cheated to get it. What would make you lie and cheat?"

"I lie and cheat all the time. I said Alis Jenkins' house was a crime scene, so that I could get her out of there. I tell suspects that we know more than we do, to trick them into confessions."

"But would you take a bribe?"

"I can't think of any reason why I would, but never say never. What's all this about, Maldwyn?"

"Bear with me. Would you cover up a crime? Not like we let those kids off dealing last year, I mean cover up something big?"

Daniel's immediate thought was no. That's why he'd joined the police in the first place. Only the answer wasn't no.

"I'd do it to protect someone I cared about if there was no other way. Or someone innocent and helpless. Now you have to tell me why."

But Mal couldn't. Not everything anyway. He squeezed Daniel's hand.

"I've met this bloke," he said, "another Manchester police officer. There's something wrong with the way he talks about criminals, as if he wants what they've got. Money, power, flashy cars."

Daniel laughed, took his hand away from Mal's, and ruffled the perfectly combed hair on Mal's head.

"We've already got that stuff, *cariad*," he said. "Well, the money goes to pay off the mortgage, and the power is a bit theoretical, but this is definitely a flashy car." Then he asked, "You think this guy is on the take?"

Mal shook his head. "I don't know."

He turned into the hospital car park and drove to the furthest corner before stopping. He pulled Daniel towards him across the seats, loving the feeling of his body, despite the discomfort of the car. *You,* he thought, *I'd protect you, only when I try, I get it wrong.*

"You're not enjoying Manchester, then," Daniel said.

"Not much. But it's important. Let's go and see what's up with Mr Kettles."

ONLY THEY WERE TOO LATE. Barry Kettles was dead.

18: NO ONE DIES IN AN AMBULANCE

They found the same paramedic who'd been in the ambulance.

"Nothing we could do," he said, "his heart just stopped. He was dead before we got here, but as I'm sure you know, no one dies in an ambulance."

"Any idea what he died of?" Daniel asked.

"If it was a teenager we picked up in town at three am, I'd say drugs and drink. Middle-aged man in the afternoon? No idea." The paramedic went back to cleaning the ambulance.

Daniel thought about Harriet Marston and Arwyn. Neither seemed like a candidate for street drugs, but street drugs were a possible cause of their deaths.

"Was Barry Kettles a drinker?" Mal asked, thinking of the whisky in the office.

"He wasn't drinking when I saw him last, and he didn't smell of drink," said Daniel, "but I'm more interested in the drugs element. We should ask Ian as well as Hector."

It started snowing as they left the ambulance bay. Everything was grey and the clouds were low overhead. The only colour was in the form of car paint and the ambulances parked by the entrance to A&E.

"We've brought the wrong car for this," Daniel said. "I'll go and see Ian, and you can get anything with Kettles' address, and talk to Hector so we can get back before it settles."

"Who's the ranking officer here?" Mal asked.

"My case. You work for Manchester. Go and see Hector. Sir."

IAN WAS UP AND ABOUT, though looking very battered and bruised.

"They say I can go home tomorrow," he said, "once I've seen the doctor again. I can't wait."

They sat in the ward's day room, trying to ignore the TV, which refused to turn off, despite all their efforts. Daniel had arrived in time for the tea trolley, so they were both drinking almost tasteless coffee and making faces at it. Daniel hoped that the shared experience might persuade Ian to tell him the truth.

"I know that you know who was behind your assault," he began, "so don't try and pretend you don't."

Ian shook his head and started to speak.

"Don't." Daniel said. "You know, and I know you know. The only question is, are you going to tell me?"

Ian didn't answer. The day room had chairs around the walls, and low tables scattered at random in the middle, with old magazines and greasy packs of cards. The TV hung from a bracket on the ceiling, where it could be seen from everywhere in the room. The floor was pale blue linoleum, polished to a dangerous shine, reflecting the strip lighting above. Through the windows, the greyness pressed in.

"I think," said Daniel, "that there is a relationship between the assault on you and Arwyn Jones falling off that ladder. I also think that there's a relationship between the assault on you, and those letting companies run from North Wales Estates. I *know* that there are a group of heavies who come and frighten tenants who don't pay their rent or who want too many repairs, and I would put money on them being the ones who beat you up. I can't prove it yet, but I will. You can help me, or you can get in my way, but I'm going to find out."

As he spoke, Daniel's determination hardened. Bethan would call it bloody-mindedness, but he preferred *tenacity*. Whatever it was called, he meant what he said to Ian.

Ian said, "I know you mean well, but you don't know what you're dealing with. And that's all I've got to say."

"Fair enough," said Daniel, "but think about it. And think about what you'd like to tell me about someone in this mess who has access to street drugs, and if you know anything about Barry Kettles that you'd like to share."

"Barry? Barry who used to run the office?"

Daniel felt another piece of the jigsaw fall into place. He couldn't see the picture yet, but he was sure that things had changed when Connor arrived, and Ian had just confirmed it.

"Barry. He's dead. That's why I'm here. I found him unconscious in his office and we followed the ambulance. He died on the way."

The blood drained from Ian's face. It hadn't occurred to Daniel that Ian could look any worse, but he knew better now. But he still didn't speak.

He gave Ian one of his cards with his phone number. "Just ring, anytime." Ian looked anywhere but at Daniel, but he put the card in his wallet, and that would have to do

Out in the corridor, Daniel rang Bethan.

"We searched the office, boss," she said. "Dozens of files on equity release cases. The only ones that are missing are Iolo Price and Harriet Marston."

Daniel asked whether there was anything that indicated

that Kettles had a family. "Because he's dead. Died on the way to hospital."

Bethan said she'd have a look.

MAL CAME ROUND the corner looking fed up.

"Hector's got nothing new, and all I've got for Kettles is an address from his driving licence, and it's in Manchester."

"Good job you're going there tomorrow then, isn't it?"

Mal poked Daniel in the ribs. "I'll add it to my list, boss," he said and poked Daniel again. Daniel grinned.

"I wish. Text it over to Bethan and let's see if she can get a phone number. Do we have a mobile?"

Mal got a mobile phone wrapped in an evidence bag from his pocket.

"Yep. Out of juice and password protected, so we'll have to leave it for the technicians."

THE DRIVE BACK WAS HORRIBLE. Mal was stuck behind a bright yellow gritter, which at least made some colour, even if it slowed the traffic down to a crawl. Daniel asked whether Hector had anything to say about the antidepressants Arwyn had been taking.

"They wouldn't have caused dizziness," Mal said, "not according to Hector."

"Helena could have bought something, some street drug, and put it in his breakfast," said Daniel. "That fall wasn't an accident."

"Well, she *could have*, but do we have any suggestion that she did? Did she even know that Arwyn was going up a ladder that morning?"

"If she gave him something that interfered with his balance, it would probably make him an unsafe driver, or impair his ability with power tools, so it would have been dangerous one way or another."

"Too many ifs for me, Dan. And that all supposes that she wanted to kill him. Or that anyone did. Don't go off on one, but we don't even know if there's been a crime here."

Daniel banged his fists together in frustration. He believed what Alis had told him. Arwyn shouldn't have fallen off the ladder. *Something* made him wobble, and that wobble had caused Arwyn's death in a way that could have been a tragic accident. If it had been murder, it had been either very clever, or very lucky.

"We need those toxicology reports," he said.

"Hector says another couple of days, and that *is* a priority," Mal said.

"This gets more complicated with everything we find out, and there's less and less to hold on to, but I *know* there was something weird about Arwyn falling off that ladder," Daniel said, "Hector is sure that there is something weird about Harriet Marston's death. And now Kettles is dead. The only thing they've got in common is a connection with one of the Flowers companies. Is it enough, though?"

By the time they got back to Melin Tywyll the snow had turned to a slushy rain and the roads had begun to clear. They thought about going back to the office, but the call of home, and a warm fire was too strong.

19: COULD YOU COME ON YOUR OWN?

B ack at the house, Daniel reheated the leftover curry and put some rice on while Mal brewed up some extra strong coffee. "I need to wake up," Mal said. "Following that gritter was sending me to sleep. That and the sleet in the headlights." He yawned.

They wrapped themselves in sweaters, and swapped their outdoor shoes for the thick handknitted socks that they wore as slippers around the house. The fire warmed the room as the meal cooked, so that they could remove a couple of layers and sit with their meal on their laps and their feet on the coffee table. The room hadn't been finished for long, and Mal still had to put most of his books onto the new shelves, but with only a couple of lamps, and the firelight, it felt like a home. *Their* home.

There was the sound of a car in the lane outside the house, and they saw the shadow of a figure pass the front window, switching the automatic lights on outside.

"Shit," Mal said, jumping up and taking their plates into the kitchen. Daniel heard him dump them into the sink with a clatter. "Shit, shit, shit."

There was a knock at the door, and Mal went to answer it. Daniel got to his feet as Mal escorted a small woman into the room. She was very well dressed, and carefully made up, *making the best of herself* as Daniel's mother would have said. Despite the foul weather, the woman was wearing high heeled court shoes, and a pale wool coat. Although her hair was streaked with grey, it had obviously once been the same very dark brown as Mal's. Daniel had no doubt who had come to visit.

"Daniel, this is my mother. Mam, this is my boyfriend Daniel, whose house we're in."

"Mrs Kent," said Daniel, holding out his hand to shake hers, "you're most welcome." He saw Mal behind her. Mal's expression said that he wasn't at all sure that his mother *was* welcome.

"Shirley, please," Mal's mother said. "It's a lovely place you've got."

Daniel thanked her and offered coffee. When she agreed, he went into the kitchen, carefully closing the door.

When he went back, Mal and his mother were sat close together on the sofa, Shirley grasping Mal's hand as if it was a life belt. Daniel couldn't read Mal's expression or body language. There was anger, but also longing, Daniel thought, as if Mal wanted his mother, but couldn't forgive her. The physical similarities between mother and son were clear to see, despite their different sizes.

"You'll have to excuse me Daniel, arriving out of the blue like this. Maldi's dad doesn't ...."

Mal said, "He knows, Mam."

Daniel smiled and said that Mal's family was welcome any time. Mal scowled.

"The thing is Maldi," Shirley said, turning to Mal, "it's the wedding."

"Of course it is," said Mal. "I was wondering when this would happen." Daniel saw that Mal had moved away from his mother on the sofa and crossed his arms. Now his body language said *bring it on.*

"It's not you, lovely, I'm pleased that Huw wants you there. I'm so pleased he's getting married, settling down, and Rhiannon is a lovely girl. It's just ...."

"I know, it's just that Dad doesn't want me there." Mal's face was set. Daniel knew that he was aware of his mother's every expression, though he stared straight ahead, seeming to ignore her.

"No, Maldi, no. But, well, there's no good way to say this, but could you come on your own?"

"It'd be different if I was proposing to bring a girl, I suppose," said Mal.

"Oh, I knew this would be awkward. It's just your Dad. You know how he is." Shirley held out her hand towards Mal who ignored it.

"You mean homophobic as well as everything else?"

"He loves you Maldi, he does, underneath. We were hoping, well I was, that maybe at the wedding...."

"If I pretend not to be gay, he might acknowledge that I exist?"

Daniel didn't think he'd ever seen Mal so angry. At the same time, Daniel though, Mal wanted his mother to stay. He wanted his mother, full stop.

"I don't mind not coming to the wedding," Daniel said, "not if it means things will go more smoothly."

Shirley looked at him with relief.

"Thank you," she said.

Mal said nothing. Part of Daniel had hoped that Mal would stick up for him, for *them,* say that Daniel had just as much right to be at the wedding as anyone else. The other part of him wanted Mal to be OK, and for him to get some kind of relationship with his mother. Mal claimed not to care about his family, but Daniel saw the love between Mal and Huw, and he saw how much Mal wanted his mother. It was there in his anger.

If he didn't care, he wouldn't be angry.

He stood up to put another log on the fire, and touched Mal's shoulder as he went past. Mal's body was as hard and unyielding as stone. Daniel felt his own anger rising, along with a terrible desire to make things right for Mal.

He's a good man. Prickly, ambitious, defensive, but good. You should see how soft he is with Bob the dog, and how he looks out for his friends. His father should be proud.

"Mam," said Mal, "Daniel not being there isn't going to change Dad's mind."

"It might," she said, "if he sees you. He's OK about Huw being in the police now. He just needs a bit of time."

"He's had twenty years, Mam. Twenty years."

"But he hasn't seen you. If he saw you, standing next to Huw ...."

"This is pointless Mam. Where are you supposed to be? Shopping? A spa day? A night out with your mates in Chester? If you can't even tell him that you're coming to see me, why do you think he'll talk to me at Huw's wedding?"

The bitterness in Mal's voice was heartbreaking. His mother had no answer to give.

What answer could there be

Daniel didn't see his parents often since they'd left to live in the Spanish sunshine. He and Megan teased them, saying they'd abandoned their children to the cold and rain, but they spoke on the phone, and visited as often as they could. Daniel's house was full of things his mother had made for him — the woolly socks he and Mal were wearing, the cushions on the sofa, the crocheted blankets all over the house. Mal had nothing from his family, apart from his relationship with Huw. He pushed his own anger away, and poured them all some more coffee.

Daniel tried to shift the conversation to neutral topics, asking about Shirley's trip, and the miserable weather. It didn't work, and after about twenty minutes of awkwardness, Shirley said she had to go. Mal walked out to the car with her, and then came back, collected his keys and said, "I'm going out for a bit," and was gone.

20: SPECTACULAR AWFULNESS

There were hours yet before it was going to get light. The bed was warm, and so was Mal, who was wrapped round Daniel like a blanket. Daniel couldn't see Mal's dark skin, but he felt it, warm next to his own, hard with muscle. Mal's nipple ring pressed into his back, and reaching backwards, Daniel felt the soft hair covering Mal's arms.

I'm never going to get tired of this.

After Shirley left and Mal disappeared, Daniel had calmed himself with housework, tidying the kitchen and sorting the washing. Mal came back after an hour, freezing cold, and shivering. "I was sitting in the car," he said, as Daniel rubbed Mal's hands between his own, trying to get some warmth back into them. The fire in the living room had started to die down, but Daniel knew that the bedroom would be warm. "Shower," he said, "quickest way to warm up."

"Only if you come too," said Mal.

They had stood under the hot water kissing and cuddling, until Mal said that he was warm now and it was time for bed. Looking down at their twin erections, Daniel had to agree. He'd intended trying to talk about Shirley's visit, but at that moment it hadn't seemed so important.

He wriggled, experimentally to see whether Mal was awake. He wasn't. Or if he was, he was pretending not to be.

Daniel slipped out of Mal's embrace and down under the duvet to pay some attention to Mal's dick.

Time to wake up he thought, *and I know just the way to do it.*

He wasn't on his own for long. Mal groaned and felt for Daniel's hair. It wasn't long enough to pull, but he loved the feeling of Mal's hands gripping his head, and the effort he was making not to let rip and thrust hard into Daniel's mouth.

Daniel sucked his own fingers as he sucked Mal, and when they were wet, ran them under Mal's balls and between his arse cheeks, teasing. Now Mal gripped his head harder and stopped fighting his desire to fuck Daniel's mouth, and Daniel was totally on board with that. He sucked harder and moved his hand faster until Mal gasped "Don't stop ... please don't stop ...."

Daniel thought about it. Slowed down. Enjoyed the way Mal tried to keep going. "Patience," he said, and pulled away altogether, sliding his hands up through the hair on Mal's chest until he came to the nipple ring. He gave it a tweak and Mal groaned. Mal reached to stroke himself and Daniel pushed his hand away. "I'll get back to it," he said.

"Please get back to it now."

Daniel grinned and stoked Mal's cock with the lightest possible touch.

"Pretty please?"

Daniel stroked harder, feeling Mal's desperation in his urgent movements.

"I'll make the coffee," said Mal.

"Deal." Daniel moved back down and took Mal's cock back into his mouth and ran his tongue around the head. Then he relaxed and let Mal thrust deep. He drew back and sucked, letting his tongue play, enjoying the sensations and the connection until he felt the moment that Mal let go.

Mal thrust harder, until Daniel could hardly breathe, and then he felt the hot rush in the back of his throat and Mal cried his name, and collapsed, tension receding in waves.

"You're just evil," Mal said, when he'd got his breath back. "Now I'm going to want to wake up like that every day."

"Life is full of disappointment," said Daniel, scrambling out from under the duvet. Mal reached for him, and things got hot and interesting all over again.

MAL THOUGHT that the route to Manchester from north Wales was a mixture of the spectacular, and the spectacularly awful. On paper, the drive should take an hour and a half, but all of it was congested with milk lorries, parents on the way to and from school, and trucks pounding their way across Britain, to connect mainland Europe with Ireland, via Holyhead. If he could lift his eyes from the traffic, he would see the hills on both sides — green beside the road, then rising darkly towards the overcast sky, brown with dead bracken. The road crossed a couple of high passes, and a snatched glance would reveal a vista of mountains stretching into the distance.

When he'd lived in London, motorways had numbers. Here in Wales, there was only one, running along the south of the country, so people just said *The Motorway*. He pulled onto the A55, which runs parallel to the north coast, in the same way that the M4 parallels the south. *The Expressway* he thought, tightening his lips. What's a fucking *expressway,* when it's at home? They can't even make the biggest road in north Wales into a motorway. He looked up and realised that he was getting too close to the car in front and took a slow breath as he eased back on the accelerator. *Calm down.*

As the satnav directed him around Chester and into the tangle of roads connecting Merseyside and the cities of north-west England, he tried to decide whether his bad temper was a result of having to leave Daniel, his mother's clandestine visit, or his dislike of the Manchester case. He knew that he was a good undercover officer. He'd been involved in more than a few drug buys around the country, pretending to be a small-time dealer. He'd 'received' stolen goods in pubs and under railway arches. This job was a step up, working his way into an organised crime group at a much higher level. On the face of it, it was the same job; pretend to be a villain and then take the real villains down. But something about it didn't feel right.

The motorways spewed the traffic into the city, and regular streets, buildings looming up, making dark canyons in the winter gloom, tramlines and bus lanes, traffic lights and endless stopping and starting. Rows of coffee bars and pubs. Litter. Mal was pleased to see people who weren't white, people he didn't recognise. *Melin Tywyll is pretty, like a postcard is pretty, No one would make a postcard of this,* he thought, *but I like it.*

At the next traffic lights, he snapped a picture of the street scene on his phone and sent it to Daniel. A raised eyebrow emoji came back. Mal smiled.

He decided to leave his car at the hotel and walk to the police station. It would give him a chance to call Andy Carter and to try to understand why he felt so unsettled about this operation. The ground floor of the hotel had floor to ceiling windows, so that passers-by could see into the bar and restaurant. Mal had to look twice at the figure lounging in a chair by the revolving door. It couldn't be Daniel, and it wasn't. As the figure got out of the chair, Mal realised who was waiting to ambush him.

"Hi," said Wade Addison. "Can I buy you a coffee?"

"I hate to use the word, Addison, but it's hardly *appropriate*." Mal sketched in the scare quotes round 'appropriate'.

"You mean that we are kind of on show here, a senior police officer and a notorious gangster? To me, those windows say we've got nothing to hide."

Mal said that he didn't have anything to hide.

"We've all got something to hide, Detective Chief Inspector."

"You more than me, I imagine," Mal said. Mal wondered how long Addison had been waiting, and how he knew where to wait. Because this wasn't a chance meeting.

"Let me buy you a coffee, and we can sit away from the windows," Addison said and Mal agreed, wishing he'd got some method of recording their conversation.

"I'm not going to beat around the bush," Addison began. "I've done a lot of illegal things in the past, and I've made a lot of money. It's time for me to get out of that game, and for that I need help. Councillor Terry might be a drunk who can't keep his hands off women, but he's a big deal on the Council. He can help me. You helped him. I want to know why."

Mal said that he hadn't been helping Councillor Terry in particular.

"I wanted to get those women out of there. Didn't need the paperwork. We caught the men with their pants round their ankles and their dicks on show. They were humiliated and that was enough."

Addison leaned back in his seat. "If you say so. I'm sure you've got an equally good explanation about why you were there at all."

Not one that either of us would believe, but Mal thought that he couldn't help liking the man, especially compared to the other big villain on his plate.

Declan Hughes wasn't complicated, or smart, or pretending to be respectable. Declan Hughes had a sawn-off shotgun and took it with him into convenience stores and bookmakers, after dark, and threatened people until they gave him the contents of the till. Not for the first time, Mal reflected that he'd be happy with more like Declan Hughes and fewer like Wade Addison. He might like talking to Addison, and for sure Declan Hughes had neither culture nor conversation. Hughes spent his time in drinking clubs and racecourses, not researching the murals in the Town Hall. Nobody needed to set up a sting for Declan Hughes, they just had to catch him. Once they had the handcuffs on, Hughes was going to jail, like his father before him. If Mal asked why he did what he did, Hughes would shrug and say, "I wanted the money." Except he wouldn't. He'd say, "No comment," because it was the default setting, even when answering the questions made more sense.

Mal wondered what Addison would say if he asked why he did what he did. Would he say that he wanted the money? And would it be the truth?

21: UNDERWATER LIVING

The building by the riverside in Melin Tywyll looked as if it had once been a shop, though now it was the worst kind of building site, rubbish spreading in a tide from the walls towards the steel mesh fencing on the pavement. Passersby had added to the heaps of trash, and every few minutes another piece of debris was dumped by someone inside. A blue portable toilet cabin, in need of emptying if the smell was anything to go by, completed the scene. But it was Ian Goldsmith's place of work, and Daniel was hoping for clues about the assault.

"Lovely place to work," said Bethan.

"Worse place to live when they finish," said Daniel. "The last time I saw this, it was underwater,"

"And it will be again. It wants knocking down."

Instead, they knocked on the mesh fence, and shouted to whoever was inside. A face appeared at what had been the shop doorway.

"Clwyd Police," said Daniel. "We've got some questions for you."

"Come in if you like," said the face.

They scrambled over towards the door, to be greeted by the smell of wet cement, and the noise of several power tools all going at once, together with the sounds of hammering and breaking wood. In the middle of it all stood a radio, music playing, unheard by anyone.

"What can we do you for?" said the face, once they were inside.

"DI Owen," said Daniel, "and my colleague DS Davies. We're following up on the assault on Ian Goldsmith on Friday night. We understand that he worked here. Who are you, sir?"

"Danny Jenkins. Foreman. And yes, Ian worked here, and yes, I heard about him being attacked, but I don't know what you think we can tell you."

"Tell us what you're doing here," said Bethan, "and what Ian's role was."

"It's going to be little flats, eight of them. Cheap rents. Ian's a sparky, he was getting started on the first fix."

"Isn't it a bit close to the river?" Bethan asked. "This area got flooded last year."

"We've cleared all that out. Dunno about anything else. Flats they said they wanted, and flats is what they're getting."

They asked Danny if he would show them round. "Not much to see." But they looked as if they were going to insist, so he led them without enthusiasm through a series of small dark spaces, stacked with building materials, and all smelling unpleasantly of wet cement and dirty water. As they went, he indicated the other workers, naming them, but not making proper introductions. At the end of the tour, Daniel asked about Danny's relationship with Ian, leaving Bethan to start talking to whoever she could find.

"He was OK," said Danny, "knew what he was doing, turned up on time, and didn't skive off doing other jobs."

"But he did work in other places," Daniel said. "He did some repairs for a friend of mine in a rented house."

"That's different," said Danny. "Same company, so they can send him somewhere else. I just meant he didn't do foreigners."

Daniel said that Ian had complained "to a friend" about having to wait a long time for his money. Danny shrugged. "He was just the complaining sort, self-employed, see, so they have to put their invoices in, and they leave it, and leave it, and then moan when the girls in the office don't get them the money the same day." Daniel asked where the office was, and Danny looked at him as if he was stupid. "The high street, North Wales Estates."

"These flats aren't going to be very big." Daniel said, and again Danny shrugged.

"They're going to be cheap. Cheap enough for people on benefits. Druggies and dossers. They don't want much, and they'll be better than the streets."

"But some of these rooms don't have windows."

"Only the bathrooms and who needs a window in a bathroom? Look mate, I build what I'm told to build. If it looks good enough for the planners, then it's good enough for me."

"And the Building Inspector comes regularly, does he?"

"Not my business. Nor yours, I think."

"Most things are my business," said Daniel, but the other man sneered.

And that seemed to be that. Daniel went in search of Bethan, noticing the poor quality of the materials he could see, and the sloppy way the workmen were using them. Sure, he was a perfectionist when he was working on his own place, and he kept his workspace clean and tidy. This site was filthy, and it would show in the finished product. These were the kinds of tradesmen who had filled Alis's broken windows with cardboard and failed to repair the roof, the sort of men that Arwyn had complained about.

But it's not police business. Unless there's some kind of crime in all this chaos.

Bethan looked as depressed by the work as he did. They picked their way out of the old shop, and back onto the street before speaking.

"Those places will be slums within six months of the first tenants moving in," said Bethan, and Daniel agreed.

"I don't know how they got planning permission, and I don't believe the Building Inspector has ever visited. He seemed to be round at my place every time I laid a brick."

"Do you think the plans in the council offices and what's going on here are the same?" Bethan asked. "Because I'd be very surprised if they were."

"But is it our business?" Daniel asked.

"I'm sure that we could find out how to make it our business," Bethan replied. "I have a cousin in the planning department."

"Of course you do," said Daniel.

BETHAN KNOCKED on Daniel's office door and he waved her in, pushing aside the monthly crime figures return. "I can't make it add up, and I can't palm it off on the DCI," he said, "but if I send it to Hart, she'll see the mistakes and think I'm an idiot."

"You are an idiot," Bethan said, "with all due respect. You should have shoved it into the DCI's briefcase before he went."

"Point. Too late now. Distract me."

Bethan looked at her notes.

"I've been on to the Council's Planning Department, and the Building Inspectors. When I'd had the official line, I rang my cousin."

"Different story?"

"No, and that's what's odd. No story at all. Planning permission granted for the flats, no discussion, went through on the nod. I asked my cousin and he said that it's the only new residential site so close to the river, all the rest is commercial. I said, what about potential flooding, and he said their reports show *no* potential flooding. I looked up the reports and he's right. No potential flooding. Then I rang a friend I was at school with ..." Daniel rolled his eyes "... who works for an insurance company. She looked it up. I quote 'No one in their right mind would insure anything within five hundred yards of that address.'"

"So, who wrote the flooding report for the council?"

"I'm glad you asked me that, boss," Bethan said. "Want to take a guess?"

"Yellow Flower Planning Consultants?"

"Almost. Goldenrod Consulting Services. Paid by the developers."

"And the building inspectors?"

"All the reports are up to date. Regular inspections have taken place and no problems have been identified. And I had to call in some favours to get that load of twaddle."

They looked at each other.

"Perhaps you'd like to see if those developers are developing any other sites around the town," said Daniel.

"Just what I was thinking," Bethan replied, "and I was going to have a closer look at the planning committee, in case I know anyone else I could talk to. If you see what I mean."

22: THAT'S NOT VERY FEMINIST

"It's got nothing to do with whether I think you're a grown up," Megan was saying, "and everything to do with the fact that he left you, and now he looks like he's doing it again."

Megan had phoned to ask Daniel to come out for coffee and a bun, and Bethan had all but pushed him out of the door, telling him to bring cakes back for their afternoon meeting. "And bring yourself some lunch," she said. "Black coffee has zero calories and that's all you seem to live on." So, Daniel had gone to meet his sister and she was lecturing him about Mal spending his time in Manchester.

"It's not that simple," said Daniel. "It's a way of him having more varied work and me being in charge here."

But he knew that where Mal worked wasn't the problem he kept having to push out of his thoughts. It was Mal's refusal to talk about the wedding, or his family. He took a deep breath and told his sister about Shirley's visit. As he expected, only the presence of a cafe full of gossips stopped a sisterly explosion.

"She did *what?*" Megan hissed. "And you offered not to go?

Sometimes I think you *like* people trampling all over you. Jesus, Dan, what are you not seeing here?"

He shrugged, because he wanted to go to the wedding, wanted to be Mal's partner at this public event, spend time with Sasha and Rhi, whom he liked, to get to know Huw. But he also wanted Mal to be able to make peace with his family, and for Huw to have both his brother and his Dad on his wedding day, and ideally, not fighting each other.

He tried to explain himself to Megan, and she put her head in her hands and said, "But you don't get it. *You* are just as important. Mal has to stick up for *you*. He has to talk to his mother and everyone else and say that *you are the one he's chosen.*"

"But he has. Chosen me, I mean." Because he had. He'd moved in, he didn't hide it at work, and anyway his family problems went way back. "I wish he'd talk to me about it, though," Daniel said.

"Which is what you said when he disappeared on you before. Or have you forgotten that?"

Daniel hadn't. He understood why Mal had felt the need to keep everyone at arm's length while he dealt with corruption in his previous job. But it had still been painful. He had wanted Mal to talk to him then, and he wanted him to talk now. He felt tears start behind his eyes and took a paper napkin from the table to blow his nose.

"I hate this, Dan," said Megan. "I want to like Mal. I want you to be happy. But I want you to understand that you have rights too — to be included in things that affect you." He looked up and Megan had tears in her eyes too. She grasped his hand.

"Get a grip," she said. "I'm going to order cake, and then we're going to talk about something else."

She stood up and went over to the counter. Daniel remembered that Mal did do a million kind things for him, including buying cake. Was he overreacting? He didn't know, and not knowing made it all worse. He had a pain in his stomach, jabbing at him, telling him that something was awry, only his mind said there wasn't. He just needed to keep loving Mal, and Mal would feel more secure and start talking. He wanted to put his head in his hands and let the tears flow, but he thought about where he was: in a cafe in the middle of Melin Tywyll, on a busy morning. It was dark inside; all the furniture was painted black, and the lighting was intimate rather than bright. The steam from the coffee machine clouded the windows, reducing the light further. But despite all of that, if he cried, the whole town would know by sunset.

Megan brought carrot cake and chocolate cake, two forks, and more coffee. "Dig in, and I'll tell you something that I promised to keep secret."

He expected a revelation about one of the kids, so he was surprised when Megan leaned closer and said, "Helena's Arwyn is having an affair. Or rather he *was* having an affair, but I don't know if it was still going on when he died."

Daniel asked how she knew. She took a forkful of chocolate cake and winked. "District nurses know everything...."

"Yeah, right," said Daniel. "Helena found out and told you." Megan nodded.

"She thought that she ought to leave him. It broke her heart, it really did. Maybe she would have left him in the end, but for sure she's grieving him now."

"So how come?"

"I know because I'm her friend, but I also know because I've dealt with her as a patient. And this is what I totally must insist you don't tell anyone ever." He nodded, and she knew her secrets were safe. "They were trying for a baby, but she kept having miscarriages, and it was making her depressed and almost suicidal. Then Arwyn had all the trouble at work, and he was depressed too, so they were just fighting all the time. I suppose this girl came on to him and he didn't say no."

"This girl came on to him? That's not very feminist."

"You're right. I don't know how they met, but she's called Lizzie and she lives in one of the houses he used to work in. And that's all I can tell you."

Daniel asked whether she thought Helena could be persuaded to tell him, not about the miscarriages, but about the affair.

"I think she'll tell you. I think she wants to talk about it," said Megan.

Daniel nodded. "I'll make an appointment to see her again this afternoon."

Because if it was true, the affair, then Helena had to be a suspect in her husband's death. Or at the very least, they had to eliminate her.

He and Megan fought over the last pieces of cake. It was time to go, but things weren't right between them. He didn't think they'd agree about Mal unless things changed a lot, and he didn't see that happening any time soon. The pain in his stomach started up again.

HE'D TOLD Bethan that they could put Roderick Marston on the back burner, at least for now, because the various Flowers companies looked like they needed more attention. But he went back to the office and asked her to come with him to talk to Helena Jones. Primrose Lettings might be responsible for the state of the River Terrace house, but not responsible for Arwyn's death. As for Harriet Marston, he couldn't make his mind up one way or the other. They chewed it over as they walked round to Helena's house, and came to no conclusions.

Megan was right, Helena was prepared to talk about the

affair. She was still crying about Arwyn, and at the same time saying what a bastard he'd been and calling Lizzie all the names under the sun. The affair was over, at least Arwyn had said so, and Helena believed him. Daniel asked whether Helena knew where Lizzie lived or had any contact details for her, and it seemed that Helena did. In fact, Daniel felt sure that Helena had made quite certain that she knew exactly where Lizzie lived, and everything about her. They took down her address and left Helena, once again drinking tea with her mother.

On the way he suggested that Helena might be a suspect worth considering in Arwyn's death.

"A woman scorned," said Bethan. "But how did she do it?" And that was the question Daniel couldn't answer.

LIZZIE LIVED on the same street as Mal's old rented house. Judging from the outside, Lizzie's home was her pride and joy. All the paintwork was fresh, and there were new windows and a new front door, all wood, all good quality. When the door opened, they could see that inside was similar: new carpets, new furniture, and the whole place smelling of paint, in a good way. Lizzie herself was a well-dressed thirty-something with glossy hair and well-done makeup. She greeted them with a smile and freely admitted to having been fond of Arwyn.

"He was a lovely, lovely man."

Lizzie kept saying how much she had enjoyed Arwyn's company. She explained that she was recently divorced, had moved into this house, and was determined to make it her own. Arwyn had been installing new radiators and they'd fallen into conversation, and then into bed.

"I know it was wrong," she said. "We were just two people with problems taking comfort from each other."

Daniel asked whether she thought Helena had known about the affair. Lizzie said, "Oh yes, at least I saw her outside this house more than once. I'm not saying she was a stalker, but she certainly wanted to know what I was up to."

Bethan asked how long the affair had lasted, and Lizzie said a couple of afternoons, well maybe more than a couple, but not long. "Because I'm worth more than that. It sounds selfish, but I don't mean it to be. I had sex with another woman's husband to make myself feel wanted. It's a bit new age, but I have to get beyond that, and learn to value myself without someone else telling me that I'm OK."

Daniel thought that it made sense, just that it would have been better for Helena if Lizzie had realised it before she started sleeping with Arwyn.

They left Lizzie and stood on the pavement outside.

"So, what do you think?" Bethan asked.

"I think Helena was badly hurt by her husband's behaviour, but I don't believe for a minute that she killed him."

"I'm almost with you, but not quite. Helena was stalking Lizzie, hanging round her house and not worrying about being seen. That sounds like she was pretty unstable."

"Sure, but if she was going to kill someone, wouldn't it be Lizzie?"

"Maybe Lizzie was next."

23: FLINGING INSTRUCTIONS AROUND LIKE CONFETTI

Daniel had four dead bodies, at least one of which was murder according to Hector, who also said it probably couldn't be proved. Plus, an assault victim who was lying about who beat him up. There was a dodgy planning decision, and some substandard housing, with even more substandard landlords. There was a tenuous connection through a series of companies named after yellow flowers. And possibly a connection to Hector's new boyfriend. Or equally possibly, there was nothing at all.

Connor could have been having a bad day when they met him in the pub. Ian Goldsmith might owe money and have been beaten as a punishment. Harriet Marston may have had a heart condition. Until the autopsy, no one knew how Barry Kettles had died. Arwyn Jones could have had too much coffee and lost his balance. Iolo Price almost certainly died of natural causes. For all he knew, the planning department was just understaffed, and the Building Inspector incompetent. Veronica had shown him bad housing, but that might be a one off. The companies named after flowers might be just a coincidence.

He could let it all go. There was no shortage of crime that was clear for everyone to see. Crime that he and the team could investigate, solve, and persuade the CPS to prosecute. Bad housing wasn't police business any more than marital unhappiness or relatives disappointed by their inheritances. If Hector wanted relationship advice he could ask.

He couldn't stop worrying that Megan might be right about Mal, because she was his touchstone as he was hers. Mal's unwillingness to talk and Megan's doubts were affecting his judgement. He couldn't concentrate, was flinging instructions around like confetti, nothing tied together, no single thread to pull on, just a tangled mess. One minute he was convinced that the Flowers companies were the centre of a mass of corruption in the town, the next he wondered if there was anything criminal going on at all.

He had his running things in the car, and there was a quick loop around the riverside path. If he pushed it, he could be back in the police station shower within half an hour. No one saw him leave. He gave himself two minutes to warm up, to lose the feeling that his shoes were filled with sand, and for every joint to tell him that this was a bad idea. Ignoring the protests from lungs and legs, he speeded up, and speeded up again, until he couldn't think about anything except keeping up the pace. He found a rhythm, counted his steps, and refused to allow his body to slow, until the police station came back into view. Sweat poured off his face, and his breath was ragged as he stretched. It wasn't his best run, it wasn't even a good run, but when he'd had a shower and dressed in his work clothes, he knew what the next step was going to be. By the end of the day, he was going to have decided, one way or the other, and he had a good idea which way it would go. He wrote a lot of notes for his colleagues, signed out a car, and set off for Wrexham and Hector.

THE FIRST THING Daniel noticed about Hector was the black eye.

"Don't tell me you fell downstairs," said Daniel, "just don't. We don't have to talk about it, but don't tell me any lies."

"It's not what you think," said Hector.

"Yes, it is," said Daniel, "but that's not why I'm here."

"It was a fight. It was stupid. Connor was stressed, I was stressed. Things just got out of hand. It's fine now. He is a great guy, but he's having a rubbish time at work, and there's other stuff."

Daniel stepped closer to Hector and pulled him into a hug. He felt Hector wince as Daniel touched sore and bruised flesh. Hector was the gentlest of men. He'd probably learned to box at his expensive school, but this wasn't the result of a boxing match, with rules. Daniel made a private resolution that it wouldn't be happening again.

"Just remember that I have a spare room, and that I'm a good cook. If you need me, call me. Or Mal. Either of us will come if you call."

Hector looked away. "I'm fine, honestly. What did you want to know? Something we can talk about over coffee?"

Hector made a mean brew, so Daniel passed him the kettle.

"I want to know about antidepressants, taking too many and losing your balance on a ladder, and I want to know about Barry Kettles."

Once the spotlight shifted to work, and away from his personal life, Hector relaxed.

"I can't tell you about Barry Kettles yet. The notes say he died of respiratory failure, but that's all. I've got the autopsy on the list for later today or first thing in the morning."

Daniel shrugged. Kettles was a suspicious death, but if he

wanted Hector to do the post-mortem, and he did, then Barry would have to wait his turn.

"So, the other person you're thinking about is Arwyn Jones?"

Daniel nodded. "Is it possible that he took a couple too many Valium or whatever, and it caused the accident?"

Hector reached for the file. "Loss of balance is a common side effect of Valium and benzodiazepines in general. But that wasn't what he was prescribed. I have ordered an analysis though."

"Could the drugs he was prescribed cause him to lose his balance?"

Hector looked at his computer for a few minutes, scrolling in search of information, then shook his head. "They shouldn't. Also, I rang his doctor, and he'd only just got the scrip. The medication shouldn't have had any effect at all by then. They take a couple of weeks to kick in. You do know that I told Mal this already?"

"I do. But I've spoken to the witness. What she describes is someone who was stable one minute and wobbling so badly that the ladder fell the next. Arwyn was used to being up ladders. I've seen where the ladder was, and it was on firm ground. No reason to fall. There were things Arwyn could have grabbed hold of if he'd had his wits about him."

"I'm sorry Daniel, the answers I gave Mal are still the same, even though it's you."

Daniel knew that he was grasping at straws, but all his instincts were telling him that Arwyn should not have overbalanced on the ladder.

"You know the most likely reason for Arwyn to be dizzy?" Hector said. "A cold. Ask your witness if Arwyn was blowing his nose or sneezing."

Daniel said he would but asked again if Hector was

checking for possible drugs, and Hector reassured him. "If you find anything else, let me know and I'll tell you if it's a possibility. But most likely thing is a cold. I know that doctors' practice and they aren't the kind to hand out serious drugs like sweeties. Nice people. Lesley and Keith Flowers."

24: HART AND FLOWERS

Daniel drove back to the station, mentally preparing for the meeting he'd called. His conversation with Hector had left him feeling that the case, if it even was a case, was getting more nebulous by the minute. He'd briefed Superintendent Hart, and although she had agreed with his assessment, he still felt the ground under his feet was in danger of collapse.

He took a tray of coffee and cake upstairs to the meeting room, and called his colleagues in. Abby and Charlie had been looking at equity release, and the many companies named after flowers. Bethan had been looking hard at their most obvious suspects, *if there were any murders at all*, and he'd asked Sophie to come along too, because she'd been there at the start of it all.

"This is a summit meeting," he said, when they all had coffee and cake. "I need to make a decision. Today. Mostly about Harriet Marston, but also about Arwyn Jones, and possibly about Barry Kettles."

"And about fraud," said Abby. Charlie nodded vigorously next to her, his mouth full of carrot cake.

"Fraud?" Daniel asked.

"Fraud," Abby said. "At least I think it's fraud. Targeting elderly people and selling them equity release."

"It's a regulated financial product," said Daniel.

"Not the way Daffodil goes about it," said Abby.

"OK then, you can start," said Daniel, but it was Charlie who grasped the baton.

"Those companies, boss, the ones named after yellow flowers, they are all connected. They're connected to each other, and they're all connected to Melin Tywyll. The registered offices are in London, but it's the same registered office as North Wales Estates, and a couple of other local businesses. And the directors are mostly the same, too. No surprises that two of them have the surname Flowers."

"Interesting, but no crime so far."

Abby joined in, cake forgotten. "Sir, I looked at the Land Registry and Probate Office records, along with the papers we got from the Daffodil office. I've matched up as many sales as I had time for, all through North Wales Estates, all owned by Daffodil, and all for good prices. None of the owners who died had any living relatives, until my Uncle Iolo and Harriet Marston."

"Still no fraud." This time it was Bethan who spoke.

"Maybe, maybe not. But Daffodil has only been going for three years, and they've had over fifty properties sold in that time — and they are just the ones I've found. What are the chances of the firm identifying fifty homeowners with no relatives, who were going to die in the next few years, and selling them equity release?"

"It's getting on for four million quid," added Charlie.

"But there might be dozens more who have bought the product and haven't died," said Bethan.

"What would you say if I told you that two of the directors of the companies are local doctors?"

There was a shocked silence. A GP would be in the best

possible position to identify elderly people in failing health, who had no relatives, and who might want extra cash.

"Not Dr Mr Flowers and Dr Mrs Flowers? I bet half the station is registered with that practice. I know I am," said Bethan.

The silence grew again.

"They wouldn't," said Bethan. "Dr Mrs Flowers is a lovely woman. I always ask to see her."

"Well, the names match up," said Abby. "There might be other Flowerses in Melin, but the directors are Lesley and Keith, and so are the doctors."

"We'd need a *lot* more information before we do anything," said Bethan and everyone nodded. "We don't even know whether any of them were the Flowers' patients." More nods.

If the doctors were targeting their own patients, then it was unethical, thought Daniel, and he needed to talk to them. But it didn't help with Harriet Marston. Or Arwyn Jones. He said as much.

Bethan took the baton.

"Roderick Marston is a nasty piece of work," she said, "and he needed money. I can't say that I took to Jennifer, but her finances look OK, and she hasn't been sacked from her job for fraud. Jennifer wanted help with the school fees, Roderick looks like losing his house. The money from his mother's estate might save it."

Abby started thinking aloud. "Harriet Marston doesn't fit the Flowers pattern anyway. She was fit and healthy, and she had living relatives."

"Only they never visited, so no one knew about them," countered Charlie.

"Tell us more about the horrible Roderick," asked Daniel, "like how come he had an expensive car outside his house and said that he had a job in sales. I know you told me, but tell everyone else."

"It's all on borrowed money," said Bethan. "The car's probably gone by now, or it soon will be. He *does* have a job in sales. He's involved in a couple of pyramid schemes selling health foods. The job he was sacked from was as a sales manager for an internet vitamins company. A good job too, only he was greedy. He was siphoning off VAT on things where VAT wasn't payable. He was going to be charged, but at the last minute, the company decided they didn't want the bad publicity, and the CPS bailed."

Daniel wondered about Harriet Marston's late husband. Was he the reason that Harriet's children were so unpleasant? Not for the first time, Bethan was ahead of him.

"I also did a bit of asking about Roderick and Jennifer's father," she said, "and it looks like Roderick was a chip off the old block. William Marston killed himself while he was on remand for fraud."

There was a collective *aha!* from everyone in the room, and Bethan smirked as she polished her fingernails on her jacket, as if to say that Abby and Charlie were not the only ones who could pull rabbits from hats. The offences for which Marston senior had been arrested were almost identical to those for which his son had lost his job — stealing from his employer by adding invented taxes to invoices and skimming them into his own bank account.

"It was over twenty years ago, in Swansea. Harriet came up here after her husband died. From what I can work out, Roderick and Jennifer were at university, and none of them ever went back to Swansea."

Bethan said she'd found out most of it from old newspaper articles and a conversation with a retired detective from Swansea. "I think we have to consider Roderick as a suspect for his mother's death," she said. "He needed the money and he's shown that he's prepared to lie and cheat to get it."

"It's a big step from fraud to murder," said Daniel, and

everyone started talking at once. Daniel drank the last of his coffee and took advantage of Charlie trying to get his voice heard to snag the last piece of cake. Could there be two fraudsters at work in one small town? If Roderick had been about to lose everything, would he go to extremes to save it? His father had killed himself, perhaps to avoid the shame of conviction. Had Roderick faced the same prospect but taken a different path? He listened to the argument around the table — his colleagues were wondering the same things, and, like him, reaching no conclusions.

"We've found out a lot in a short time," he said, "and well done for it all, but I'm not seeing a single strong lead. Lots of maybes, and could-bes, but nothing holding up a big sign saying *Follow Me.*"

Sophie looked up and caught Daniel's eye. He held out his hand to invite her to speak. He saw that she'd been making notes. The rest of them could have been any corporate types, he and Charlie in suits, Abby and Bethan both in dresses with jackets, but Sophie's black and white couldn't be anything but what it was. She had slipped her jacket over the back of her chair, but the black trousers and white shirt still shrieked *uniform.* There were detectives who thought their uniformed colleagues were second-class citizens. He wasn't one of them. Uniform or not, she was an experienced police officer, and she looked as if she had something to say.

"This is all to do with *houses,*" she said. "Someone has seen how the market in this town is working and they are cashing in. Four million pounds from the equity release scheme, cheap houses and flats rented out and not maintained, with heavies coming in to threaten tenants who don't pay. All being run from an estate agent, and all tied in to those Flower companies. All perfectly legal, at least on the surface.

"I know I've only been here a few days, but I think there's

something behind it all, and it isn't Roderick Marston. It seems bigger than that to me."

Bethan didn't look happy at that.

"So where would you start, ma'am?" she said.

"With the Flowerses," Sophie replied, "the doctors. Because why would a couple of GPs own an estate agency?"

25: NOT A BAD WORD

Daniel had not spoken to anyone who had a bad word to say about either Dr Lesley Flowers, or her husband, Dr Keith. He'd told Superintendent Hart that he needed to talk to them, and she'd agreed. While telling him how nice they were.

Given the universal esteem in which the doctors were held, he shouldn't have been surprised to be invited into their house with what appeared to be genuine warmth. He found the house up a long, tree-lined drive; a flat-fronted eighteenth century beauty, with multi-paned windows, a shallow pitched roof, and four tall chimneys. It was a simple design, but the proportions were perfect. He was led through an oak-floored hallway, strewn with pale silk rugs — no suggestion of taking his shoes off here, he noted. The living room was big enough for three enormous sofas, what looked like dozens of occasional tables, vases of flowers, cushions, lamps, more silk rugs, swags of fabric around the windows, an ornate mirror over a marble fireplace, and all of it looking as if it had been styled for a magazine. A silver coffee pot waited on a tray, with bone china cups and homemade biscuits on dainty plates.

The two doctors were all smiles, Keith pouring the coffee and offering the biscuits, Lesley asking if he had had any difficulty finding them. When the fussing died away, they looked at him.

"What can we do for you, Inspector Owen?" Keith asked.

"I'm interested in Daffodil Equity Release, Primrose Lettings, and all the associated businesses," he said. "I'm investigating a number of incidents related to those businesses, and I'm hoping you can help me understand them."

Lesley and Keith looked at each other. Daniel thought that he saw puzzlement on both faces, but also some distress.

"We heard about Iolo Price and Mrs Marston, and we've returned their money," Keith said. "But it was all legal, the agreements, I mean."

Daniel nodded. "So why return the money?"

"We didn't want the fuss," said Lesley. "Really, equity release is supposed to help older people, not cause problems. Most people who sign up don't have close relatives, you see. But we don't manage the business that closely. The manager does that."

Daniel decided that the preliminaries had gone on long enough. Yes, they had been welcoming, but he was certain they'd been passing information about their patients to Barry Kettles.

"I've spoken to your manager," he said. "Barry Kettles. He tells me that he gets his 'leads' from someone else. It seems to me that doctors are in a good position to supply the names and addresses of older people who might be interested in equity release."

"It's not illegal," said Keith.

"So, you are passing names on to your manager?"

There was no answer. Maybe it wasn't illegal, and maybe those elderly people did want some extra money, but Hector was sure that Harriet Marston had been murdered.

"Are you perhaps passing on the names of people who aren't in the best of health, and who don't have close relatives to make a fuss? Because that would be the most profitable, wouldn't it? Buy a house for half its worth and double your money a few months later."

"Really Inspector, nothing we've done is illegal, I assure you," said Keith.

Which was an answer, but not to the question they'd been asked. He looked round the over-styled room, paid for by their careful sorting through patient records, and Barry Kettles' sales ability.

"The police pathologist is not happy with how Harriet Marston died," he said, to see how they reacted. They didn't, continuing to sit on their big sofas, with half-smiles. "Is that perhaps the reason you didn't want her children making a fuss?"

"I don't know what you're getting at, Inspector. I hope that you're not suggesting that we had anything to do with her death, because if you are, I will be calling my solicitor."

"That's your right at any time, of course," Daniel said as blandly as possible. "Can I ask you about Primrose Lettings?" He hoped the sudden change of subject would disconcert the two doctors. It didn't. Or if it did, it didn't show.

"Of course. Although we have nothing to do with the day-to-day running of the business."

"So, you would be surprised to hear that one of your properties has been condemned as unfit for human habitation? That another has electrical fittings that are hazardous to life? That several of your tenants have been threatened in their homes by men representing your company?"

"Very surprised. And shocked," said Keith, sounding as if he was reading from a script.

"If those things are true, we need to investigate," said Lesley, with an equal lack of emotion.

"I have investigated," said Daniel, "and so have various council officers. I assure you that what I'm telling you is true. Some are civil matters, and I have no doubt you will be hearing about them in due course. But the threats are my business."

"You surely don't think we would countenance threats to our tenants?" Lesley asked, with the first bit of animation he'd seen. So, he told her the truth.

"I think that if you don't know about the threats, and the appalling conditions of some of your properties, then it's because you have *chosen* not to know." He wasn't sure whether they knew, or if they were deliberately remaining ignorant. Either way, they owned the properties, and their money had paid for thugs to visit Casey and Jemima. They could sit in their beautiful home and pretend none of it was anything to do with them, but they weren't going to avoid it forever. Their next move, he thought, would be to throw Connor and Barry Kettles under the bus. He was right.

"We rely on our managers," said Keith, "perhaps too much. We had no idea such things were going on. Rest assured we will be looking into these allegations."

"Can I ask how you came to employ Mr Byrne-Jones and Mr Kettles?" Daniel asked.

"I can't remember exactly, the usual way I suppose," said Keith.

"The usual way?"

"Adverts, interviews, that sort of thing."

"And you could provide me with the records of the recruitment process? Where you advertised? Application forms?"

"I don't see why we should."

"I think I'd like to see what your managers' qualifications are for the kind of work they're doing. If, as you seem to be implying, they are responsible for the things I've just told you."

Keith mumbled something about looking for the paperwork and sending it to him. Daniel thought it was time for a Come to Jesus talk.

"Dr and Dr Flowers, you are the legal owners of some of the worst housing I have ever seen. Your tenants are being treated like animals. You are using your patients' information to make money. Some of what you have done may indeed be legal, but I don't think you will have much of a reputation left when all this gets out."

"We didn't know about any of this, Inspector," said Lesley. "What can we do?" He didn't warm to her plaintive voice.

"It's Detective Inspector, and it's not for me to tell you what to do. Maybe finding out what you own and visiting it might be a start. And definitely some good legal advice."

Then Keith blew it.

"Isn't there some way we can work this out together? Without people having to know? Something you need, perhaps?"

His wife's expression told Daniel that she knew he'd made everything ten times worse.

"I look forward to receiving details of how you recruited Byrne-Jones and Kettles," he said. "Tomorrow would be good. Plus, a full list of all your properties, your tenants, your tenancy agreements, all your dealings with the local authority and your employees in the property businesses. Failing that, we will be seeking a search warrant for these premises, North Wales Estates, and your place of work. All further conversations will be held at Melin Tywyll police station, under caution. Do you understand?" They both nodded. Keith opened his mouth to speak, and Lesley hissed, "Be quiet."

Daniel was tempted to leave without telling them about Barry Kettles, because he was certain that as soon as the Flowerses knew of his death, everything would turn out to be Kettles' fault. But they were going to find out soon enough.

"I need to tell you," he said, "that Barry Kettles died yesterday. We don't know how, yet. It would be helpful if you could provide me with any and all information you have about his next of kin, and his address here in Melin Tywyll."

He watched as the blood drained from both their faces. "We don't know anything about him," Lesley Flowers said.

Daniel thought that they

"Then I suggest you find out and add it to the list of things to bring to the Police Station tomorrow. Shall we say two o'clock?'

Daniel stood up, put the delicate plate and cup back on the tray, and left, hoping he was headed the right way to the front door.

26: MY SCHOOL FRIEND, THE GANGSTER

The Wade Addison in Mal's files had become as familiar as a school friend. Mal needed to know Addison inside out, to be able to predict what he'd do next. So far, he'd surprised Mal twice, and Mal thought that he couldn't afford to let him get away with it a third time.

Addison had been born and brought up in Manchester, where he'd won a scholarship to the famous boys' grammar school. Mal knew that Addison's parents had divorced, that he had two full siblings, and two half-brothers, from his father's re-marriage to a Cardiff woman. He knew that Addison had left school at sixteen with stellar exam results, and much to his teachers' dismay. His first arrest had been at age fifteen, for possession of cannabis. He could have been arrested for dealing, but the school queued up to tell the police about his good character and he got away with a caution. It was the beginning of a long line of narrow escapes, and the development of his reputation as untouchable. He was forty-three, the same age as Mal. His family was respectable and middle-class, and nowhere was there anything to suggest why he'd chosen crime as a career.

"Who knows? Who knows why any of them turn to crime?" Andy Carter said.

"But that's it," Mal replied, "we mostly do know. It's what their family does, like Declan Hughes, or they need money quickly, or they live somewhere where crime looks like a way out of poverty, but there's nothing here to say what motivated Addison."

"Maybe he just likes it," Andy said. "A way to use his brains. You know: lots of money, influence, power, nice things, that kind of stuff." There was something about the way he said it that made Mal uncomfortable. Andy smiled as if he was being funny, but Mal didn't think the smile was honest. He supposed that constant undercover work did no one any good.

On the other hand, there was something likeable about Wade Addison. He reminded Mal of Hector at his most puppy-like.

None of which was going to stop Mal bringing him down.

Andy Carter had a long list of operations that involved Addison's organisation, where Mal was supposed to disrupt the police response. He saw that brothels featured again, as well as intelligence about a car moving a large quantity of cash. Mal's role was to divert the traffic cops and allow the car to get away.

"It's all going to make you look bent to Addison, but not so bent that there isn't plausible deniability to your colleagues," said Andy. "Then we set up the sting."

Except I don't trust what I'm being told, thought Mal. The operation depended on Addison's realising that Mal was prepared to bend the rules, and why would he realise that unless someone told him? *Addison isn't the only one being set up here.*

Mal wanted to talk it through with Daniel, but that meant admitting that he'd lied. So Mal went back to the files and the newspaper cuttings and focussed on the thing Addison seemed to care about most — old buildings.

Addison had three major developments, all in the city
centre, and Mal visited them in turn to get a sense of the kinds
of projects that Addison liked. What they had in common was
that they were all rundown nineteenth-century buildings, two
coated with grime, and looking as if the For Sale signs had been
erected in long-vanished hope. The third was almost finished
and had a sales suite. Mal went in and was shown round a "loft
apartment" with bare brick walls, arched Crittall windows, and
twelve-foot-high ceilings. A mezzanine bedroom gave views of
post-industrial Manchester. The finishes were all up to Daniel's
standard, though Mal thought Daniel would hate everything
about it. There was a gym in the basement, and half the
building had been converted to a multistorey car park,
disguised by keeping the street façade intact.

"It's impressive," he told the saleswoman, because it was. It
was the kind of place he would have loved to have owned when
he worked for the Met, and, if he was honest, the kind of place
he would love to own now. He wondered for a moment about
commuting between Manchester and north Wales. People did
it. He fantasised about a city pad for the week, then home to
Daniel at the weekends. Then he remembered the reality of
police work, and its sad lack of reliable weekends.

Back at his desk he stared at the information about the theft
of building materials. He thought about organised crime and
the difficulties that big crime groups had turning vast amounts
of cash into something that they could spend. He wondered
how much it would cost to convert an old warehouse into the
kind of flats he'd just visited, and he started making phone
calls. Then he went out into the office and called the best
dressed DC into his office.

"I need you to go down to the Walker Wallace Building on
Oxford Street," he said, "and go into the sales office. Ask to see
the show flat, and photograph *everything*. I want the brand
names of it all. Don't let the saleswoman work out what you're

doing. Let me have the list as soon as." The DC nodded and left. An hour later, Mal had a list of high-end fixtures and fittings, some with brand names, some without, like the *Extra Wide Solid Oak Board flooring,* a truckload of which had been stolen last November and never recovered. The same was true for a container full of Villeroy and Boch sanitary ware and tiles, stolen the month before. He smiled to himself as he recognised the kitchen taps. Daniel had the same one and had blushed scarlet when he'd told Mal how much it had cost. "I just loved it," Daniel had said. "I admit that it's ridiculous to fall in love with a tap, but once I'd seen this one, none of the others would do." A load of super-expensive taps was also on the missing list.

Correlation doesn't equal causation, he told himself, and after thanking the DC, went back to his phone calls.

All the local builders' merchants would be happy to take cash for very large orders. "How large?" Mal asked.

"Sky's the limit, mate. S'all money, innit?"

None of them was prepared to say whether they had done so recently.

And they still hadn't found Declan Hughes.

Andy had another brothel raid on his list for the afternoon. Mal texted him to say he'd been sent on another job and walked back to collect his car from the hotel, via the Burns and Wood building, the most rundown of Addison's projects. As he approached, a truck was reversing into the alley alongside the building, warnings beeping as it edged into the narrow space. Mal couldn't see what the load was, but he noted the name of the company *Batterbee Building Supplies.* He took a quick picture and cursed under his breath.

Wade Addison was crossing the road towards him.

28: I THOUGHT YOU'D BE INTERESTED

"I want to show you something," Addison said to Mal, when he was safely across the road," something that I hope will convince you that a leopard can change his spots. It's the Burns and Wood building," Addison pointed across the road, "It won't take long."

He was full of it, desperate to show Mal round, to convince him that Addison-the-gangster was being superseded by Addison-the-property-developer. He talked about meetings with the Mayor, apprenticeships, preserving the city's heritage.

"Like it or not, Maldwyn, I'm a legitimate businessman with a disreputable past. Every year I'm more legitimate and less disreputable. I'm leaving the past behind and embracing a brighter future."

They had their backs to a flight of steps onto a road bridge over the canal. Tall, ornate buildings dominated the wide streets. "These were all warehouses," said Addison. If it hadn't been for his three am reading, Mal would have assumed that they had been offices and banks, though most now seemed to be either flats or bars, and one was a gym.

The main entrance to the Burns and Wood Building was on the corner of the street opposite.

There were six or seven wide steps up to a colonnaded doorway at least fifteen feet high. The heavy double doors looked as if they were last opened in the 1980s, and the CCTV camera was hanging drunkenly from its bracket. A notice warned of a regular guard dog patrol. Addison led Mal to the side of the building down a bin-lined alley. The delivery truck had gone.

"Some of the inside is pretty much as it was built — the stairs, all tiles and marble — and we'll turn that into flats and workspace, maybe a restaurant. But we're starting with the basement. I love a basement nightclub, don't you?"

"I've not been to a nightclub for a while," Mal said.

"That can change. I'll be sure to send you an invitation when we open."

The alleyway ended in a large yard, much bigger than Mal had expected, with a set of wooden doors, now propped open, and to the left a set of steps leading downwards to a metal door marked Fire Escape - Do Not Obstruct. A new neon sign leaned against the railings.

"We'll go in this way. This is where the orders were dispatched when it was a warehouse," Addison said, headed towards the open doors. "I want you to see the main staircase. It's a bit gloomy, and a bit of a hike to get there, but it's worth it, I promise.

"I've made myself an office by the front door, so we've got to go past the stairs to get there. Watch yourself, the builders just leave stuff everywhere."

They left the service areas of the building, getting away from the smelly bins and soggy sleeping bags abandoned by the homeless. There were bags of plaster, radiators, reels of wire, and yards and yards of copper pipe, stacked against the walls, and Mal wondered how much of the material had arrived on a stolen truck, and how much had been paid for with cash from drug deals. The walls themselves were a riot of ceramic tiling: fake panelling, barley twists, Greek key patterns, stripes and flowers. Most of the tiles were shades of brown and gold, interspersed with white, but when Mal looked closely, there were blues too. Towards the front of the building, tiled columns with roman arches held up an ornate ceiling.

Wade kept pointing things out — cast iron supports that made the building fireproof, that the tiles were properly called *faience*, and that the building was converted to offices after the war. "And now I'm converting it again."

Mal looked down at the floor — his feet crunching in the debris covering yet more tiles, this time in Celtic designs. Doors stood open to the left and right, some of the rooms filled with office furniture, others with cardboard-wrapped sanitary ware. The rooms were lighter than the corridors, but the glass in the windows was obscured with the cobwebs of decades and smeared with dust and rain. Mal heard water dripping and smelled rot and plaster.

The staircase was as magnificent as Addison had promised. It rose the full height of the building, curving extravagantly up to a stained glass cupola above the top floor. If anything, the ceramic tiling was even more flamboyant, but it was hard to make out much detail.

"This floor was the showrooms, and upstairs were offices where manufacturers could sell their stuff. The top floors were for packing the orders, and then there was a hydraulic system to take them down to the basement and bale them up," said Addison. "It's a privilege to bring it to life again. There were only ever a few offices, and they mostly closed in the eighties."

Addison gestured to an open door. "Look," he said. "I'm thinking restaurant." The room was vast and high ceilinged, divided at regular intervals by arched columns. The tiled floor had been roughly swept, and the huge windows meant the colours — blue, terracotta, and light grey — could be seen more clearly. "I've seen old photographs, there would have been display cabinets and counters. You can see where they were from the tiles on the floor." Addison pointed out where the tiling pattern followed the outlines of the missing cabinets. Mal found himself imagining the room full of tables covered in white linen and sparkling silverware.

Up the first flight of stairs, Addison opened another door. "This is interesting," he said, "some of the old display cabinets are still here, where the rooms weren't converted into offices." Mal followed him down a long corridor away from the light of the staircase, and through a 1980s fire door. On the far side was a second, far less ornate, staircase, and a series of doors still labelled. Mal read, "Shattucks, Importers" and "Silks of India" before Addison opened one to reveal a beautifully panelled space, lined with cabinets and shelves in polished mahogany. Not looking so polished now, but Mal could see where some-one, maybe Addison himself, had rubbed away at the dirt to show the glowing wood beneath. Addison was glowing too.

"You really love this place," Mal said, and Addison smiled. Mal had to work hard not to fall under the spell.

"I do. Let me show you one more thing."

"This is where I want to live," he said, "when it's all done, but there are a lot of stairs...."

Addison led the way up the second set of stairs, up to the fourth floor, which had lower ceilings and smaller rooms, but still plenty of light. He pointed out that on this floor the windows were let into the roof and explained that they'd put a temporary lift on the outside of the building to bring up mate-rials to the upper floors. Then it was back towards the middle of the building and the grand staircase, which was still grand, despite the top floors being for packing and dispatching orders.

"But it doesn't go up any further," Addison said. "This is the secret floor." He produced a key from his pocket and unlocked a door on the gallery at the top of the staircase. Behind it was a set of wrought iron spiral steps. On each side arched windows opened onto the roof, and at the top, a series of small rooms with no apparent purpose. There were more arched windows, plain plastered walls, and wooden floors. Even in the January gloom, the space was full of light, and in the room furthest away from the stairs, the window had been used to give access to the roof.

"I shall have a garden there," said Addison pointing at the flat area outside the window, "and spend summer evenings looking out over the rooftops. I can get up here with the builder's lift now, but once that's gone, there's only the secret stairs, and this part of the roof will be all mine."

"This lot must be costing millions," Mal said, impressed despite himself.

"Costing millions and taking years. I want it restored, not ripped apart. We've got to put lifts in, and utilities, but I'm not creating rabbit hutches out of these big rooms. The numbers are scary now, but when it's done, I'll have enough to start another one.

"You see a derelict building, but what the City Council sees is an employment opportunity. They're happy to pay for people to get jobs and training, and I'm happy to take their money. Where the City hands out grants, the banks queue up to lend — even to someone like me."

"And the City gives you grants because you know where the bodies are buried?"

"Perhaps that is how it started, Mal, but these things build up their own momentum. When people are making money, or winning votes, they have very short memories."

"Don't you worry that their memories will grow longer if you stop being successful?"

Addison shrugged. "I don't worry about much to be honest."

Mal believed him. *Is this what a psychopath is like?* he thought. *Because this man cares about these buildings, but not about anything else, including his own safety. It makes bringing him down more important. I'm not an FBI profiler, but even I know that psychopaths come unglued and that's never a good thing.*

"Why did you bring me here?" he asked.

"I thought you might like it," Addison said.

He knows that I'm not a bent copper. Now all I have to do is convince Andy Carter and the DCC.

BY THE TIME Mal got to his car, the traffic out of the city was solid, and it was almost eight when he parked behind Daniel's Land Rover. The house was empty, though the shower still smelled of Daniel. The boxes of books called out mutely, demanding to be shelved, to provide their colours and textures to the empty spaces. Daniel had built the shelves, it seemed only fair to fill them. Mal went into the kitchen for a knife to start opening boxes.

The shelves filled the entire back wall of the living room, opposite the French doors with the view of the valley — or what would be the view of the valley if it wasn't dark. A few lights twinkled in the distance, but the moon and stars were hidden by cloud. With the lights on, the windows reflected the room, and Mal bending and stretching to empty the boxes and fill the shelves. He'd packed the books in the order he wanted to unpack them, and numbered the boxes, much to Daniel's amusement. The memory made him smile. He picked up his phone to find out when Daniel would be back, but it rang before he could call up Daniel's number. When Mal answered, he heard Hector whisper something, and then there was a shout in the background.

"I'm scared, Mal." This time the whisper was clear.

"I'm on my way," he said, and ran out to the car.

29: UNHAPPY HOUR

Daniel had enough time to get home, get changed, and get back into town before the estate agent closed. He put on his skinniest jeans, a tight T-shirt, and one of Maldwyn's leather jackets. He had an extra close shave and splashed the cologne with a heavy hand. He took the unmarked police car back into town because he didn't think the Land Rover supported his image as someone who had come into money and was ready to trade up.

North Wales Estates was as trendy as it got in this area of the country, which is to say that it was about ten years behind everywhere else. It had a laminate floor, rough white walls, and everywhere photographs of beaches, mountains, stunning country houses, and attractive people walking chocolate labradors along paths through the autumn leaves.

Daniel took the chair in front of Connor's desk.

"Hi," he said, "it's good to see you. I'm here because I've had a bit of good fortune, and I wanted to keep it in the family so to speak."

Connor looked at Daniel with his eyes bright and licked his

lips. "I'll help you any way I can," he said and licked his lips again.

"Just some housing advice for now," Daniel said.

"If you're sure that's all you want, then that's what I'll give you, and a coffee too, if you ask nicely."

"Coffee would be great."

The flirting wasn't obvious, but it was there in the licked lips, and the way Connor looked straight into Daniels eyes. Daniel looked right back. As Connor went to get coffee from the machine, he brushed past Daniel, trailing fingers over his shoulder.

When they were settled again, Daniel said, "I was thinking about what you said the other night in the pub. I own a little smallholding, and I'd like something bigger."

"Bigger is always better, don't you think? But you're talking about a house, right?"

"For now," said Daniel. "I'm looking for a bit more land too."

Connor looked at his computer and beckoned for Daniel to join him on his side of the desk.

Daniel scooted round and was careful to sit a little too close to Connor. Connor scrolled through the properties that he had for sale, talking them up, and pointing out where a deal could be done. Then he started talking about properties that might be coming onto the market, suggesting that with a little inside knowledge, Daniel could save on estate agent's fees. "Better for everyone." Daniel was fairly sure that one of the properties was Roderick Marston's house.

"Let me print you a few things out," Connor said, sending a couple of sets of the most luscious particulars to the printer on the other side of the room. Daniel took the opportunity to swap their coffee cups, finishing Connor's drink and putting the empty cup gently into his jacket pocket, where he'd stashed an evidence bag. He added a couple of Connor's pens to his haul for good luck. When he looked over to the printer, Connor was having trouble.

"It only wants paper," said the woman from the other desk. "I'll do it for you, but then I'm off."

"Me too," said another female voice, from a desk in the far corner that Daniel hadn't noticed. "We were going to aerobics, but the wine bar is having a happy hour." She giggled.

"Easy choice," said Connor and they all laughed, though Daniel thought that the two women looked less relaxed about it than Connor.

"There," said the first woman, slamming the paper drawer shut. The printer started to churn out glossy pictures of houses Daniel would never be able to afford, unless he was promoted to Chief Constable. The two women left, and Connor slid the pages into an even glossier folder, and the folder into Daniel's hands, caressing his fingers as he did so.

"Come any time, Daniel," he said.

Daniel smiled, holding the folder carefully.

"Don't worry," he said. "I'll be back soon."

BACK AT THE STATION, he found Sophie. "I need fingerprints off this lot as soon as you like," he said, handing over the glossy folder, the coffee cup, and pens.

"Should I ask what they're for?" she said.

"Catching a con-man I hope," he replied and explained.

She called a PC and sent him off to photograph the prints.

"You scrub up well," she said.

"I'm off to happy hour at the wine bar to see if I can pick up some girls."

"Maybe I should come too."

IN THE WINE bar Daniel spotted the two women from the estate agency easily. They had found a table and were sipping from glasses of wine and eating olives and what looked like artisan bread with a dip of olive oil and balsamic vinegar. Everywhere was very busy. Daniel ordered himself a beer and wondered over in that direction.

"Hi," he said. "I heard you talking about the happy hour earlier on, so I thought I'd call in."

The two women were already starting to get a bit drunk.

"Come and join us," the taller one said.

"I'm Daniel," he said. The two women giggled.

"And I'm Danielle," said the taller of the two women, "and this is my friend Ceri." Daniel found a chair and sat down.

"Do you come here every week?" Daniel asked.

"Only when that bloody job drives us completely mad," said Danielle, "or rather when Connor drives us completely mad."

"Careful," said Ceri. "He's a client, remember."

"Yes, but that didn't stop Connor making an exhibition of himself. Daniel can see what we have to put up with every day."

Daniel grinned. "He is a bit full on."

"Do you really want to buy a bigger house?" Ceri asked, "Or did you come in to flirt with Connor?"

Daniel thought maybe these women weren't as drunk as they were pretending to be.

"I'm not against buying a new house," he said, "but mainly I wanted to see what was available and what I can afford. I'm already spoken for in the boyfriend department. Not against a bit of flirting, though."

"You're as bad as Connor. He's got a lovely bloke. Much nicer than he deserves." This from Danielle, who possibly was as drunk as she appeared.

"That's how I know Connor," said Daniel. "Hector is a friend of mine."

"Then you know that he's too good for that twat."

"Danielle, shut up!"

"I won't. He is a twat. He's a bloody liar too, and everyone falls for it." Danielle got up rather unsteadily and headed in the direction of the Ladies.

"Sorry about her," said Ceri. "She hates Connor because she thought she was in line for the manager's job, and then he appeared from nowhere and now we work for him."

"We all know how that feels," Daniel said, "but is he any good at it? Being manager, I mean."

Ceri might not be drunk, but she seemed prepared to spill the beans on Connor. She thought for a moment. "He's a bloody good salesman, I'll give him that. Mind, the other guy was a good salesman too, even if he was as ugly as sin. Connor's public school accent is fake. He's from the back end of Cardiff when he's on the phone and he thinks no one's there."

She dragged the first syllable of Cardiff out, in an imitation of the accent: *caaeyerdiff.*

The noise level in the bar was going up, and Daniel had to lean closer to Ceri to hear her.

"He's up to all sorts of stuff off the books, too. I don't know what, but we're doing lots more lettings, and some of the places are awful. Some of the people who come into the office ... let's just say I wouldn't want to meet them down a dark alley. But profits are way up, so I dunno. Anyway, you're not interested in all this."

Oh, but I am.

Daniel had questions forming a queue in his mind, but he sensed that it was time to back off. He moved the conversation on to the state of the property market in the town. Ceri confirmed what he'd been picking up everywhere else — too many people looking for somewhere to live, not enough houses. The ease of the drive to Wrexham and Chester was bringing wealthier buyers, and some people were even commuting from Liverpool, because it was cheaper than the traditional Merseyside suburbs. Daniel told her about Sophie, who'd wanted to rent, but couldn't find anything, and Mal, whose rented house was constantly having to be repaired. Somewhere along the way, Danielle reappeared with another bottle of wine. He needed to go back to the police station to see if Connor's fingerprints had been identified, but he didn't feel that he could just walk out. Rescue came in the form of a group of women, even more drunk than Danielle, who scooped up the two, and he made his escape.

THE COLD AIR hit him like a bucket of water to the face. A few flakes of snow had begun to fall, caught in the light spilling out of the bar. He pulled Mal's jacket round him and stepped away from the knot of smokers. He saw that his phone had been taking messages while he'd been inside, and he called his voicemail.

Sophie's voice said, "Lovely fingerprints, Daniel. Anyone would think you were a detective. They belong to a Colin Bryson Jones, wanted for questioning by our colleagues in the Met. Convictions for fraud. Most recently for taking deposits on a flat he didn't own. Plus, a suspended sentence for possession with intent to supply a Class A. See you in the morning."

30: LEAVING

The phone call from Ian Goldsmith came as Daniel was walking back to the car.

"I'm leaving town," said Ian. "And if you want me to talk before I go, come and meet me in the co-op carpark straight away. I've parked my van round the back near the delivery doors. I only want to talk to you though."

Daniel wanted to smile at the cloak-and-dagger arrangements, but he told Sophie where he was going, and set off for the co-op carpark. Ian was exactly where he said he would be, and Daniel drew up next to him in the unmarked police car. Daniel saw that Ian's van was packed to the roof. He wasn't kidding about leaving town. He pushed open the passenger door of the car and beckoned. Ian came and sat next to him. He was still looking bruised, with bandages around his neck and face, but he had obviously found the energy to pack up his whole house and find somewhere to go. He looked round as if he were afraid that the three thugs would pop up from behind one of the Paladin bins.

"Where are you going?" Daniel asked.

"To work on a building site in the West Midlands, but I'm not going to tell you where, and I'm changing my phone number."

"But you've got something to tell me," said Daniel, "about the men who beat you up."

Ian said, "I'll tell you, but there is no way I'm going to court, no way I want those guys to know where you got your information from. I don't want them to know where I'm going." Daniel thought that it would be very easy to track Ian's van, but he didn't say anything. If he thought he was safe he might tell the truth.

"So, who are they, then?"

"I don't actually know very much," said Ian. "I know that one of them is called Jeff and another one is called Alun. I saw them once in a green Fiesta and I think they come from the coast. But they make an effort not to talk to anyone except each other, and they do everything they can to hide their faces."

"So, who calls them? Who tells them where to go, and who to threaten? Why did they beat you up?"

"They beat me up because I was complaining about not getting paid. I'm working on those shitty jobs like the one down by the river. I've said too many times that the building inspector must've been bought off because we never saw him. I said those flats would flood in the next heavy rain. Danny told me to shut up and I didn't take any notice. And then I lost my temper with Connor because the money was taking so long to come through."

"So, it's Connor who calls them?"

"Sure, but he's not their boss. I don't know who is, but Connor's a minion just like the rest of us, a minion in a suit."

"So, who is behind them?"

Ian turned his palms upwards in the gesture of "I don't know".

Daniel thought he probably didn't know but it was worth

asking a few more questions. "Have you come across a man called Barry Kettles? He works for another one of those flower companies."

"He used to do what Connor does now, organise the repairs and take the invoices."

"So, he is part of it?" Daniel asked.

Ian nodded.

"What about Dr Flowers? Have you come across either of the doctors in anything to do with all this?"

Ian shook his head. "Nope sorry." There was a silence, but Daniel thought Ian had more to say so he waited. The silence stretched on for a bit, but Daniel could be patient. In the end Ian spoke.

"It's Arwyn," he said. "That wasn't right, him falling off the ladder like that."

"What do you think happened?" Daniel asked. "Our witness says there was no one else there, the ladder just wobbled and he fell."

Ian shook his head again. "I don't know, but I think he must've been drugged, because he was a surefooted as a cat. When I worked with him, I always made him go up ladders or onto the roof. That's the main reason I'm going. I'm good at my job, I don't need to be short of work, but I don't like these people and I want to get away from them." Ian started looking round again, reaching for the door handle, wanting to get away. But Daniel hadn't finished.

"Why would anyone want to hurt Arwyn? Everyone seems to have liked him."

"These people ... the Primrose Lettings people, Connor and that, they aren't nice. They seem OK, like, professional, but there's something wrong, like it's all an act." Ian came to a hesitant stop.

"How did you come to work for them?" Daniel asked.

"Might have been through Arwyn, maybe. Someone told

me they were new, and on the lookout for good tradesmen, gave me a number. I met that Barry Kettles, and it looked like a good gig. Regular work, regular money. He said they were buying more places in the town, so if it worked out, there'd be more work. It's not easy being self-employed, a little bit here, a little bit there ...."

Daniel thought about his own struggles to find tradesmen when he started renovating his house, and how he'd found it easier to learn how to do most jobs himself. If Ian was a decent electrician, he should have had as much work as he could handle. But perhaps he wasn't good at marketing himself.

"So, you and Arwyn agreed that Primrose Lettings wasn't a good firm to work for?"

Ian nodded.

"So why didn't you just stop working for them?"

In the silence that followed, Daniel wondered if this was the first time Ian had considered it. Then he remembered what Mal had said; the company owed Ian too much money for him to risk leaving. Helena had said the same.

"Did they owe all their tradesmen money?" Daniel asked.

Ian looked round again, and Daniel thought that was it. Ian and Arwyn had been trying to find out if other people had the same problem, and the beating had been the result. Ian confirmed it. "We asked too many questions," he said. Then he took a deep breath. "Not just about our money, or the building inspector. Down at the flats we got deliveries. Of building materials, like."

Daniel nodded.

"They come on those trucks with a hoist, bricks on pallets, or bags of cement, that kind of stuff?" Daniel nodded again.

"Then other stuff comes in a van — toilets, cabling, light switches — you don't need a truck for them." There was a pause. "But the thing is, the driver was always the same guy. So, we had deliveries that were supposed to be from Travis Perkins or Brickability, and deliveries that were supposed to be from Victoria Plumbing or All Star Electrics, lots of different companies, all in different vehicles, real delivery vehicles, but always the same driver. And I think he might have been one of the men who beat me up."

Ian looked frightened, just remembering, and Daniel was tempted to offer a reassuring arm rub, but instead asked, "Who did you talk to?"

"No one. Well, I said *you again, mate* to the driver one time, and I might have said something to Danny, but the only person I talked to was Arwyn. I did think about talking to that other policeman, but then I got beaten up."

"And what did you think was going on?"

"Same as you, I should think. They'd nicked the trucks and got one of their blokes to bring them to site."

That was exactly what Daniel had been thinking. He'd also been thinking that this was trouble he *could* investigate. That stolen building materials might explain Ian's beating, if not Arwyn's death. How they tied into equity release he couldn't imagine, except that Barry Kettles had been involved in both.

"You said you thought the men came from the coast, I'm assuming Rhyl or Prestatyn, rather than Anglesey? What made you think that?"

"Accents maybe? Or maybe I heard them mention somewhere. It always took them a while to arrive when they were called, so maybe I thought that they couldn't live in the town."

"And why do you think Arwyn was drugged? Have other people been drugged?"

Ian blushed. Daniel said that he knew there were plenty of drugs around the town, but was there something specific about Primrose Lettings or any of the companies around it?

"I just thought it, OK? I was looking for an explanation about why he would fall, that's all." And this time Ian did reach for the door handle, opened it, and got out. He got back into his own van, put it into gear, and drove away. Daniel noted the license plate number on his phone. Then he called into the office and asked for the ANPR cameras to track where Ian was going. He thought that he'd need to speak to Ian again, and knew that he'd feel very stupid if he lost him.

31: CONNOR GOES POSTAL

"Why don't you mind your own fucking business?"

"Because you've been hurting my friend. He asked for help. That *is* my business."

They were outside Hector's house, the blue light in Mal's car still flashing, his headlamps lighting up the hedgerows. Connor had rushed out as Mal's car door slammed, and he stood between Mal and the house.

Connor swung for Mal. Mal saw the punch coming, and moved, so that Connor caught his upper arm, not his face. Connor wasn't prepared for Mal to grip him by the arm and shove him hard against his own car.

"You've just assaulted a police officer. How do you see this playing out?" Mal said.

"You assaulted me, you bastard. You don't know who you're dealing with."

Connor pulled his arm to try to get free from Mal's grip and failed. Mal stood like a rock, absorbing Connor's struggles, pushing his face into the roof of his car, and looked over to the house, hoping Hector was OK.

"Carry on like this and it's handcuffs," said Mal.

Connor jerked his arm but couldn't get free. "Don't be fucking stupid," he said. "Let me go."

"Or? Only if you promise not to hit anyone else."

"Or I'll make some calls and you'll regret messing with me."

"I don't think so."

"Your mistake. Anyway, he started it," Connor said.

"I don't believe you, and to be honest I don't care."

Connor kept yanking at his arm, swearing and jabbing at Mal like a street brawler, until he was almost free. Mal noticed that the Home Counties accent was slipping. He kicked Connor's feet from underneath him, shifted his grip on Connor's arm, twisting it up his back, so as Connor fell, Mal had to bend over with him for fear of dislocating Connor's shoulder. Connor screamed in anger and pain, giving Mal the break he needed to pull the handcuffs out of his pocket and fasten them round Connor's wrists. The temptation to kick Connor was great.

"Don't think Hector will be grateful, *Maldwyn*. He was hoping for the sainted Daniel to come flying to his rescue."

"Listen, sunshine," said Mal, "I'm going to take these cuffs off on condition that you get in your car and go. You do anything else, and you're nicked. OK?"

"I'm going. But don't forget that your boyfriend and mine have a history."

"You don't have a boyfriend anymore," said Mal, "and you don't deserve one."

"You're in the way, mate, same as me. Did he tell you that your precious Danny-boy is planning on selling up?" Mal's mystified look answered that. "Thought not."

"Go," Mal said, "before I change my mind." He undid the handcuffs and Connor scrambled towards his car, got in, and was gone.

He went into the house. Hector looked frozen, stood in his kitchen holding onto the back of a chair. He had a cut on the side of his face and dried tears on his cheeks. Mal put his arms round his friend and disentangled his fingers from the chair. Hector started shivering. "I'm cold," he said. "What if he comes back?"

"You won't be here," said Mal, "because you're coming home with me."

BACK AT THE HOUSE, Mal got the fire going, and fetched a spare blanket. "You're in shock Hector," he said. "I'm going to make some tea, and warm you up."

Hector managed a feeble smile. "I shouldn't have let this happen. I know better. You can say *I told you so* if you want."

"I don't want," said Mal. "Connor is clever, and manipulative, and you are a decent human being. It's not your fault."

"He wouldn't let me go," said Hector, and started crying. "He kept saying that I didn't want him, that I wanted Daniel, and every time I objected, he slapped me."

Mal felt tears in his own eyes and turned to the kettle and tea bags.

"I should have hammered the bastard into next week," said Mal. "None of this is down to anything you did."

He made two mugs of his favourite bright orange, sugary tea, and decided that he was going to ignore everything Connor said about Hector and Daniel.

"Drink this," he said. "We've got a brand new spare room, and when we've drunk the tea, we'll go and make up the bed. I'll even find you a hot water bottle.

DANIEL WAS EXHAUSTED by the time he got home. But there were lights on in the house, and a shiny black Audi parked by the door. The fire was lit and Mal was asleep on the sofa. He woke up as Daniel closed the front door and held his arms out. Daniel kicked his shoes off and then he was lying on top of Mal, feeling those big arms wrapped round him so tightly that he could hardly breathe.

"You came back," Mal whispered into his ear, "and I am so glad to see you."

Daniel felt the warm current between them, loving Mal's hard body underneath him. He put his hands on Mal's cheeks and kissed him, sliding his tongue between Mal's lips, as Mal ran his hands over Daniel's back, his arse, and then up to his chest to help Daniel shrug out of his jacket. Then he felt Mal's hands under his T-shirt, fingers marking off each vertebra down his spine and the muscles on either side.

"I do believe you are wearing my jacket," Mal said, "and those jeans are very tight." Daniel thought that his jeans were getting tighter, and so were Mal's.

"I've been out on the pull," said Daniel.

"I guess you got lucky, coming in at this time."

"It's a long story."

"Keep it quiet, we've got a visitor. Hector's upstairs asleep."

Mal explained about Hector's panicked call.

Daniel asked if it was too late to make something to eat and open a beer "because I can't remember the last time I ate, and there's a lot to tell you. Like how Connor was flirting with me an hour before he was hitting Hector, and how he isn't Connor at all."

Over frozen pizza and beer Daniel told Mal about Connor's real identity.

"Only there's more," Daniel said, and told Mal about Ian Goldsmith's revelations. "The fake delivery driver could be one of the heavies who beat up Ian and frightened those two young women. And Connor's in the middle of it somehow. Lots of things changed when Connor arrived. Barry Kettles stopped managing the repairs, they started work on that horrible riverside building, and two people with noisy relatives were sold equity release policies. But most of it was in place already. Connor didn't set this all up, and I don't want to pull him in until I know who did. So, thank goodness you didn't nick him."

Mal got up and put another log into the stove. It wasn't necessary but he needed time to think. He asked Daniel if he wanted another beer, and then went to the kitchen and got them both one anyway. He knew that there wasn't a choice. He had to tell Daniel what he'd found out in Manchester.

"I think I know who's behind everything here."

Daniel's face said *What?*

32: WE ARE TRAINED

"I haven't been buying drugs in Manchester," Mal said. "I've been trying to convince an organised crime boss that I'm a bent copper." He explained about Wade Addison and the stolen building supplies. "Addison is an octopus, tentacles everywhere. How likely is it that there are two gangs hijacking building materials and sending them straight to site? Connor might be the face of it here, but I'd put money on Addison being the banker, and funding equity release to launder a bit more cash."

As Mal was talking, Daniel felt his anger bubbling up like hot lava. Then the lid blew off.

"Run that past me again," he said, "the bit where you told me that you were involved in a straightforward drugs operation, with lots of back up, while you were really all on your own, deliberately making enemies inside the police force, and making friends with someone who has already killed one police officer? The bit where you say that this villain, this Teflon-coated Wade Addison, suspects that you aren't bent at all, and where you carry on meeting him because your handlers don't want to listen. The bit where you admit that you don't really trust your handlers. Which is why you were asking me all about what would make me cover up a crime, because you think someone you're working with is bent. Are you *trying* to get killed?"

"No, but ...."

"No, but nothing. You lied to me, Maldwyn. Everything about this operation sounds dodgy as fuck and you didn't tell me. Because you *never tell me anything.*"

"Daniel, listen ...."

"No, *you* listen. You never talk to me. You lie to me about what you're doing, you won't talk about the wedding, or your family, like you wouldn't talk to me about what was going on in Glamorgan. That's not how it works. You live here. With me. You say you love me and then you keep everything important a secret, like I'm not good enough to be told what's going on in your head."

"It's not like that."

"It *is* like that. If you won't tell me about a dangerous job, how can I trust you about *anything?* How do I know that you won't disappear again, just like Megan says?" As he spoke, Daniel thought that mentioning Megan was a mistake. But it was too late. Mal's face had turned to stone.

"I have to go." Mal got up and headed for his shoes and the front door, but Daniel was quicker.

"No, you don't get to walk out on this," he said, getting between Mal and the door.

Mal tried to push him out of the way but Daniel didn't budge.

"Move."

"No."

"Get out of my fucking way."

They pushed and shoved against each other, neither willing to give way, but equally unwilling to do more.

"You're not going anywhere. It's the middle of the night and you've been drinking. Sit down and stop being a dick."

"*I'm* being a dick?"

They didn't realise how much their voices had risen until they heard the spare room door open, and the sound of feet coming to the top of the stairs. Hector looked down, befuddled with sleep, and the bruises on his face stood out against his pale skin. Daniel wanted to go to his friend, but he was too afraid that Mal would leave.

"Sorry, Hector," he called, "go back to sleep." Then he looked at Mal. "Look, I'm sorry. Let's just go to bed and sort it out tomorrow." He wasn't sorry, except he wished he hadn't brought Megan into it. And if he could get over his anger, he thought that they had every chance of dealing with an organised crime group. He could see Mal fighting with himself, so he held out his hand and pulled Mal towards him. Mal gave in and stopped trying to get to the door. They were both still angry, but it was a start.

There was an icy gap down the middle of the bed. Anger had kept them from their usual bedtime cuddles, but at least Mal was still here, Daniel thought. Daniel didn't know if Mal was awake, but he couldn't sleep for thinking about what he'd learned. He wanted to look at the canvass of Harriet Marston's neighbours again — had Connor been one of her visitors, or did anyone see Barry Kettles? He wanted to set up a watch on the riverside building site, to catch the next delivery. He wanted to set the team looking for a thug called Jeff, and another called Alun, possibly from the north Wales coast. They didn't have much to go on, just two first names and a car, but they might get lucky. They needed to check out Barry Kettles' address in Manchester, because *a good salesman, even if he was as ugly as sin* sounded like Kettles. Was he the face of North Wales Estates until Connor arrived? If so, *why* had Connor arrived?

Daniel turned over, desperate to put the light on and start

writing notes of all the things he had to do. Mal was snoring, very quietly, and Daniel decided that he was definitely asleep, and a light would wake him. So, he slipped from under the covers, and pulled his thick socks back on. He'd lived in the house long enough to find his way downstairs without a light. There was still some heat in the living room stove, and he had a fleece on the back of the sofa, as well as a crochet blanket. He booted up his laptop and started sending emails — to set up the surveillance, to find out about the thugs, to ask for a check on the house-to-house, to find out more about Kettles. An hour later, he thought that he'd done enough, and he closed the computer. He was about to go back to bed when he heard a noise.

"Wassup, Hector?" Daniel asked, as his friend sat down next to him on the sofa. Daniel saw that Hector had been crying. He reached over for Hector's hand and said, "Hey, it's going to be OK."

Hector leaned into Daniel, buying his face in Daniel's chest and sobbed. Daniel stroked Hector's hair and whispered all the comforting things he could think of. After a while, the sobs eased, then stopped. Hector looked up, wiped his eyes, and blew his nose. "Sorry," he said.

"Nothing to be sorry for," Daniel said. "You've had a rubbish time."

"I'm nearly as big as him, and I let him hit me."

"Because you're too nice to hit people. It's nothing to be ashamed of. Not hitting people is a good thing."

Hector blew his nose again.

"Mal hit him. I just froze. He'd come at me and I just froze. But Mal could hit him, and I bet you could too."

"But, Hector, we're trained to hit people if they're attacking someone. It's our job. And Mal goes to the gym most days, and to all sorts of martial arts stuff. You're a doctor."

"I go to the gym."

"I know you do. But policemen *expect* to be attacked. We learn how to defend ourselves. You don't need to know how to do that, any more than I need to know the names of all the bones."

That raised the tiniest smile. "I was glad Mal hit him. I wanted Mal to hit him some more, to be honest. And I feel guilty for that too."

Daniel smiled. "I wish Mal had hit him more too. And I don't feel guilty at all." They sat together quietly for a while, Hector resting his head on Daniel's shoulder, Daniel's arm around him.

"I need your help, Daniel," Hector said, "or Mal's. Connor has been leaving stuff at my house, and he wants to come and get it in the morning. He sent me a text and that's what woke me up."

"And you want company? No problem. That's what friends are for." Daniel kissed the top of Hector's head.

Neither of them heard Mal come to the top of the stairs and look down at the two figures cuddled together on the sofa, talking quietly, and just visible in the last light from the stove.

Mal told himself that what he had seen was nothing. That it was no different to when he had held Hector in his own arms. That anything Connor said was by definition untrustworthy. That Daniel and Hector had sex *once* and that it was before he and Daniel had got back together. That Daniel had asked him, Mal, to move in. That Megan would probably dislike anyone Daniel lived with, even someone as obviously reliable as Hector. That Hector was a *friend*. None of which helped him to sleep, though he pretended when Daniel came back to bed.

In the morning they were polite. Daniel said that he'd be setting up the surveillance and trying to identify the thugs, and that he was going to go round to Hector's so that Connor could get his things. Mal said he was going back to Manchester. When Hector was in the shower, Mal said that he thought

Daniel was right about not picking Connor up just yet. "If Wade Addison is bankrolling things here, we want them both."

Daniel's face was pale and tight. "Please be careful."

"I'm in meetings all day. Not with Addison or Andy Carter."

Mal didn't say when he was coming back, and Daniel didn't ask.

33: EYE OF SAURON

Mal hadn't been lying when he told Daniel that he had a day of meetings, and that none of them were with Wade Addison or Andy Carter. He also needed to make some decisions, to *think*. Visiting the show flat in Addison's block of flats had given him a shock, forcing him to admit to himself just how much he hated living in a small Welsh town. Melin Tywyll was beautiful, and he loved all the hill walking, surfing, country pubs, and working with Daniel on the smallholding. He loved Daniel, didn't want to imagine life without him. But the city gave him a buzz, sharpened his wits, made him think faster, work faster, even walk faster. He liked his colleagues in Clwyd Police, liked them a lot, but even the best of them were small town coppers, and he was a big city boy. He'd told himself for years that he'd left Wales to get away from his father, and it was true. But it was also true that London had pulled him towards it, like gravity, like Manchester was pulling him now, even though people were lying to him, and nothing was what it seemed. You can reinvent yourself in a city, he thought. Country mice and city mice.

The traffic in front of him slowed for a set of roadworks.

Never mind rugby, what we do best in Wales is roadworks. There was a lay-by with a tea and coffee stall, made out of a converted caravan, so he stopped for a cup of builder's tea. It came in a thick mug, orange and milky.

"Put hairs on your chest, lovely, that will," the stallholder said with a grin, leaning down at him over the counter and pushing the sugar dispenser his way.

"I know. I've been drinking it all my life — can't you tell?" He showed the woman his hairy arms, and she cackled with laughter.

"It hasn't worked on my husband, and I've been making his tea for thirty years." And she cackled again. "But he's got his good points, bless him."

The exchange brought Mal out of his reverie and he smiled a thank you to the stallholder, though she probably thought it was for the tea. Which was made exactly how he liked it. For the first time, he saw that the grey clouds had gone, and the sun was rising behind him, turning the sky pink and yellow behind the leafless trees. There were a few snowdrops hiding under the hedge by the tea stall, and he could hear birdsong, even over the noise of the traffic. He gave himself a mental shake and imagined himself folding all his thoughts about cities and Daniel like sheets of paper and tucking them away in a box. He'd come back to them later. For now, work. The work dilemma was equally difficult, just not so painful. Mal finished his tea, returned the mug, and got back in the car.

Daniel had arranged to pick Hector up, so that they could be round at his house to meet Connor by half past ten, which didn't give him enough time to check everything he wanted to check. He chose to revisit Harriet Marston's neighbours and trust his colleagues for the rest. For now.

The original house-to-house records were complete but didn't answer his new questions. Now Daniel knew the main players, it was time to check who had been seen visiting Harriet, and in a perfect world, *when* they had visited. Everything pointed to Connor having ousted Barry Kettles, and taken over sales of equity release as well as managing the lettings from the estate agency. Had Connor realised that it had been a mistake to sell a policy to Harriet, who would probably outlive them all? Had he decided to get the profit earlier, with murder? He was tired of people telling him that he and Connor looked alike, but he thought that it might be useful today. He began with Harriet's friend Angharad from number ten.

Angharad's house was a clone of Harriet's. Same colour scheme, same under-stairs shelving unit, gateleg table, small sofa, and chairs. Only the family photographs were different. If the two women were alike in personality, Daniel thought, then Harriet must have been the nice woman everyone described. Angharad welcomed him in with offers of coffee, even though she was visibly distressed by the death of her friend.

"I still can't believe it," she said. "We'd only been speaking the day before."

Daniel refused a drink, apologising that he didn't have very long.

"I wanted to know about Mrs Marston's visitors," he said, "whether one of them was a shortish man with a kind of squashed-up face and auburn hair?" Angharad shook her head. "He sounds like someone you'd remember," she said, face lifting into a smile at his description.

Daniel looked over at the window. There a slatted blind, the kind that it would be easy to angle so that someone inside could watch the street and not be seen. Angharad saw where he was looking and giggled. "You've caught me," she said, "The Miss Marple of Melin Tywyll."

"If you are," he replied, "you're not the only one, and we

couldn't manage without you. So, if you didn't see the man I've described visiting Mrs Marston, who did you see?" He mentally crossed his fingers and *Bingo!*

"She had a couple of visits from someone who looked a bit like you, though not as tall, and nowhere near as handsome," a wink and more giggles, "When I asked Harriet who he was, she changed the subject, so I left it alone."

Daniel asked whether she had seen the man on the day Harriet had died, but she hadn't. "Sunday, I went over to my sister's and Monday I do all my washing, so the first time I looked out of the window properly, there was a policeman there, and they were saying Harriet was gone." Angharad reached for a tissue from her pocket and blew her nose to cover her tears.

Daniel chatted for a few more minutes, finding out who the other Miss (and Mr) Marples were in the street. *If you murdered Harriet Marston, Connor, we will find out.* He visited three more houses, all people identified by Angharad as likely to have been peering through the net curtains. None of them recognised his description of Barry Kettles, all of them had seen "someone who looks a bit like you." And two of them had seen the man who looked like Daniel on the day of Harriet's death.

The misery Daniel had taken to out with him after the row with Mal began to lift. The net was closing around Connor. He had time to go back to the office and organise for proper statements to be taken and then he went to collect Hector.

DANIEL SAID that Hector should just give Connor his stuff at the door, but Hector showed his upbringing, and let Connor into the house, for a few minutes of stilted conversation. When he left, with his bag of clothes and toiletries, both Daniel and Hector breathed out. Daniel hadn't realised that he'd been holding his breath until that moment. They finished the extra strong coffee Hector had made to wake them up after their disturbed night.

"I'm so sorry mate," Daniel said.

"It wasn't all awful. Some of it was fun. It sounds insane, but part of me is sorry he's leaving, at least like this." Daniel thought Hector might have tears in his eyes. He wrapped his arms round his friend and hugged hard.

"I'll get over it. Whatever doesn't kill you, right?" Hector said, and they both did their best to smile.

"I'll come back tonight, just in case," said Daniel.

"No need, it'll be fine."

"I'll bring food."

"He won't be back. And if he does come, the doors are locked, and my neighbours are in..."

But Daniel said he was coming over anyway. No arguments. Mal was probably going to be in Manchester, the case was proceeding nicely, and they could both do with a night hanging out in front of the TV.

"So, I'll see you about seven."

Hector gave up.

"I'd just stay, but work calls." He didn't say that the work was finding more evidence against Connor. Hector didn't need to know that Connor was guilty of more than domestic abuse. And wasn't even called Connor. Not yet anyway.

Hector waved him away. "Clear off. I'm going to lock the doors, put sad music on, and feel sorry for myself for a bit. I'll be fine."

BACK IN THE LAND ROVER, Daniel drove towards the first set of roadworks, beginning to turn his mind to work, and away from Hector's problems and his own row with Mal. Sophie had organised a watch on the riverside building site, and Everyone else was trying to find out more about Alun, Jeff and Barry Kettles.

His phone rang, and it was Sophie, with news.

"There's a Screwfix van at the building site," she said, "they're unloading a mountain of stuff, and my guys say they're drinking tea and chatting, so we've got a few minutes."

"Get them, Sophie. Arrest the driver, impound the van. Don't let them get away. That van is stolen."

He heard Sophie saying something else, something loud and even angry.

"What?" he asked.

"Van's driven off, but we've got Traffic after it." He could hear the crackle of the radio calls between Sophie and Traffic, amplified by his phone. The calls blurred together, numbers and call signs, none of it making any sense, though his brain told him that he *should* understand.

He knew that it was vital that the van didn't get away, but for the moment he couldn't quite remember why.

"Mustn't get away," he said firmly.

The car felt stuffy, even in the January cold. He cranked the handle to roll the window down, wishing for the little switch in Mal's Audi. And the air conditioning. And the heated seats. Better still, Mal driving, and not angry with Daniel for saying stupid things about Megan.

The phone rang again, and he realised he must have cut Sophie off.

"We've got the van, but the driver saw the traffic cars and legged it."

"Get him. Dogs," Daniel said and thought of little Bob. *Bob knows best.*

He felt the Land Rover bump over the cat's eyes in the middle of the road and Daniel pulled it back. *Concentrate. Like Mal says, this car is a choice.*

He slowed for the first roadworks, the red light staring at him like an eye. *The eye of Sauron* he thought, and giggled, realising that he'd stopped far short of the Stop Here sign. The phone was ringing again, but he couldn't remember how to answer it, and anyway, he had driving to do.

He pulled forwards and stopped. An indignant Beep! behind him jerked him back to see that the light had turned green. As they exited the roadworks, a white van roared past, ignoring the blind bend. *Idiot.*

The trees beside the road leaned towards him, ivy coating the branches like fur. They reached towards the Land Rover, brushing the sides and roof. *That shouldn't happen* he thought and felt his wheel hit the muddy verge. He corrected the car back onto the road, but the hairy limbs stretched out across, trying to grab him in their dusty clutches. It was horrible. He shivered and began to crank the window back up, making the car veer again.

He saw the next set of roadworks. STOP! DANIEL! read the sign, so he obeyed. *It doesn't say that.* He looked again. It said:

PAN WELWCH OLAU COCH SEFWCH YMA
WHEN RED LIGHT SHOWS WAIT HERE

But as he watched, the letters rearranged themselves.

ARE YOU FEELING SLEEPY?
BETTER STOP FOR A WHILE

He blinked, and the sign went back to normal. *But I do feel a bit odd.* He wound the window down again as the lights changed back to red. Then back to green. He drove very carefully through the roadworks and thought that maybe he'd stop at the next lay-by and take a nap. All the road signs were blurring now, and he was glad of the high hedges on each side. The white lines were very clear, almost glowing, in the centre of the road. Perhaps it would be easier to follow them - a wheel on each side - and slow down a bit. It took him too long to see the milk lorry coming straight towards him, but muscle memory turned the wheel and they missed each other by a coat of paint. *Maybe not such a good plan.* He tried to keep to the left of the glowing white lines and kept hoping for somewhere to stop.

Faces looked out of the hedges at him. Leering. Mouths opening and closing. Talking to him. Telling him that there were things he should know. "What things?" he shouted, but the faces just smiled. The next roadworks were ahead and he stopped with relief, carefully not looking at the signs in case they moved. He felt nauseous enough. On the other side, the hedges retreated, and he could breathe again. Only a thin tracery of branches sketched lines across the bright blue sky. *Watch the road.*

On his right, the hillside was orange, where the trees had been cleared. On his left, a drop to the river, waiting for its concrete reinforcement to keep the road in place. *Next month's roadworks.* Out of the corner of his eye he saw a trickle of red earth down the hill on his right. *The trees have been cleared too soon.*

The trickle turned into a flow. He had to look. Quickly he turned his head. The earth was sand, running down towards the road, faster and faster, like lava from a volcano. *This is NOT REAL.* He turned back to the road, fixing his eyes on the carriageway and forcing himself to drive as he had been taught on his police driving course, saying aloud what he was going to do, before he did it.

There is a right-hand bend 100 yards ahead. I am going to brake and slow to 30. Or 20.

I am going to accelerate out of the bend and increase my speed.

But the whole hillside was moving, rushing down towards him, soil carrying the remains of the trees, dead vegetation jumbled with moss and leaves, rocks and stumps ... he *couldn't* not see it, *couldn't* pretend it wasn't real. He snatched the wheel to the left before he was buried in mounds of choking earth and braced himself as the Land Rover left the road and headed down, down, down, into the river. Bouncing on the rocks, breaking trees, a thick branch slamming into the windscreen turning it to stars, a branch through his open window, slicing through his face. He felt himself land. The seatbelt made bruises on his ribs and scored into his neck. He closed his eyes. He heard someone scream. He vomited. He heard someone laugh. Time passed.

MAL STARED AGAIN at the spreadsheet. There was enough here to open an investigation into Wade Addison's warehouse developments, and their relationship, if any, with the theft of building materials. His problem was he didn't know who to talk to. He was sure that Addison was behind Connor, and that Connor was in the middle of Daniel's case in Melin Tywyll. He had to get over himself and talk to Daniel. Only not yet, because he had a pile of work a yard high, and a team to manage.

His phone rang and it was Sophie.

"Sir? I know you're not officially here, so to speak, but I have a problem, and I can't get hold of the DI."

"Tell me," he said, glad to stop wrestling with his dilemma.

"The DI ordered a watch on a building site by the river," she said.

"I know about that," he replied.

"We got lucky, sir, and a van turned up. I rang the DI and he said arrest the driver and impound the van. Only he sounded a bit strange, like he was drunk, almost.

"Anyway, we did what he said, got the driver, and the van's

in the yard. Now we've got this bloke downstairs, kicking off about false arrest, and the foreman from the building site threatening us with who knows what for nicking his materials, and slowing up his job. I don't know where the DI is, but it's somewhere without a signal."

"The van is almost certainly stolen," Mal said, "so you can find out for sure, and arrest the driver for that. What's his name?"

"Jeffrey Coates."

"Then get onto Veronica Brown ..." Mal's office door flew open. "Guv, we've got a bead on Declan Hughes. He's been spotted at his mother's."

"Sorry, Sophie, I've got to go," said Mal and ended the call, following his DC out into the office to begin organising an armed response team, the forensic team, transport, and all before Hughes went to ground again.

34: INTERVIEW SUSPENDED

"Maldwyn? it's Megan. Daniel's sister."

"Hi, Megan, sorry but now isn't a good time."

"Look. You're going to think this is weird, and maybe it is, but do you know where Dan is?"

"He's at work," Mal said, a spike of anxiety flaring in his gut.

"That's just it. He isn't. Bethan says that she was expecting him back ages ago. He's not answering his phone. Something's wrong. I always know when something's wrong with Dan. It's a twin thing."

Megan was gabbling. His team were looking at him for guidance, he needed to sign tickets for weapons to be issued and ask for drone and helicopter support.

"Calm down, I'm sure it's fine."

"No really. I have a really, really bad feeling. Like, I'm going to ring the hospitals bad feeling."

Mal knew about the *twin thing*. He envied it, was jealous of the close relationship, of the way that Daniel turned to Megan when something was wrong. *And OK maybe I deserve it.* He knew Megan didn't like him, and maybe he deserved that to, but if she was ringing him, there was something wrong. The anxiety in his gut flared up again, stronger this time.

"I really can't talk now, Megan, but I'll ring you back as soon as I can."

"Fine. Don't help."

And the call ended.

SHIT, shit, shit.

There was nothing Mal could do until Declan Hughes was either in custody or had escaped yet again. Hughes was a violent, serial offender and they needed him off the streets. They were going to go into a residential area, armed to the teeth, to arrest someone who was known to be stupid enough to shoot at police officers. Mal needed his head in the game or people might die. He pushed thoughts of Megan's worry to the furthest corner of his mind and headed for the armoury.

One after another, firearms officers claimed their weapons and donned their protective gear, turning themselves into robots. Mal swapped his leather jacket for a protective vest but didn't get a gun even though he was trained to use one. If he was close enough to need to shoot anyone, they'd have lost control of the situation altogether, and it would be too late.

The convoy set off in unmarked cars and vans, blue lights clearing the way until they were close to the address where Declan's mother lived. Then it was lights off and all out of the vehicles. The house was a small terrace, with an alleyway down the back, parallel to the street. Four of the armed officers headed that way with the rest waiting at the end of the street until they were in place. Mal was well back from the group who went to bang on the door, though not so far that he couldn't see the small, middle aged woman open it, and begin arguing with the armed officers on her doorstep.

"She's giving him time to hide," Mal said, "get in there, and be careful."

But he was wrong. Declan's mother was giving him time to get out of the back door, and into the alley, where he ran into the waiting arms of the armed officers, wearing only his underpants and a T-shirt. If that wasn't enough, the search team found a sawn-off shotgun in Mrs Hughes' knitting basket, so they had the pleasure of arresting her, as well as her son.

Mal left a forensic team searching the house and got back into his own car, thankful that no shots had been fired. The case against Declan Hughes was solid, and they had an illegal firearm off the streets. He could allow himself five minutes to ring Daniel. The call went to voicemail. He rang Bethan.

"We don't know where he is," Bethan said, "we were hoping you might know."

BETHAN WASN'T the only one wondering where Daniel was. Sophie found her in the CID office. "Can we talk?" she asked, and Bethan nodded towards the DCI's empty room.

"I need help." Sophie told Bethan about the surveillance Daniel had asked for, arresting the van driver on Daniel's instructions, and about contacting Mal because she couldn't get hold of Daniel. "The van *is* stolen, but the driver isn't talking, except to ask for a solicitor. I have no idea what I should be asking him, and there's no sign of the DI. Does he often disappear in the middle of a case?"

"It's been known," Bethan said, "but we came in this morning to pages of notes. Things are happening and he's usually in the middle of it."

Bethan led Sophie back to her own desk and showed her Daniel's notes of his meeting with Ian Goldsmith.

"This Jeff that Goldsmith refers to could be our Jeffrey

Coates," said Sophie, scribbling away, "and the DCI said to get in touch with Veronica Brown, before he was cut off. Do we have any clues about that?"

Bethan scrolled through Daniel's notes until she found the trip to the dangerous flats. "Our man could be one of the thugs who threatened those young women."

They smiled at each other. "That's one thing off the list," said Bethan, "we know what to ask our guy downstairs."

"Maybe those young women will be able to identify him," Sophie said, happy for an excuse to ring Veronica.

Sophie saw that there were also notes from Daniel's visit to Connor, and her own identification of him as Colin Bryson Jones, wanted man. Bethan scrolled down the page of Connor/Colin's arrests and his few convictions: possession of Class A drugs, suspicion of dealing Class A drugs, mortgage fraud and most recently the conviction for taking deposits for a flat he didn't own.

"I've met him," Sophie told Bethan, "and I didn't like him at all."

"Now we know why. He's a drug dealer and a con-man who arrived here six months ago and was up to his old tricks straight away."

The final set of notes were a long audio file, describing Daniel's visits to Harriet Marston's neighbours.

"Does this Colin Bryson Jones look like the Boss?" Bethan asked.

"Superficially. Tall, thin, fair hair, blue eyes. But not a nice face. Handsome, but somehow not attractive, if you see what I mean."

"So, what the DI seems to be getting at is that Bryson Jones visited Harriet Marston before she died. Hector Lord says it was murder, and the boss is putting Bryson Jones in the frame." Sophie nodded.

"That's how I see it too. It's a CID case, but I'll do anything I can, starting with calling Veronica to contact those two young women to ID our driver."

"Cheers. Finding the boss is your other job I think."

~

SOPHIE STARTED with Dai in technical support — could he track Daniel's phone? Then she asked for any ANPR pings on Daniel's car, and for Connor slash Colin's car too. There were no pings and Daniel's phone was switched off.

"Where was it last?" she asked.

"A call to you, ma'am, just before ten this morning," followed by a set of co-ordinates that she marked on the map on her office wall. She called PC Morgan and showed him. "Is there anything round there? Should we be calling the hospitals? Is it a mobile dead spot, do you know?"

PC Morgan shook his head. "Everyone's avoiding that road at the moment, ma'am, it's one set of roadworks after another, spending the budget before the year-end."

"Then maybe we'd better send someone over there to talk to the road workers and see if they've seen the DI."

Then it was time to try Veronica. Sophie was nervous, but it was only work, right? She hadn't been attracted to anyone for a long time, but Veronica's passion for her job sparked a reaction in Sophie. And, Veronica had a smile that could light up a room. She rang, and asked Veronica if she could take a picture of their arrested driver to show to the two young women Veronica had introduced to Daniel.

"I'll come with you," said Veronica, and Sophie's heart lifted.

~

DANIEL FELT COLD, damp and sick. He lay very still, hoping the nausea would pass. It didn't. He tried closing his eyes, but the world spun, and he felt even sicker. He opened them, and the floor moved underneath him in waves. He tried to brace himself, but he couldn't move his hands. Nothing made any sense. He felt bile rising in his throat and heaved. Not much came out, but he let the heaves come until he was exhausted. Afterwards he didn't feel so sick, and he could try to take stock. He began by wriggling away from his vomit.

He was lying on his side, on the floor of a dark room, on a cheap carpet, that smelled of dust. His hands were secured behind him and when he jerked his head up, he saw a cable tie round his ankles. He thought it was probably a cable tie holding his hands together. He lay still and listened. Nothing. He sniffed. Damp dusty carpet, plaster, bricks, building site types of smells. He looked. The room was a big one, with dirty windows set high in the walls. One end of the room had a stage. Moving his head to look round made the nausea return, but all he had left were dry heaves and a raging headache.

He looked at his clothes. Work suit. Torn and filthy. He waited. Nothing got any better. It just got darker, and colder. His arms ached. Very slowly, a thought entered his mind, creeping past the pain and the sickness. *Move your arms to the front. It'll be better.* It took a lot of wriggling, but wriggling was one of his superpowers, and he was right, it *was* better. With his arms at the front, he could move. He crawled around the room, looking for something to cut the cable ties, stopping often to listen. There was nothing.

There is a nail clipper in my pocket.

But without his hands free he couldn't get it. So, he started chewing. The plastic was hard. He couldn't get a good angle, but it was dark, silent, and what other choice did he have? After an eternity, the plastic seemed to stretch a little. He pulled his wrists apart until every muscle cried out for mercy. His shoulders throbbed with pain and his wrists felt slimy. He told himself it was sweat. He knew it was blood. The plastic stretched another half millimetre. He chewed some more. Now his tongue could feel a tiny bit of stretched plastic and he ran his teeth over and over and over it. And pulled his wrists apart, and chewed, and pulled, and chewed and pulled until it broke. He was shaking, but he found the nail clipper and sawed his way through the cable tie on his feet. He put both the ties in his pocket. He didn't look at the blood.

The room was almost black now, only the faintest slivers of light coming through the windows. He still had no idea how he had come to be where he was, but he was very sure that whoever had tied him up didn't mean him any good. He wanted to be well out of the way before that person came back. He stood up and set off to walk round the room. There would be a door. More than one door.

He listened again, and this time he heard voices.

BETHAN ASKED Charlie to come with her to interview Jeffrey Coates. She would have liked to have waited until she had the positive ID from Veronica Brown's two young women, but she had the stolen van, and that would have to do for now.

Jeffrey Coates and his solicitor were cut from the same template, just dressed differently. Short men with long bodies and dark hair brushed straight back from their foreheads. She could see them crammed into the pub, pint in hand, shouting at the TV as Wales played in the Six Nations, bursting into song with every point. The solicitor was in a navy suit with drooping pockets and a button missing. Coates was in a well washed rugby shirt and jeans.

Recording set up in the nastiest of the interview rooms, the one with the flickering overhead light, she began.

"Mr Coates, you were arrested this morning with a stolen vehicle. Would you like to tell me about that?"

"No comment."

"You were seen helping unload building materials from the van and carry them into the flats being built next to the river. Were those building materials stolen with the van?"

"No comment."

"We have a witness statement saying that you have been delivering materials to that site in a number of other vehicles. Were those other vehicles stolen?"

"No comment."

As Bethan continued, the solicitor took endless notes, though what he could be writing, she had no idea. They would get a copy of the recording, and all his client said was the same two words. She decided to change tack.

"Mr Coates, do you know a man going by the name of Connor Byrne Jones?"

There was a hesitation before the "No comment."

"Mr Byrne Jones was based at North Wales Estates on the high street. Perhaps you knew him from there?"

Jeffrey Coates said his "No comment," but he had begun to look annoyed. Bethan was used to career criminals' sneers of No Comment, their pride in being able to keep the game going for hours, knowing that a refusal to give an inch gave them a chance of getting them back on the streets. But this was different. Bethan didn't think Coates was annoyed with *her*, she thought he was annoyed at the thought of Connor. So, she kept going.

"Did Connor Byrne Jones manage the building site by the river?"

"No comment."

Which was interesting, because how would he know who managed the site? Jeffrey Coates' job was surely to deliver the stolen materials and dump the van or truck.

"Connor Byrne Jones managed a number of properties for rent around the town. Did you have any involvement in any of those properties Mr Coates?"

Coates swivelled to stare at his solicitor, who took the cue.

"This is a fishing expedition, sergeant, nothing to do with the offence for which my client has been arrested."

"We may be considering other matters in relation to your client, but I'll leave it for now. Mr Coates, when you left the site in the stolen van, where were you going?"

"No comment."

She was right. Coates was back in his comfort zone. She needed Veronica's girls to make the identification, and she needed to find a way of bringing Connor back in. She asked a few more questions about the van, and then,

"Do you know a man called Barry Kettles?"

And she was there.

"What's Barry got to do with anything?" Coates said, before the solicitor could open his mouth.

"Mr Kettles is dead, in suspicious circumstances."

"The fucking bastard! *The fucking bastard.*"

"Who, Barry Kettles?" she asked, trying to keep the snark out of her voice.

"Don't be stupid. Connor buggering Jones."

There was a knock at the door. Charlie went to answer, slipped out into the corridor and was back a moment later. "Sarge. You need to hear this."

Bethan looked daggers at him. She'd just got Coates talking. If they stopped now, he'd remember to keep his mouth closed.

"Sarge, really."

"Interview suspended."

In the corridor, one of the civilian staff from the front desk was looking worried, *as well she might.* "This had better be important," she said.

"There are two doctors here, Sergeant Davies, and their solicitor. They say they have an appointment with DI Owen."

34: I HAVE SOMETHING YOU WANT

Declan Hughes' arrest created at least a day of solid paperwork, all of it necessary to ensure that he was charged, remanded in custody, and in the fullness of time, convicted. As well as that, Mal had a gun-crime prevention strategy meeting to prepare for, attend and speak at. He told himself that Daniel was somewhere with no signal, following a lead that only he had seen, and that would turn out to be the one thing that they needed to know, and that Megan's imagination had got the better of her. He had almost convinced himself when Bethan rang.

"Sir, Keith and Lesley Flowers, and their solicitor have shown up at the station, saying that they had agreed to meet the DI. But we can't find him. Inspector Harrington is coordinating a search, based on the last location of his phone."

"Go straight to Hart," Mal said, "I've got a meeting, but let me know what's happening." He tried not to sound desperate, but Bethan would see straight through him.

"I'm sure he's fine, sir," she said.

The meeting was in full flow when Bethan rang, and Mal couldn't answer. He was the only non-executive officer present, and Major Crimes was depending on him to push their concerns. He had pages of carefully argued notes, supported by solid data, and the issues were important. But his heart was racing, and he felt the sweat break out under his arms. He wanted to reach for water but was afraid that he would knock it over with trembling hands.

He felt the phone vibrate with the arrival of a text and he couldn't look because he was talking about guns and gun crime. He had to listen while the DCC made an interminable response, but that was it. As the DCC finished, Mal stood up and excused himself. He had to know.

Sgt Davies: DI's LR found near Pentrefelin. Seems to have driven off the road on sharp bend and straight into the river. No sign of DI. River not deep at this point. Some blood in LR, not significant amount. Also vomit. LR being recovered. Area being searched. Witnesses being sought.

Mal rang Hector. "Is Daniel with you?"

Hector sounded half asleep. "No, why?"

"Wake up, Hector. Daniel's Land Rover has been found in the river not far from your house, and he's not in it. Tell me when you saw him."

"He went about ten. Connor collected his stuff, and a bit later Daniel left. I crashed out."

Mal's next call was to Bethan. "You need to find Connor Byrne Jones and bring him in," he told her. "Ask him about Daniel and don't let him go, whatever he says. And get Hart to authorise a helicopter and dogs to look for Daniel."

"All done, sir," she said, "Byrne Jones' car has pinged ANPR cameras on the way into Manchester, and he's not in his office."

"I have to go back into my meeting," Mal said, but what he wanted to do was think. The last thing he needed was to talk to Megan, but she had a right to know. He told her about the Land Rover being found, the blood, the search, the helicopter and the dogs.

"Can't you come and look for him?"

"Bethan and Sophie are doing everything that I'd be doing."

"He's in trouble. Bad trouble. You should be here, be looking for him." Megan was sobbing.

"That's not possible, Megan, but trust me, we're doing everything we can."

"Words, Maldwyn, empty words, that's all you are." Megan rang off.

He wouldn't be able to do anything more from Melin Tywyll than he could do here, but Mal wanted to be there, if only to make sure. He told himself that he could keep the façade up for a few more hours, but he felt as if he was being slowly and painfully torn down the middle. The job was important, hell, this *meeting* was important. Getting Declan Hughes off the streets was important. And he was almost certain that there was enough information to start pursuing Wade Addison for the theft of vehicles and their contents, and that might tie in with some of the things going on in Melin Tywyll, but for that he needed to speak to Daniel — and there he was back again, thinking about Daniel and being torn in half again. In the end, he did what he always did. His job. It felt like the wrong choice.

Mal contributed his thoughts to the meeting, and he gave them with conviction, not like someone whose boyfriend was missing. He looked out of the window, and saw the sky start to darken and the lights come on.

What if he's lost in those woods, injured, in the dark?

The executive officers congratulated Mal on finding Declan Hughes, and he smiled, and insisted that the praise was due to the people who'd been monitoring things long before his arrival. He smiled, and shook hands as the meeting closed, having made good decisions.

Why hasn't Bethan been in touch about the helicopter and the search dogs? What's going on with the Flowers? Why has Connor come to Manchester? What did Hart have to say?

The meeting room emptied, and Mal thought that he could make his calls and find out, but he didn't get the chance. His phone rang first.

"Maldwyn? I have something you're looking for, and I'm ready to trade."

Mal felt the ground rushing up towards him. He groped for the nearest chair and managed to sit down before he fell.

BETHAN WAS OUT OF IDEAS. She'd been about to make a break-through with Jeffrey Coates, but she couldn't ignore the doctors. And this was an appointment Daniel wouldn't have forgotten. She went to see Superintendent Hart and laid it all out in front of her. Hart was decisive, as always.

"You and I will talk to the Flowerses, Bethan, or rather you will talk to them, and I'll look like a senior officer who's taking everything *very seriously*. Get Charlie to tell Coates that he'll have to wait for an hour. Lock him up, give him a cup of tea and a sandwich. That'll give him time to think, and us time to get those two young women to identify him.

"Do you think Inspector Harrington is doing a good job on the search for Daniel?"

"Yes ma'am," said Bethan.

"Then we can leave that to her."

THE BIGGEST AND best of the interview rooms was crowded with five of them, but at least, Bethan thought, no one's going to say *No Comment*. She hoped. The Flowerses solicitor was an alto-gether different beast — very smart suit, hair trimmed with precision, and no sign of a notebook, just a smartphone. His only affectation was a pair of enormous tortoiseshell spectacles. The Flowerses looked like what they were, a couple of middle-aged country doctors.

Their solicitor began with a prepared statement.

"My clients would like to offer every co-operation to Melin Tywyll Police in their enquiries. They were asked to bring certain documents with them today, and they would like to explain why that isn't possible. Put simply, some of those documents don't exist. There are no employment records for either Mr Barry Kettles or for Mr Connor Byrne Jones."

They had brought everything else Daniel had asked for — the full list of properties owned by the Flowers companies, tenancy agreements, plus the most recent accounts.

"Detective Inspector Owen also asked about a property my clients are converting into flats, and their contacts with the council's planning department. Unfortunately, we don't have those documents either. Those matters were all dealt with by Mr Byrne Jones."

Bethan had read Daniel's notes of his meeting with the Flowerses. The big question, she thought, is how did two respectable and respected country doctors employ a crook like Connor? So that's what she asked.

"Connor Byrne Jones is an assumed name," she said, "His real name is Colin Bryson Jones, and he has convictions for drug dealing and property related fraud. Paperwork or no paperwork, I'd like to know how you are allowing this man to run your businesses."

Lesley and Keith looked at each other. Keith had beads of sweat on his forehead. He looked at the solicitor, who held up his hand in an 'over to you' gesture. In the end it was Lesley who spoke.

"We're not proud of any of this, but we never intended for things to go the way that they did. We just wanted to make a bit of extra money and Buy to Let seemed like the way to do it. We talked to people — friends — and a couple of them already had little portfolios of property already. One said that they had this brilliant manager who they would introduce us to, and they did." Lesley paused for a drink of water.

"That was Connor Byrne Jones?" Bethan asked.

"Oh no, his name is Wade Addison." Bethan heard Hart gasp and looked at her boss. Hart's face was blank.

"Please go on, Dr Flowers," Bethan said.

"Wade is a Manchester property developer, very interested in old buildings. He'd helped our friends get their Buy to Let business off the ground, and he offered to do the same for us. This was a few years ago now. He said that he was considering opening an estate agent in the town and it would be a good base for a letting agency too. So that's what happened."

Hart leaned forwards. "Did you do any kind of due diligence on Wade Addison before you went into business with him?" she asked. Bethan's antennae were twitching overtime.

The solicitor stepped in, eyes blank behind the ridiculous glasses.

"My clients have only recently become aware of Wade Addison's less than savoury past. However, all their business dealings with him were quite legitimate."

"That's not what I asked," said Hart.

"We trusted him," said Lesley, "he had made money for our friends, he set up the estate agents, and we owned the properties we were letting, so we weren't in business together, not at first."

"So, you bought properties to let out, and Addison managed them?"

"Yes. Well, Barry Kettles managed the office, we didn't see Wade very often. And we did make money, it was a good investment."

"What about the equity release?" Bethan asked.

"It's perfectly legal," said Keith.

"So I understand," Bethan replied, "But whose idea was it for you to supply clients' names?"

"Wade Addison's." Lesley said, "and he was the one who told us to look for people with no relatives, and who were, well, older, and less healthy, patients."

"So that you would get your money back quickly?"

"Yes." Lesley said, and she sounded defiant, chin up and looking Bethan in the eyes, "It isn't illegal, and those people had some money to spend on nice things before they died. I'm not sorry."

No, because you made a fortune out of it.

Hart stirred in her seat. "Tell me, Dr Flowers, the lump sums that you provided to your equity release clients, where did that money come from?"

Lesley Flowers looked puzzled. "From the company."

"But where did that money come from? According to our research, you lent over a million pounds in the first couple of years of the scheme, and a lot more since then. Did the company borrow the money?"

"Barry Kettles did all that," was the only answer that they got. Bethan thought that she could see a pattern beginning to form.

"Going back to Connor Byrne Jones," she said, "how did he come to take over?"

"I think he's some kind of relative of Wade's" said Lesley, "they look a bit alike anyway. Wade just rang us and said he'd be working in the office instead of Barry."

Hart pushed her chair back. "I think we have enough for the time being," she said, "but we will want to talk to you again." She reached across Bethan to turn the tape off and called for someone to escort the Flowerses and their solicitor out of the building. Then she beckoned for Bethan to follow her.

"Wade Addison is a major league criminal," she said, when they were alone and out of earshot of everyone else, "and DCI Kent is on an undercover operation, trying to get close to him."

"HE'S ALIVE," said Addison, "Probably doesn't feel very well, but he's alive. On the other hand, he could die easily."

"Who?" Mal asked, although he knew. He was shaking so hard that he struggled to stay on the chair, terrified that one of the other officers would have forgotten something and return to the meeting room. But he couldn't stand, not even to lock the door.

"Don't play games Maldwyn. Your Inspector. Your boyfriend. The man Clwyd Police have been wasting their time searching for, like you've been wasting your time trying to convince me that you're a bent copper. That game's over my friend. If you want him back, I need something from you. Not much. It isn't a hard thing, and it'll solve a lot of problems for you, close a lot of cases. Think about it. Don't try to trace the call — I'm dumping this phone."

Mal tried to speak but Addison was gone. The phone number was unobtainable when he tried to ring back.

Procedure told Mal to report the call. Recuse himself from any part of the investigation because he was emotionally involved. Stand aside while others set up a team and arranged negotiation. He should go back to Melin and hold Megan's hand, and drink tea while they waited for the phone to ring. That's what he would advise anyone else to do, because he knew that the procedures worked. They'd been researched and evaluated. People like him had spent hours looking at statistics and case studies. Procedures save lives. Being too emotionally involved with a case means making mistakes, and people can die from mistakes. Not following procedure ends careers.

Following procedure was the right thing to do, and Mal had no intention of doing it.

The police *never* give kidnappers what they want, not even for one of their own. Mal knew that Addison wanted to negotiate with him and no one else. He could deny any phone calls and just kill Daniel, hide his body and no one would ever be able to trace it back to him.

But Mal didn't want to. He didn't want to take Addison on, Addison was too clever, knew too much. Addison was no Declan Hughes, running and hiding at his mother's house. Addison had friends in the police, friends who knew what Mal had been trying to do, who knew where Mal was, and even when Mal was going to be on his own to take the call.

Mal felt watched, certain that one of the officers he'd been talking to was working for Addison. He was afraid of making mistakes and letting Daniel die. He wanted to hide, let someone, anyone, else deal with it. Daniel would know what to do, Mal thought, would jump in with both feet and just do it. Daniel made intuitive leaps, and more often than not he was right. Mal sat in the empty meeting room, with its etched glass doors, abandoned coffee cups and uneaten biscuits, and thought that he had followed procedures since he had first joined the police, that he was a plodder and a reader, and a note taker. This felt like stepping off a cliff, into Daniel's way of doing things. He needed to know what Addison wanted before he asked for it, and how Addison knew he was being set up. He needed help, but not here in Manchester, where he didn't know who he could trust, and where they would take the case off him.

All he was sure about was that Daniel was in Manchester. He might have been kidnapped in Wales, but he was in Manchester now. Manchester was Addison's territory, and Connor had brought him here.

He texted Megan. *I'm going to find Daniel.*

He could do this. It was the job he'd been trained for, that he'd been doing for years and doing well. He thought of the boy who had killed himself after being raped in the cells in Cardiff. I couldn't save Ethan, Mal thought, but I'm going to save Daniel.

I might not be intuitive, but I am stubborn.

The shaking stopped.

35: SPECIAL K IN EVERY CUP

Mal went into the to the first café he came to. It had its wifi password written up in chalk behind the bar. He ordered coffee and soup, found a table in a corner, got out a pad and a pen, and called Hector.

"Did they find him?" Hector asked, and Mal said no.

"I'm in Manchester," Mal said, "and I think he's here too. Im fact, I'm sure he is. I think he was kidnapped when he left your house this morning. I need you to tell me everything that happened, every detail."

Hector described Daniel taking him home from the small-holding, Connor arriving to pick up his stuff and leaving, then Hector telling Daniel to go.

"So, Connor knew Daniel was going to be at your house?" Mal asked.

"Daniel made the arrangement," Hector said, "I was there, it was my phone, but Daniel talked to Connor."

"When did you arrange it?"

"First thing this morning. Connor texted in the middle of the night. Daniel said I needed to reclaim my house, not give Connor any more reason to visit."

"So, what? Sevenish?

"Maybe earlier."

Connor had plenty of time to set up the abduction. Mal made a note on his pad. But he couldn't have done it on his own. Daniel was bigger than Connor, and a trained police officer. Connor had no chance against Daniel on his own. Mal made another note. He thought of Arwyn wobbling at the top of the ladder.

"What were you and Daniel doing when Connor arrived at your house?" he asked Hector.

"Drinking coffee. I'd packed Connor's stuff and he wasn't there, so I brewed up."

"Your usual high strength hand ground beans, made in a French Press?"

"Of course."

"So, you were drinking coffee when Connor arrived, and you were still drinking it when he left?"

"Yes. Though I don't see ... you think he drugged the coffee?"

"Could he have done?"

Hector didn't answer.

"Hector?" Mal said.

"I don't remember that he was on his own with the coffee. But he might have been. It was all awkward. We were sort of all moving round each other." There was a pause.

"Daniel wanted to stay, but I made him leave. I was just so tired and miserable. I should have let him stay ..." Hector's voice trailed off. Mal told him that none of it was his fault and asked what he did after Daniel had gone.

"I crashed out. Didn't wake up for hours. Till you rang earlier. I haven't washed the coffee pot. Haven't moved off the sofa in fact. I'll send it for testing. Take some of my own blood."

Mal asked Hector what he thought they were drugged with and Hector didn't hesitate.

"Ketamine. There's ketamine everywhere. Easy to get hold of, wouldn't taste it in coffee, knocks you out. Could be lots of other things, but my money's on ketamine."

Mal thought that it was worth asking the question that had come into his mind earlier.

"If that builder who fell off the ladder had just had a mug full of ketamine enriched coffee, would that explain it?"

"Oh yes. I sent a blood sample for testing, but they take ages. You were both on at me to try to speed it up." Mal made some more notes. He was following in Daniel's tracks. Someone needed to check if Arwyn had been into the North Wales Estates office before he died, and if so, had he had a coffee with Connor?

"Hector, what did Daniel tell you I'm doing when I'm away?"

"Just working for another force. You're working for Manchester Police now, right?"

"Do you know what I'm doing for them?"

"No idea."

"And this is the big question, did you tell *Connor* where I was working?"

"And happily, it's a big question that I can answer. No."

The soup arrived and Mal stirred it with hungry desire. His coffee cup had mysteriously emptied, so he asked the waitress for more. She asked if he wanted anything else, and he thought that yes, he did, because he had more calls to make. He asked for a toasted cheese sandwich.

Mal didn't know whether to be relieved that Connor hadn't found out about his undercover role through Hector. They knew that there must be a connection between Connor and Addison, but now Mal knew that Addison must have told Connor about him, not the other way round. He put his spoon down and made another note.

Connor drugged Hector and Daniel. Hector crashed out;

Daniel crashed his car. Connor, or someone else, found Daniel and abducted him, and brought him to Manchester, to use as a hostage, to get Mal to do something. What? Mal needed to know, to get ahead of Addison, because people like Addison don't leave loose ends.

Now Bethan knew about Mal's undercover job, she returned to interview Jeffrey Coates with determination. She was starting to be afraid for Daniel, aware that Hart had gone to make high level calls, and was as worried as Bethan. They were wading into some very deep water.

For a wonder, Coates had taken the time to think, even before he found out that Veronica Brown's two young clients could identify him.

"My client is prepared to give a statement in exchange for consideration of any charges being dropped," said the solicitor. Bethan told him that wasn't how it worked, as both the solicitor and Coates knew perfectly well.

"Let me tell you what I think, Mr Coates," said Bethan, "you work for a Manchester gangster called Wade Addison. You drove a stolen van to the building site this morning, and we have evidence that this isn't the first time. You also act as an enforcer when called upon, such as when tenants complain too much, or don't pay their rent. I think that you and two others attacked an electrician called Ian Goldsmith, because he had been asking too many questions. All of this is entirely consistent with your past criminal record, and of course we have witnesses. When we spoke before, you seemed upset that Connor Byrne Jones had taken over the reins from Barry Kettles. Perhaps you could explain why that was?"

"I'll tell you," he said, " but I want protection. Addison doesn't take prisoners."

"If you tell us enough to put Addison away, protection is a definite possibility." Bethan knew she had no authority to make any such claim, but from what she'd learned, it wouldn't be a problem if the information was good. It was. Coates had turned from no comment-man to let me tell you everything-man.

"IF ADDISON HAD LEFT Barry Kettles in place, we'd still be in the dark. Bringing Connor in is what caused all the trouble." Bethan and Charlie reported to Hart.

"But why did Addison spoil a good thing, by bringing a useless dick like Connor in, sorry, ma'am." Charlie wanted to know.

"I might not have put it quite like that Charlie, but it's a fair question," said Hart. "I've asked Inspector Harrington to join us, and we'll have a conference call with DCI Kent, and pool our knowledge. Thank you, Charlie."

"Ma'am." Charlie's shoulders dropped as he left, passing Sophie on his way out.

36: WHY WOULD HE?

Mal got the call as he was wiping grease from his cheese toastie off his notebook. He belly was full, but his notes were making him feel ill. There weren't enough pieces of the jigsaw to make a finished picture. He knew Daniel was in Manchester, but it was a gut feeling based on his knowledge of Addison. He was morally certain that Andy Carter was Addison's man, but who the others were, or even if there were others, he couldn't tell. He was sure that Hector and Daniel had been drugged, and possibly so had Arwyn, Barry Kettles and Harriet Marston. He had a suspicion about what Addison wanted, and why he wanted it, but if he was right, there was no chance that they could comply, even if they were willing.

Hart put her phone on loudspeaker. "We need to pool what we've got, Mal," she said.

"Ma'am"

"Wade Addison has gone out on a limb for Connor slash Colin," she began. "According to the Flowers, and to the van driver, Jeffrey Coates, everything was going smoothly until Addison brought Connor in, and pushed Kettles to the sidelines. Connor sold equity release to the wrong people, stopped doing repairs to the rented properties, and started bribing council officials to allow that development down by the river. He used Addison's heavies to threaten or beat up anyone who objected. It was a perfect, almost legal money laundering operation, and Connor blew it. Why would Addison do that?"

Mal thought about the upcoming wedding, and Huw's decision to risk upsetting their father by asking Mal to be his best man. "I think that Connor is Addison's brother, ma'am. Or more accurately his half-brother. My guess is that Addison heard about Connor's trouble in London and offered to set him up with his operation here. Then Connor started doing his own thing, and now Addison needs to get him away."

Mal had to decide. If he told Hart and the others that Daniel had been kidnapped, he'd be told to stand down. If he didn't, he could miss vital information.

"I think Connor drugged Hector and Daniel this morning, ma'am. Hector slept all day, couldn't wake up, and Daniel drove off the road. Hector says he thinks it's Ketamine, and he's testing for it."

"So where is DI Owen?" Bethan asked, and to Mal's relief Sophie answered,

"Connor's car was pinged all the way into central Manchester," she said, "could he have kidnapped Daniel and taken him to Manchester?"

Hart began, "Why would he do that?", but Bethan interrupted, "Coates said that he and his mates were supposed to go to the Burns and Wood — is that right — for some *boxing practice* tonight. *Boxing practice* being the euphemism for beating people up."

Hart said again, "Why would he do that?" Mal was sure that Hart knew the answer.

He said, "The Burns and Wood building is a warehouse that

Addison is converting into flats. The building is empty, although Addison has an office there. Ma'am, do you know anyone trustworthy in Manchester Police? Because perhaps you should call them. I need to go." And he ended the call. He had the final pieces of the jigsaw. Hart would order him not to go, so it was better that she didn't get the chance. He had to trust that she'd have his back.

THE VOICES WERE GETTING CLOSER. They might be coming to rescue him, though Daniel didn't want to take the chance. His eyes had begun to adjust to the gloom, but there wasn't enough light for him to see across the big space for a fire exit, or anything that would help him get out of here before the owners of the voices arrived. He started to move away from the direction of the sound and was brought to a stop by the stage. Stages had doors, he thought, but this one didn't seem to. He could see steps in front of him, the steps performers must have used to get onto the stage.

Like the ones in the scout hut. That we had to move so we could use the area under the stage for storage.

He pulled. The steps moved. He pulled some more until there was room to wriggle underneath the stage and as he pulled the steps back into place, he heard a door open, and the owners of the voices came into the room.

"What the fuck?"

Daniel recognised the voice, and he knew who had brought him here, if not why.

Through the minute gaps between the steps, Daniel could see torchlight on the floor of the big room, and hear footsteps moving round. He was glad there was no electricity, flooding the place with light. He was sure his hands were bleeding, and a bloody handprint would show them where he was. If they only had torches, he might get away with it. He hoped neither of them had been in the scouts.

"Unconscious and tied up? Great job Col."

"He was. Enough Special K to put him out for hours. He was right there in the middle of the floor."

"Well, he isn't right there now, is he?"

"You can see where he was though." Daniel supposed that they were looking at where he'd thrown up. "And there's blood." He wanted to get further away from the steps, to hide deeper under the stage, where their torches wouldn't reach. But if he moved, they'd hear him.

He was lying on cables, and bits of wood and who knows what other nameless protrusions digging into his flesh. His head ached, his wrists and ankles were sore, and he just wanted to sleep. Only he'd learned two things, and if he could manage not to get found, those two things would solve at least one of his cases. Connor had drugged him with Special K, aka ketamine. Suddenly he remembered trying to drive away from Hector's, the hallucinations and the tiredness. *That's what killed Arwyn. Now all I have to do is get out of here and tell Mal.* He remembered that Mal was angry with him and wanted to weep.

The voices stopped. Daniel couldn't hear anything. The torchlight was still flickering through the gaps in the steps, but he couldn't look without moving.

There was a cry of pain.

"Wade? That hurt."

"It was supposed to. That's your fucking insurance policy that you've lost, you halfwit. Get Carter and get looking, because if he's got away, you are going to jail and there's fuck all I can do about it."

"Jesus Wade, I'm bleeding."

"Good. Get going."

Daniel heard the footsteps recede, and then the slam of a door. He didn't move. After a while, he reached underneath his back and as quietly as he could, removed whatever it was that was setting his bones on fire. Then he lay still, counting his breaths and listening. Time passed. Perhaps Mal would be looking for him. Megan would know something had happened. He could stay where he was and hope someone came. His mind started to clear.

Connor had drugged him, and probably Hector too. He'd been brought here as some kind of "insurance policy" for Connor. The other man must be the Wade Addison that Mal was supposed to make friends with, the man Mal thought was behind Connor and his schemes in Melin Tywyll. He remembered that Sophie had rung him when he was driving, and he thought he remembered that they'd caught the delivery driver. But everything after that was a blank. He risked another tiny adjustment in his body, and it helped with the nail boring a hole in his hip. But it didn't help with the cold, which was seeping in under the steps, rising from the floor and blowing in an arctic draught across his face. He put his arms across his chest and his hands underneath his armpits. He felt his neck getting colder and stiffer, and only wriggling his toes assured him that he still had feet. He started to try to warm his muscles in turn without making a sound — toes, feet, ankles, shins, thighs, buttocks, stomach, arms, face — clenching and unclenching. If he got out of here, he would have to be able to move.

He heard a sound, perhaps a cough, and froze. Then a voice, Wade's voice. It sounded soothing, and reasonable.

"I know you're here. You may as well come out. You must have had enough by now."

He can't know I'm here. If he was sure, he wouldn't have sent Connor away.

"Props to you for working out that I hadn't left. Thing is, your boyfriend will be here soon, and I need you."

Mal? Mal is coming?

Daniel was tempted, but if Mal was on his way, then it was worth hanging on a bit longer.

"Of course, if you aren't there as a negotiation item, I won't have any reason to be nice to the lovely Maldwyn, will I?" Daniel's heart was banging so loudly in his chest that he thought it would break his ribs.

Suddenly, there was a crash. A new voice said "Boss? Kent's across the street."

Wade said, "Perfect timing. I suppose I'd better go and meet him. Keep watch here."

"Boss."

Daniel heard footsteps receding and a door close. Then there was a thump above his head. Daniel used the exchange and the crash of doors opening and closing to move further under the stage, and to turn onto his side. A crack in the wood allowed him to see out. He could see a man's ankle in front of him, and hear as the man shuffled, trying to get comfortable sitting on the edge of the stage. Daniel asked himself how much damage he was prepared to do to another person, but he didn't think about it for long. He measured the crack in the wood with his eyes, and then felt gently around the floor by his body until he had the metal coat hanger in his hands. Under the cover of the man's fidgeting, he straightened the curve of the coat hanger and stabbed it through the crack and into the flesh of the man's ankle driving it in as far as he could then twisting.

The man shrieked in agony as Daniel pushed the steps aside and got to his feet, blood rushing away from his head and making it spin. He kicked the man, hard, in the ankle he'd just stabbed, and there was another scream of pain. As he ran for the door, he felt the man grab at him. Daniel punched, and felt the punch connect. He was at the door, barely visible in the darkness, but he felt for the handle and turned. Nothing happened.

He heard a gasping laugh behind him and spun around.

"Give me the key," he said.

"Fuck off."

Daniel took a step towards the man and saw the gun. They were so close together that Daniel imagined that he could see the bullet at the end of the barrel, poised and waiting.

"You're not going to shoot me, because your boss needs me alive," he said, and waited a split second for the man to contradict him. As the man opened his mouth, Daniel kicked him again, this time in the balls, and as he gasped and grabbed his crotch, Daniel kicked him on the still bleeding ankle, then body slammed him into the stage. The man still held the gun, but it was trapped underneath his body. Daniel grabbed his hair and banged the man's head against the wood of the stage, hearing the crack of cartilage as his nose broke and blood flooded out.

"Key." Daniel said, and banged the man's head on the stage again. The man grunted. Daniel put his hands round the man's neck and began to squeeze.

"MALDWYN," said Wade Addison, "I was expecting you."

"Here I am," said Mal, "What do you want?"

"I want you to do me a small favour, and in exchange I will return Daniel to you, and at the same time, rid your little town of some major criminals. Major by small town standards anyway."

And Mal knew he had been right. Addison was bankrolling Connor, Addison had set up the letting companies and the equity release scheme, with Barry Kettles to run it for him.

"Why did you let Connor wreck all your hard work?" Mal asked. "You were making millions on that equity release scheme, steady money, perfectly legal, laundering dodgy cash, and he came in and fucked it all up."

Mal saw the mask slip. Only a tiny amount, and only for a moment, but Mal saw anger behind the bland expression.

"You don't need to answer," Mal said, "I know why you want to save him, but he'll only screw up again. How long was he in Melin? Six months? Where are you going to send him this time?"

The mask slipped again. "It doesn't matter. Do you want Daniel alive or not?"

The noise came without warning, from beneath their feet. Shouting and a single gunshot, unmistakable. Then silence.

37: YOU CAN KEEP HIM

Daniel found the police ID in Andy Carter's pocket, along with the key to the door, a smashed phone and a couple of useful cable ties. Daniel had let go of Carter's neck before he lost consciousness and grabbed the gun while he was gasping for breath. Carter had held on, so hard that Daniel thought he might have to break the man's fingers, but then the gun had gone off, the bullet hitting the ceiling and bringing down a shower of plaster. The shock had given Daniel control.

"Let's take a walk," said Daniel, "because I am so sick of this place."

He prodded Carter in front of him up a set of stairs to what looked like the service entrance. It too was locked, and Daniel knew Carter had no more keys. He thought about trying to shoot the lock until it opened, but he remembered reading somewhere that it wasn't as easy as it looked in the movies. There must be another way out. Also, if Mal was here ... The corridor was dark, but Daniel could see light ahead, so that's the way they went, Carter in front, stumbling on his injured leg, face covered in blood. Daniel knew he should feel regret. He felt none.

There were two people standing in a lighted area, at the bottom of a magnificent staircase, and one of the people was Mal. When the other one spoke, he realised that it was Wade Addison.

"Ah, Daniel, I knew you must be around somewhere."

"I've brought your tame cop back."

"You can keep him."

Mal looked at Daniel and thought *whatever it takes, we're both leaving here.*

"Sorry he's a bit battered, like," said Daniel, "but he is yours. I don't think Manchester Police will want him."

Suddenly, Addison took a step forward and pushed Andy Carter to the ground.

"I *said* I didn't want him." The gun appeared in Addison's hand as if by magic, and he shot Andy in the head without hesitation. He stepped backwards, and pointed the gun at Mal.

"Now then, we've got that out of the way. You both needed to know what you're dealing with. I'm really not a nice man, though I can put on a good show if I have to. I'm here to negotiate. Colin's records disappear, Colin disappears and you two can go home and play house together. It's that simple."

"It isn't," said Daniel, "there's an arrest warrant out for Connor slash Colin from the Met, see. We can't make that disappear. Our own records, sure, but he's got a suspended sentence, and he does keep murdering people, and the courts don't like that."

"There's only so many times a person can change their name," added Mal, "if they will carry on committing the same offences, and leaving their fingerprints everywhere, then they're going to get nicked."

"And I hate to bring it up, but you just shot a policeman. Not an honest policeman, but still a policeman, and you did it in front of two witnesses. It's going to be hard for us to forget that." And Mal knew that Daniel was telling the truth. Neither of them was going to forget it. Though if something didn't change, they wouldn't be remembering for very long.

"We seem to have reached an impasse," said Addison, "I have a gun, and Daniel has a gun. He can't shoot me before I can shoot Maldwyn. It's also possible that I can shoot both of you, because as I've demonstrated, I can do it. I'm not sure about Daniel."

"I am," said Mal, "he'll shoot you if he has to. Also, you haven't taken into account that there's an armed response unit outside this building. This building that you showed me round, so that I could describe it in great detail to my colleagues, inside and out."

Addison laughed. "Now I know you're lying. Andy Carter might have been a useless tosser, but he has been following you since you arrived in Manchester. You haven't told anyone."

"The laugh's on you, mate," said Mal, "I told Clwyd police, not Manchester. Have a look out of the windows, but try not to give them a head shot."

A voice called down the stairs. "Wade. Wade, the place is crawling with cops."

Addison's gun hand never wavered, but his eyes looked up to where Connor was shouting from above. Daniel saw the movement and took a wild shot up into the roof, and Mal took the chance to dive at Addison's legs. It almost worked but Addison was quick, his shot going into Mal's shoulder, burning every piece of tissue and bone it struck on its way through. But he had knocked Addison down, and before he could recover, Daniel kicked him in the head. Then he grabbed Mal and pulled him away from the staircase into another dark corridor, and then into the big room Addison had shown Mal as a possible restaurant.

"Where did he get you?"

"Shoulder. Jesus but it hurts."

"Get me your phone, I need to look."

With the light from Mal's phone, Daniel could see that while the bullet had missed vital things like heart and lungs, it was a bad wound, and Mal was losing blood fast. He ripped off his jacket and then his shirt "Hold this against it", he said, doing his best to tie the shirt around the ripped flesh. "Now who am I ringing?"

"Sophie, Bethan, Hart, any of them. They called out the cavalry."

Daniel hit the first name he came to, and Hart spoke. "Kent?"

"No, ma'am, Owen. Mal's been shot. Shoulder injury, lots of blood loss. Addison is here and he's armed, and he's killed one man already. Also Connor Byrne Jones, aka Colin Bryson Jones. I don't know if he's armed. Mal needs urgent medical attention, ma'am."

"There are ARUs all round the building, Daniel, but they won't come in until they know where the suspects are."

"I understand that ma'am, but I don't know where they are, and Mal needs help now."

"I'm giving this number to Chief Superintendent Salt ..."

Suddenly the lights came on and Daniel could see the huge empty room, with its intricate tiling, iron columns, and sculptured ceiling. And nowhere to hide. He heard shouts from the corridor, and doors slamming. He threw his tattered jacket back on, ended the phone call and shoved phone and gun into his pockets, and then, as gently as he could, helped Mal to his feet.

"Keep breathing, Maldwyn, and try not to bleed any more. We've got to get out of here without leaving a trail."

Daniel had seen two doors on the far side of the room. One of them, he hoped, would lead to another dark corridor, or better still, a way out. Mal was grey, but he kept moving. The first door they tried was an enormous store cupboard, the second led to another corridor, lit, but with the shouting getting louder, they were out of choices.

They ran down the corridor to a fire door. On the other side, the corridor was in blessed darkness.

"I know where we are," Mal whispered, "there should be some stairs along here," and he quickly described how the stairs led to another corridor and the gallery around the main staircase, "and maybe the way out."

"Let's hope."

The torch on Mal's phone lit the way past more open doors to the showrooms Mal had seen with Addison, and finally to the stairs.

Daniel put his arm round Mal's waist. "Lean on me, and *don't bleed*" he said, and Mal tried hard to smile. "I know, you're doing your best," Daniel said, "but I've seen you look better."

At the top of the stairs was another dark corridor with rooms on either side. Light showed around the fire door. They stopped and listened. Nothing.

"We should try the next floor up. Maybe no lights," said Daniel, "We need to call Hart again."

Up the next flight they went, and seeing another fire door with light showing underneath, up again, and this time, the whole floor was dark. Daniel breathed a sigh of relief. They could choose one of the rooms, barricade the door and they'd be safe while they decided what to do next. He guided a visibly sagging Mal into one of the rooms and found that it still had a key in the lock. Even better, the key turned.

Mal had slid down onto the floor, his back to the wall, barely managing so sit up. With the light of the torch, Daniel could see that the makeshift bandage was soaked with blood, and that there were beads of sweat standing out on Mal's fore-head. He sat down next to Mal, so Mal could lean against him, and got out the phone. There were missed calls from Hart, from Wade Addison, from Megan and from an unknown number. Before he could choose, the phone vibrated with the unknown number.

38: NOT A SALES CALL

"Owen," Daniel said, hoping it wasn't a Chinese woman trying to tell him about a parcel delivery. "Chief Superintendent Salt. What can you tell me?"

"That my colleague is seriously injured, and that I have no idea where any of the suspects are, sir."

"That's not helpful, Owen."

"No, sir. Sorry, sir."

Mal took Daniel's hand and squeezed. Daniel could read his expression which said *co-operate.* Daniel imagined the dozens of armed officers outside the building, hot coffee and donuts on tap, and the two of them, trapped here in the dark, too afraid to move. Andy Carter's death was on his conscience and would be for a long time. But Mal was right. He took a breath.

"Sir, we're hiding in a room on the top floor of the building. I figured that we'd be harder to find in the dark, and all the other floors are lit up. We last heard the suspects on the ground floor, just after the lights came on. We haven't heard anything since. I don't know if there are more people than Addison and Connor slash Colin. Addison has a gun, and I have the one I took from Andy Carter. I'm not firearms trained, but I think Mal, sorry, DCI Kent is." Mal nodded, "He is, sir."

"Are you on the street side of the building?"

Mal nodded. And then went very still. "Yes, sir."

"Then come to the window and show a light."

Daniel did, and then went back to sit with Mal. The window was cracked in several places and the cold was starting to bite.

"Right then, Owen, here's what you need to do. As far as we can tell, there is only one entrance to the building, at least only one that's in use. It leads into the basement and it's locked. There's also a hoist up the outside and onto the roof, used for building materials. If you can get to the hoist, we can use it to bring you down. As far as we know there's only the two of you Addison and Bryson Jones. We stopped two other people trying to get in, and they're in custody. Once you're out, we can wait until Addison gives himself up, or it gets light. There's no way we're coming into that labyrinth in the dark."

Daniel didn't want to leave the safety of the locked room. If Addison spent the whole night searching, he might find them, but they had a gun, and they could defend themselves. The armed officers knew where they were. Except that as long as they were in the building, there was the chance that Addison could use them as hostages. And it was cold and getting colder. The place was filthy. Mal was bleeding, if not as badly as before, and they had nothing left to use as bandages. Mal was already in shock, and the longer he stayed here, the worse it would get.

"We have to go, lovey," he said, "and I can't carry you."

"No problem," said Mal, "but you might have to help me up."

"We are getting out of here," Daniel said, "you and me. We just have to get onto the roof and round to the back and they'll get us from there."

"S'OK," said Mal, "I know the way. You and me."

He told Daniel about the door onto the roof from the top of the main staircase. "Then it's mostly flat to where the hoist comes up. Lots of big chimneys." He hoped that Addison was holed up in his comfortable office downstairs, rather than in his rooftop eyrie.

Turning the key in the lock of the door was one of the hardest things Daniel had ever done. Everything inside him was shouting *we're safe here*. He put his left arm round Mal's waist, gave Mal the gun, to hold in his good hand, and he held the torch. They stepped into the corridor, and Daniel switched off the light.

"If you see anyone, Mal, shoot them. Don't warn them, just shoot them." Mal nodded, then wished he hadn't as his left shoulder exploded in agony, again.

The corridor was lit at intervals by the light of the city through dirty windows, where doors to the empty rooms were open. They stood for a while to listen, and to get their eyes used to the darkness without the light from the torch. As long as there are enough doors open, we'll be OK, Daniel thought.

Their progress towards the central staircase was slow. They could barely see, and in places the floor was slippery where birds had got in and left their droppings. In other places, they could just make out mushrooms growing in the wet wood and feel blasts of cold air where the windows were completely missing.

Addison hadn't brought Mal to this part of the building on his tour, and Mal could see why. Addison had stayed where he could describe his vision of a grand refurbishment, ignoring the reality of decay beyond repair. Some of the rooms downstairs might look as if they just needed a good clean up, but this? This needed more than imagination and a few stolen toilets.

As they reached the central staircase, the corridor brightened, the glow of light coming from below. They stayed in the dark while Mal pointed out the door onto the roof and the 'secret floor'.

"If he's up here, that's where he'll be hiding," whispered Mal, "But there's no lights, and he's got a warm and cosy office downstairs."

"But he's also mad," Daniel whispered back, "I guess we'll find out."

Keeping as close to the wall as they could, they circled the grand staircase to the door, then stood and listened. All they could hear was the sound of the wind outside. Daniel turned the handle and pushed the door with his arm outstretched, so he wouldn't be a target against the dim light. Nothing moved.

Daniel stepped through the door, still holding Mal round the waist, feeling the weight more, as Mal became weaker. Mal followed, and they were on the roof. Mal pointed with the gun, between the chimneys and the entrance to Addison's hoped-for future home.

"There," he whispered.

They started towards the other side of the roof, stepping into the shadow of the row of chimneys. Daniel felt Mal struggling to breathe, sagging against him.

"Wait," he said. Then he steered Mal into the deepest of the shadows and lowered him onto the roof, crouching next to him. "I'm going to tell them to bring up the lift, and it'll make a noise. If it brings Wade and Connor, I'll distract them, and you'll have to shoot them. Just don't shoot me. Are you going to be OK?"

Daniel saw Mal gather his last shreds of energy. "I'll be fine."

Daniel texted Chief Superintendent Salt. *We're on the roof. Bring the lift up. No sign of suspects.*

They didn't need an OK. to know that the message had been received. The clank and whine of the hoist heaving itself into action told them it was on its way. In less than a minute, a louder clank told them that it was at the top.

Salt's text read *get onto platform, close gate, and press blue button to descend.*

Mal tapped Daniel's arm with the gun. "Heard something." They waited and listened. Nothing. But Daniel remembered how long Addison had waited in silence in the basement. If he was there, and they stepped out of the shadows together, he would kill them. The only way to be sure that they were alone was to try to draw Addison out.

"Can you shoot him, if you see him?" Daniel asked Mal, not knowing whether he meant *can you kill someone* or *are you physically strong enough to pull the trigger?*

"Easily. Go." He tried to put more confidence into his voice than he felt.

Daniel needed to move fast enough to get behind the next set of chimneys without getting shot, because if Addison was hidden behind the door to his secret storey, he would have to come out of hiding to shoot *and then Mal will kill him.*

Daniel exploded from behind the chimneys and ran. He didn't reach the second set of chimneys.

"Bastard!" yelled Connor, leaping across the roof for Daniel. "You're a fucking dead man!" They went down in a tangle of legs and arms, Daniel underneath and Connor determined on revenge for everything he thought Daniel had done to ruin his life. Connor landed blow after blow as Mal watched, unable to help.

He had to watch, and wait, as Daniel tried to get enough purchase on the roof to throw Connor off balance, and somehow, he had to get to his feet, because Mal knew that Connor was only the distraction. That if — when — Daniel won the fight, Addison would step out of the shadows, and Mal wanted to get there before he had the chance.

And then he saw Addison. Silhouetted against the city sky,

leaning over the railing, sending the hoist back down, cutting off their escape. The noise covered Mal's grunts as he got to his feet, and shuffled as close as he dared, before raising the gun. He aimed for the middle of the body, as he'd been trained, and missed. But it was enough. Addison spun round and lost his balance. Mal fired again as Addison staggered, and then he was gone, over the edge of the roof. He didn't scream.

As for Connor, it was all over bar the shouting. Daniel was holding on to Connor, as Mal had done at Hector's house, arm twisted up his back.

"There's a cable tie in my pocket Mal," Daniel called, "or you could just shoot him."

The adrenaline from Addison falling was enough to get Mal over to Daniel's side, and feeling in Daniel's pocket for a cable tie. Somehow, between them, they tied Connor's hands behind him. Daniel got the phone out and called Salt.

"Send the hoist up again please, sir, and someone with a set of handcuffs for a prisoner."

39: GROWING ROOM

Mal was discharged from hospital with his shoulder bandaged and strapped, a warning to take it easy for at least two weeks, and a bag full of painkillers and antibiotics. Daniel had collected Mal's clothes and car from the hotel and drove them back to Melin Tywyll with great care. The house was warm, and Megan had left mountains of food, and a promise to visit the next day to check Mal's dressing.

They ate on their knees, looking out of the windows at the crocuses starting to come up in the garden. The sky was a hard, bright blue, and they could see across the valley through the silhouettes of leafless trees.

"I ache all over," said Daniel, "I don't think there is any part of my body that doesn't hurt." He didn't want to talk about his aches and pains, but he didn't know how to talk about everything that had happened. He wanted to, but he couldn't think how to start. "Do you want some builder's tea?" he asked Mal.

"No. Yes. In a bit. I want to say sorry first."

Daniel looked at Mal, unshaven, smelling of the hospital, and sitting twisted on the sofa so that there was no pressure on his wound. Mal's eyes looked dark, and his expression was troubled. He reached for Daniel's hand. Daniel moved everything out of the way and leaned against him.

"Sorry? What for?"

"Lying about the job. Putting you in danger. Getting shot. Not telling my mother to take a hike."

"That's a lot. I've got a list of sorrys of my own."

Mal tried to smile.

"I thought we were going to die, and it would have been my fault," Mal said, "Once he shot Andy Carter, I was sure he was going to kill us too. He was mad, and I didn't see it. I knew he was a crook, and everyone said he was violent, but I didn't see that he was mad. I told myself that we would get out of there, but I didn't believe it. I hoped that Hart would call out the cavalry, but until Connor said he'd seen them ... If I hadn't lied to you, it wouldn't have happened."

Mal sounded defeated, which was how Daniel felt. As if he'd been training for a race for months, been posting brilliant times, and then come second. He took a deep breath and looked into the fire, away from Mal.

"I hurt Andy Carter. Badly hurt him, and I hate myself. I can't stop thinking about it. That's why I didn't try to shoot Addison when I had the chance. I might have missed, probably would, but I didn't even try. So, he shot you. And I was afraid to leave that room and go onto the roof, and I hate myself for that, too."

Bleakness had entered Daniel's soul. That was the only word for it. He had no interest in anything except staring at the garden and waiting for the time to pass. Mal was silent. Daniel had thought that if they talked, he might feel better. It hadn't worked.

The sun was shining, neither of them was dead, and yet they sat in defeated emptiness.

When Mal's phone rang he looked and rejected the call. It

rang again, and again, and the third time, he answered, "Huw. Now isn't a great time."

Mal looked at Daniel. "He'll be here in five minutes. He says there's something he wants to tell us." They had the same thought. *Great. So, neither of us will be going to the wedding.*

But when Huw arrived he laughed at them. "Don't be fucking stupid, you're both still invited to the wedding. I've come to take you out for a posh lunch in Chester."

They didn't want to go.

"Look, you're going. You look like shit, but I've promised Rhi and Sasha that I'd bring you, and I'm not turning up without you. Get changed. Have a shave, brush your hair. Ten minutes."

Huw collapsed on to the sofa and started playing games on his phone.

"Go on." He waved them away.

When they returned, Huw was chatting to Hector, who had dropped in for a chat.

"Hector has been telling me what's been going on here," said Huw, "and not just the edited highlights that I saw on the police email." He turned to Hector. "I think you deserve a posh lunch in Chester too, mate."

Hector tried to protest, but Huw bulldozed the objections away.

Daniel thought that it was the second time he'd been kidnapped, and the gloom lifted a tiny bit, enough to notice what a beautiful day it was.

"Jesus Daniel, if anyone had told me that getting married was such hard work, I'd have told Huw to stuff his ring where the sun don't shine." Rhiannon had been trying on wedding dresses all morning.

"Nothing any good?" Daniel asked.

"They're all bloody gorgeous," said Rhiannon, "but seriously, a grand for a dress? That I'll only wear once? Go to Chester they said, much more upmarket than Cardiff, they said, much more expensive too, they didn't say."

Rhiannon's sister Sasha was looking at the menu. Both the sisters were tall and thin, unworried by the thought of three courses of Italian food and a bottle of wine.

"Well, if they are all gorgeous, why not just buy the cheapest?" Daniel asked, his face as innocent as he could make it. He remembered the stress of Megan's wedding; the endless shopping trips, the decisions about who to invite, who would be offended if not invited, who wouldn't come if someone else turned up. For something that was supposed to be a 'small' wedding, it had taken the logistical effort of moving a tank battalion across the Grand Canyon. With the Colorado in flood.

Sasha looked at her sister. "You may as well tell them Rhi. It's going to be obvious by May anyway. She needs *growing room* in her dress." And winked heavily.

Daniel grinned. "Hey! Congratulations Rhiannon. And Huw."

"That's why I made you come," Huw said, "We were going to do a proper announcement, but as usual Sash gets in first."

Mal smiled too, at the thought of being Uncle Mal. He had other nephews and nieces, but he'd never met any of them, but this one, he just might get to know.

Rhiannon blushed, then grinned too. "It's ace. We're so excited I can't tell you. It's due two months after the wedding, can you believe it? My day as a princess, and I'm going to look like a barrage balloon, but I don't care.

"You are both still coming? You haven't come to lunch because you're not coming?"

"Mal's going to be there," said Daniel, "Not sure about me."

Their joint shriek caused every eye in the restaurant to swivel in their direction. It was only a small place, in a chi chi area of Chester in between a bicycle shop and an artisan bakery. It was simple and elegant, mid-century wood, chrome and glass. There was a *very* upmarket wedding dress shop on the next street.

"It's alright," Sasha said, a little too loudly, "they're taking us back to the locked ward after lunch." All the starers looked down at their food, and the waitress wondered if they were ready to order.

"Sorry," Sasha said, "bit of bad news. Antipasti all round, not all meat, those two don't eat it, then lasagne for me and a glass of Prosecco. A big glass." She looked at the others expectantly. They ordered quickly and then the assault began, though more quietly.

Daniel explained about Shirley's visit, and how he'd offered not to go to the wedding.

"You're going," said Mal, "Or I'm not. Both or neither. I should have told Mam when she came to visit, but I'm a coward. Sorry, Huw."

"But your Dad?" Daniel said, thinking that Mal might be many things, but a coward wasn't one of them.

"That's up to him. It's Huw and Rhiannon's wedding, they can ask who they like."

"And we asked *you, both of you,*" said Rhiannon.

"That fucking," Sasha began then lowered her voice and leaned forwards, "your fucking family, Maldi, are a fucking nightmare. My way or the highway, that's your dad, and bloody Shirley goes along with it. Young Dai and Lewis are just as bad, and the girls both married Cardiff boys and drag them back every Sunday for lunch. I'm surprised any of them are going to the wedding at all to be honest."

"Huw's not like the rest of them," Rhiannon said, "but maybe I'm biased. Sorry love, it's your family, I don't get to diss them." But Huw smiled at her as if she could say what she liked.

"I think," Sasha said, "we can't please all of the people all of the time."

Their starters arrived, and served as a distraction. Daniel thought that it couldn't be more awkward. Huw was a police officer, a uniformed sergeant, but Mal's father refused to forgive Mal for joining the Met, after the way London police had treated striking miners in the 1980s.

"He can be a bit of a bully, big Dai, I mean, but he is Huw's dad," said Rhiannon.

"And Daniel is your friend, the one who introduced you to Huw, remember?"

"I haven't forgotten, Sash." Rhiannon turned to Daniel. "We want you there. *I* want you there." She reached for his hand. Daniel blinked hard.

"It was Mal's choice," he said.

"And I made it," said Mal, in his best *I'm not talking about this anymore* voice.

The rest of their food came and fulfilled its billing as *a posh lunch*. Mal had ordered pasta that he could eat one handed, because of his shoulder. They talked about everything except weddings and crime. Daniel entertaining them with his efforts to build enough wardrobes for Mal's clothes, Sasha and Rhiannon relating their battles with the council's 'Child Literacy Scheme'. "I said, how does closing the library help more children to read?" Sasha said. "It's like 1984. Doublethink. I said that too. Most of them didn't know what I was on about." She shook her head in despair. Then she looked up at Hector, who hadn't said much since being introduced.

"What about you, lovely, how come you know these two? We've made you sit through Maldi's mad family, Daniel's adventures in flat pack furniture and mine in twenty first century literacy."

Hector swallowed hard and took a fortifying swig of his wine.

"Hector's a pathologist," Daniel said, diagnosing heartburn from Hector's anguished expression.

A grin spread over Rhiannon's face. "Astrology is bollocks," said Sasha.

"Of course it is, but it was right today — Madam Arcarti told you to be open to a serendipitous encounter."

"She has this stupid app on her phone. Madame Arcarti. I ask you. She doesn't believe in it, but I have to listen to the prediction Every. Single. Fucking. Day."

"OK, I'll bite," said Mal, "how is meeting Hector serendipitous?"

"Because I've just been to an Open Day, and I'm applying to study Biomedical Science for September. I think it's totally fascinating, but I'm the only person I know that does. I'd love to see an autopsy."

"That can be arranged," said Hector, "What are you interested in, particularly?"

"Brains. And cells. And nutrition. All of it. How it fits together. But mainly brains. I was reading this thing about Alzheimer's and there were these amazing images."

"I see a lot of the effects of Alzheimer's in my work, but we need to be able to see into the brains while people are still alive."

"So, tell me about what you see when they are dead."

Hector pulled out his phone and started scrolling through his bookmarks. Huw stood up. "Maybe we should swap places Sash, because those are *so* not things I want to see when I'm eating."

Huw took Hector, Daniel and Mal back after lunch, and Daniel thanked him for making them go. Hector had promised Sasha an autopsy visit in Cardiff as soon as he could arrange it, and on the way back in the car, Daniel had teased him about what an excellent first date *that* would be. In the front seats, Huw and Mal were talking about the wedding, Huw saying that he had no problem if none of the rest of the family showed up. "And if they do come, they'd better behave." Tension had eased as they'd eaten and laughed, though Daniel could see that Mal needed rest and more painkillers.

But the bleakness had gone.

40: PLUS ÇA CHANGE

"Well, if you weren't so stubborn about taking painkillers, you'd have slept properly," Daniel said, "and then you'd be in a fit state to go to work."

"Watch my lips. I'm coming to the office."

"Only if you take some painkillers. You are not going to get addicted in the next week."

Daniel poured Mal another coffee and popped two of the tablets out of their blister pack. He put them on Mal's plate and waited. Nothing happened.

"No painkillers, no office."

Mal sighed and swallowed the tablets.

To be fair, Daniel had been awake most of the night too. He ached all over, and he hadn't taken any painkillers either. It was as if they were paying for Wade Addison and Andy Carter's deaths with their own pain, which Daniel knew was ridiculous, but knowing it was ridiculous didn't stop it.

They were due in Hart's office at ten. Daniel hadn't expected to see Chief Superintendent Salt there too, looking at home with a cup of coffee and a biscuit. Hart was in her usual suit and blouse combo, dark grey and teal today. Salt was a tall man, with sparse grey hair and drooping jowls. He looked as if he'd had as little sleep as Daniel and Mal.

They sat down and Mal started speaking. "I take full responsibility for what happened on Friday night," he said, "the mistakes were all mine."

Hart smiled. Salt took out his wallet, extracted a £10 note and placed it on Hart's desk. She weighted it down with a heavy glass paperweight. Daniel wasn't sure what he was seeing, but he wasn't letting Mal take all the blame. "Ma'am, Sir..."

Salt held up his hand. "Stop there Owen, before I lose any more money. We aren't here to allocate blame, we're here to find out what happened, and to bring you up to date with the investigation. First things first, I can't be upset about Wade Addison's death. Yes, it would have been better to have him in custody, but I can live with it." Hart nodded throughout this speech.

Daniel knew that Mal had expected them both to be suspended, but he had hoped that they would find out what was happening with the case before they had to leave. It looked as if it might happen.

"First things first," said Hart, "you are both on desk duty until the investigation into Andy Carter and Wade Addison's death is complete. I want the first two weeks taken as sick leave, no arguments."

"Ma'am," they said simultaneously.

"Secondly, ballistics tests show clearly that Andy Carter was shot with Wade Addison's gun, and that Wade Addison was shot by a firearms officer stationed on the building next door to the Burns and Wood. You will both be required to make statements about what happened, but for now we just want you to talk us through it."

Salt put his phone pointedly on the desk, with the microphone app showing.

Daniel described the drive away from Hector's, the hallucinations and waking up in the basement of the Burns and Wood, hiding under the stage, listening to Wade saying that Mal was there, and attacking Andy Carter.

"I needed to get out of there, ma'am ..." Daniel didn't want to think about how he'd injured Andy Carter, how he'd deliberately inflicted maximum damage on a fellow human and done so as efficiently and cold-bloodedly as he could.

"He was armed, Daniel," Hart said, "what you did was proportionate to the threat."

The words didn't make Daniel feel any less miserable.

Mal said "We never expected Addison to kill Andy Carter. But I knew he had the reputation for extreme violence. Daniel didn't."

"Enough." said Salt, "I *said* we're not allocating blame, we just want the story. DCI Kent, how did you come to go to the Burns and Wood building?"

Which was exactly the question Mal didn't want to answer. It must have showed on his face because Hart said that she had been wondering the same.

"Addison called me," Mal said, "he said that he had Daniel, and that he would kill him unless I did a "small favour" for him." Mal added air quotes. Then the words rushed out — how Mal knew he shouldn't go after Addison himself, but that he was afraid for Daniel, that Addison wouldn't negotiate with anyone else, and that he suspected that Andy Carter was corrupt, "so I thought that there might be other corrupt officers, sir."

"But you expected that Superintendent Hart would call us out to help you?"

"I was fairly certain that she would understand, sir. We'd talked about the operation, and I'd shared my doubts about it with her."

"Did you know that we arrested two men on their way into

the Burns and Wood building, both carrying illegal weapons, the two men that Jeffrey Coates was supposed to be meeting with?"

"Things might have been different if you hadn't, sir," said Mal. He looked at Daniel, who felt sick. Four people might not have been enough to search the whole building, in the dark, for Daniel and Mal, but they couldn't have fought off four people on the roof.

"In view of the outcome, it is unlikely that any serious disciplinary action will be taken against you, DCI Kent, but it won't be my decision," said Salt, "Between ourselves, Manchester Police are very happy to be rid of Addison, although less keen on the turf war that will happen to fill the vacuum."

"Can I ask about Connor?" Daniel said, and both Salt and Hart looked unhappy.

"You may ask," said Hart, "but I'm not sure that you'll like the answers."

"He's back in custody," said Salt, "and the toxicology has finally come through on both Arwyn Jones and Harriet Marston — both had ketamine in their systems, as did Hector and his coffee. Arwyn has been identified as having visited the North Wales Estates office on the morning of his death. We have statements placing Connor slash Colin in Harriet Marston's street the day she died. Barry Kettles had ketamine in his system too, but there is nothing to put Connor slash Colin anywhere near him. The CPS are thinking about it. No one *saw* anything. And we may think he was behind all the housing scams, but as of today, *proving* any of it looks like it's going to be hard work."

Daniel said that surely the combined testimonies of the Flowerses and Jeffrey Coates would sway the CPS.

"You'd think so, but don't hold your breath." Salt said.

"The good news is that the Flowerses are falling over themselves promising to bring all their properties up to standard," said Hart, "Veronica Brown alerted a whole bunch of people, and the Flowerses have come over all co-operative." Hart sounded cynical, and Daniel thought that the Flowerses owed far more than they would ever pay out.

"Melin Tywyll isn't the only place where these scams were going on," said Mal, and Daniel nodded.

"Only most of it isn't illegal, and the things that are illegal aren't our business," said Hart, "We might know that the equity release was money laundering, but Addison is dead, and there won't be any more deals made. There will be some hard questions asked in council offices, here and in Manchester, but we won't be involved in those investigations for months, if at all."

A few minutes later Daniel and Mal were on their way home, having been told not to return for at least two weeks, and then only if medically cleared.

Mal was exhausted, thought Daniel, although he wouldn't admit it. Daniel made lunch, and as they were eating Megan turned up to give them both the once over, and to bring more food for their freezer.

"You both need to *rest,* she said, "and take your painkillers. God. Misery is not attractive." She watched them swallow the tablets and gave Mal an additional lecture. "I know my brother is stupid, I thought that you were the one with some sense. I'm expecting to see an improvement by tomorrow. Promise, or I won't tell you the latest."

They promised.

"The Doctor Flowers are selling their practice, and their house, and leaving Melin. Rumour is they're going to live in Devon. It turns out that they own half the town, and that's all up for sale too. With Jenkins and Jenkins. There's a Closed Until Further Notice sign on North Wales Estates."

Daniel added the job losses of the two women who worked there to his pile of guilt.

He unpacked Mal's suitcase from his stay in Manchester

and found the leaflets from Addison's completed "Loft Apartments". He showed it to Mal.

"Is this what he wanted for the Burns and Wood building?" Daniel asked.

"I think so. Only I don't think he would ever have been able to pull it off. I think that parts of the Burns and Wood had gone too far to renovate. He showed me round, but just the best bits. If I'd seen the rest, I might have guessed just how mad he was."

"Do you like these flats?" Daniel gestured to the leaflet.

"Yes, I do. It's like being in the heart of things. Life going on all around you."

"That's how I feel about being here," Daniel said.

The next day brought another visit from Megan with news that Arwyn's funeral had been arranged for the following week, and that Megan had been forced to stop Helena going round to Lizzie's house to tell her not to dare attending. Megan said that she'd been herself, and that she'd liked Lizzie a lot. "I told her about the funeral, and she said she wouldn't dream of going and upsetting Helena. Nice woman."

In the afternoon, Hector turned up, "to see how you are." They told him they were fine, and he laughed. "Not you're not. I did train as a doctor remember. I wasn't always dissecting corpses." He'd been in touch with Sasha, and she was going to see an autopsy in Cardiff, carried out by one of his friends. He thought that he might go along too.

By the time of Megan's next visit, they were going stir crazy. She gave them permission to visit the pub, "but only shandy, and not too much of it with those painkillers." Daniel rang Sophie to ask her if she wanted to come along and bring Bob. She brought Veronica as well, both wearing shy smiles at being together. Mal claimed Bob straight away, stroking the dog with his good hand, and trying not to wince too obviously when Bob rolled onto his bad arm, by accident, trying to get a belly rub.

"So, Bob was right about Connor?" Sophie said, "To be

honest I can't stand those books with talking cats, or crime solving dogs, but I have to say that Bob was right on the money with Connor." She'd taken over Daniel's work on domestic abuse, and something in her manner suggested that she would be continuing with it. Daniel remembered the way Sophie had looked at Harriet Marston's body, and thought *this is personal.*

Sophie also told them about North Wales Estates closing, along with two other estate agents — one in Llangollen and another in Prestatyn. "And I saw Bethan, and she says that those flats you went to see by the river seem to have been abandoned. No workmen there for a week."

Veronica had news from the council. "A couple of suspensions in Planning and Building Control. Very hush, hush, lots of rumours."

A visit from Bethan brought information about Roderick Marston. "Wife's kicked him out, and he's looking at going bankrupt." Bethan said, with some satisfaction.

The doctor told Daniel that he could go back to work if he insisted but advised another week at least. "Why not go somewhere warm?" Daniel asked Mal if he wanted to go and lie on a beach somewhere. "No, he said, "but what about going to see the pyramids?" So that's what they did, and the desert sunshine warmed Daniel through to his bones. He was overwhelmed by Cairo and retreated to the shade of their hotel courtyard and pool, while Mal wandered through the city, coming back with photographs and souvenirs. The crush of people, the endless noise of car horns blowing, the shouting, and begging, and offers of things for sale, seemed to energise Mal as much as they enervated Daniel. But the evenings eating under the palm trees and glittering lamps, then strolling back to their hotel in the warm darkness, were things Daniel wouldn't forget.

They got back to find the turf war over Addison's empire in full swing, and that Barry Kettles had been a longstanding and active member of Melin Tywyll golf club and was much missed.

Hector kept mentioning visits to Sasha, before finally admitting that he was going to be her plus one at Rhiannon and Huw's wedding.

Mal's shoulder took a long time to heal, so Daniel drove him to Manchester to give evidence about Declan Hughes' arrest, and the search that led to the discovery of the gun in the knitting basket. Daniel sat in the public gallery as and watched Mal, in one of his best black suits, and his arm in a sling, tell the court about Hughes running away from his mother's house in his underpants. Afterwards, they had lunch by the canal, and walked past the Burns and Wood building, daring themselves without speaking. It was as abandoned as the riverside flats in Melin Tywyll. A new For Sale sign stuck out from the facade above the door.

"Salt offered me a job," said Mal.

"You didn't mention it." Daniel replied. They'd been talking more, since Egypt, about things that mattered, but still, a job offer was a big thing not to have mentioned.

"I'm mentioning it now," said Mal, "mainly because I've turned it down."

"So, you wouldn't have told me if you'd said yes?"

"No, you idiot, I'd have asked your opinion. I didn't need to think about it. I think this is a great city, but everything about it reminds me of that night. I thought I'd lost you."

"Salt didn't offer me a job," said Daniel.

"Actually, he did. Or rather, he sounded me out about whether you'd consider leaving Clwyd. I said I'd ask. So, I'm asking."

Daniel looked around. It was warm, and the sun caught the water of the canal and lit up the rainbow flags flying from the bars and cafes. The streets were busy, people starting to wear more colourful spring and summer clothes. Where they were, many of the buildings had been cleaned, and there were bay trees in pots, and tables with umbrellas, along the pavement.

He could hear music from the bar nearest to them. It was urban, and civilised. There were great concert halls, libraries and art galleries. There were sports facilities fit for international competition. He'd loved being a student in Manchester.

"There are no owls here," he said, "and the trees are in pots."

"That'll be a no then," said Mal.

"I'm a country mouse," said Daniel.

41: MR DARCY

The sun rose on the day of the wedding, and it wasn't messing around. The past few days had been chilly, but this morning the temperature was headed for high numbers, so Daniel couldn't help a small giggle as he straightened Mal's pale grey waistcoat over the wing collared shirt and bow tie.

"I am going to *boil*" Mal said, "and you will be in white linen, white linen that *I have ironed.*"

"You only have to wear the coat for the actual wedding," Daniel said, "I don't think that the photographs will take longer than an hour, and they won't *all* be in the sun."

Rhiannon had chosen an empire line dress, to hide the growing bump, and as it made her look like a Jane Austen heroine, had insisted on Huw and Mal wearing morning dress. Sasha had a similar dress, though as she complained, loudly and often, not the cleavage to match her pregnant sister.

"You look exactly like Mr Darcy," said Daniel, "but sexier." He went to put his arms around Mal, who pushed him away.

"I am not ironing that shirt again, Daniel," he said.

"Linen creases."

"Not before the wedding it doesn't."

Huw pushed the door open with a crash, demanding to know if they were ready.

"Two Mr Darcys," said Daniel, fanning himself.

"Never mind that, I'm not risking being a second late. Show me the rings."

Mal produced the rings, and put them back in his waistcoat pocket, making sure Huw saw him do it. Then Daniel helped him into the tailcoat and took a photograph of them both, against the linen fold panelling of the bedroom. Only the "Bridal Party" had bedrooms in the main house — everyone else was in a modern annex.

The ceremony would take place in the vast hall at the bottom of the curved stairs, allowing the bride to walk slowly down, with every eye upon her, to be met by Huw and escorted to the registrar.

Rhiannon kept them waiting for a carefully timed ten minutes, then she and Sasha, and Sasha's little girl Arwen, walked down the stairs, hand in hand, Rhiannon and Sasha's daughter holding flowers. There was a collective gasp of admiration from the crowd, and Huw's eyes filled with tears. Rhiannon's mother was openly sobbing into her husband's handkerchief. Of Mal's family there was no sign, but Daniel thought that it didn't matter. Huw only had eyes for his bride. He whispered "Wow," to Hector, who whispered "exactly." Hector was not looking at Rhiannon. Daniel nudged him. "The bride, look at the bride."

The ceremony was simple, sweet and short. There were poems, and a pianist. And champagne. The photographs were mercifully quick, and everyone had time to wander round the gardens before getting ready for dinner. Rhiannon insisted on Jane Austen outfits over dinner, and the first half an hour of dancing, "and then you can wear what you like. Except Huw.

Because I'm keeping this dress on, until the coach turns into a pumpkin."

It was warm enough to sit outside on one of the blankets provided by the venue. Mal lay with his back against a tree and Daniel leaned on him with a bottle of champagne in a cooler between them.

"Is this a bee-loud glade?" Daniel asked, taking a sip of champagne.

"There are bees," Mal replied, "but we're in Wales, and your name isn't Maud. How much of that champagne have you had?"

"Not enough. Because if you open your eyes, you will see that a convoy of handsome dark-haired people has just arrived and are making their way towards the happy couple."

Mal opened his eyes, saw his family and pulled Daniel closer. "Don't look," he said, "kiss me instead, and I won't complain about getting creases in your shirt."

"Don't you want to go and talk to them?"

"Honestly? No. If they come and talk to me, fine, I'll be polite. But it's a beautiful day, you look unbelievably sexy in that shirt, two lovely people just got married, Hector is playing with Sasha's daughter, and later there will be dancing. I'm leaving it up to them."

"Not even your mother?" And for the first time, Daniel thought Mal would answer and it would be OK.

"Nope, not even her. She's chosen not to upset my Dad, and that's her choice. My choice is to let go of feeling terrible about it. I'm glad they came for Huw, but I don't think they'll stay long, and I don't think Huw and Rhiannon will be joining the rest of them for the compulsory Sunday lunches round at Mam and Dad's. Huw's talking about looking for a transfer."

"And what about you, Maldwyn? Are you looking for a transfer?"

"If I did, would you come with me?"

"If I said no, would you stay?" Daniel asked

In answer, Mal took and handful of Daniel's shirt, and pulled him into the kiss. The champagne coursed through Daniel's blood, and the sunlight warmed his skin. He moved so that he could lie next to Mal, enclosed within his arms, their two bodies exchanging messages of love, and desire. They lay there together until they heard people begun to move back towards the house. Daniel propped himself up on one elbow, so that he could see. The dark-haired people were saying goodbye to Huw and Rhiannon.

"Your family are leaving," he said.

"Let them leave," Mal said, "I've got what I need right here."

IF YOU ENJOYED LEAVINGS

If you've enjoyed this book (and I hope you have) please tell other people by leaving a review. Two sentences is more than fine, no need for an essay. Until I started this self-publishing malarkey, I had no idea just how important reviews are, both for authors and other readers.

If you find an error, please tell me. I'm only human and errors are easily corrected (a great advantage for self-published ebooks).

You can email me at ripley@ripleyhayes.com

Or contact me on Facebook at Ripley Hayes Author

You can leave a review at:

Amazon.com

Amazon.co.uk

Goodreads

If you'd like bonus chapters and advance notice of the next books in the series, please sign up for my newsletter.

Sign up here

For pictures of places that may or may not be featured in the books, information about the other books in the series and other good stuff, have a look at my website at ripleyhayes.com

Big Thanks are due to: Denise Hayes, Austin Gwin, Bill Millward, the Octopeople, with special thanks to Jo Rabbani, and Lou Sugg.

Also thanks to everyone else who has taken time to be encouraging, on the interwebs and IRL. Shout out to 20books-to50k, as just one of the many encouraging groups on Facebook.

Cover Design by Pixel Studios

Copy Editing by Gillian Rodgerson

PLACES IN THIS BOOK

The Daniel Owen books are set in Wales. The towns and landscapes are typical of places in Wales, but these are novels, not guidebooks. You can visit stunning forests, mountains, beaches, towns and villages that may remind you of the ones in these books and you will find that they are almost crime free and full of friendly people, independent shops and cafes serving good food. But none of the places in the books exist except in my imagination.

The Welsh language is spoken all over the country. In some places you will hear more Welsh than English, in others, English is the default. The language is *debated* everywhere. 'Discussions' like those that Daniel and Mal have about Welsh are common. Legally the two languages have equal status, signs and official documents are in both, and every Welsh schoolchild either has Welsh lessons or is taught entirely through the medium of Welsh. The Welsh Government encourages adults to learn. I'm a Welsh learner, dividing my time between one area where Welsh is the default, and one where it is English. All these books have a few words in Welsh which I try to make clear in the context. I double check all the Welsh I use, but any mistakes are mine and I apologise for them.

Manchester has a plethora of textile warehouses which have been converted into flats, offices, bars and gyms. The descriptions of the Burns and Wood building are based on visits to the public areas of several of them. There are also still a few for sale, though I've never been inside a derelict on except via the internet.

Manchester Town Hall is *stunning*. The murals in the Great Hall are real and can be visited virtually.

Place Names

Melin Tywyll (phonetically something like Mellin Too-uth) is an imaginary town in north Wales. The name means Dark Mill, a hint to its past. It is set in the Black River Valley (Cwm Afon Ddu, phonetically Koom Avon Thee), also entirely imaginary.

Heddlu Clwyd (Hethlee Kloo-ud) is an imaginary north Wales police force. Clwyd is the traditional name for the area of north Wales covered by the modern counties of Wrexham, Conwy, Denbighshire and Flintshire.

Glamorgan Police (Heddlu Morgannwg, Hethlee Morgann-ug) is an imaginary south Wales police force. Glamorgan is the area of Wales covering the south coast from Cardiff to the Gower, and the Valleys to the north.

BOOKS IN THIS SERIES

1 : Undermined

Why don't the local police want to find out who dumped the body in the woods? Just how unpopular will DI Daniel Owen be if he investigates the murder himself? Why is DCI Kent always there when Daniel needs rescuing, and why is he so hostile the rest of the time?

The abandoned mine shafts give Daniel the creeps, especially when he finds another dumped body.

No one wants Daniel around. And no one wants DCI Kent around either. Unless the two men work together the murderer will go free.

2: Dark Water

It's not a good Monday for DI Daniel Owen. A body in a wheelie bin. Missing teenagers. His ex turning up as his new boss.

A secretive teenager, a nosy secretary, an idealistic social worker, and a dodgy fruit and veg salesman all have pieces of the jigsaw.

If Daniel and Maldwyn can trust each other again, they can put the pieces together. But time is running out, and at least one child's life is in danger.

It's been raining for weeks, and the flood waters are rising, threatening to engulf them all.

3: Leavings

Setting up a new home with Mal was all fun and flat pack furniture for Daniel. Until Mal disappears on an undercover operation, leaving Daniel on his own to deal with three dead bodies, and trying to help a friend escape an abusive relationship.

A man is violently assaulted in town and Daniel is warned that if he investigates, he'll get the same treatment. He knows the three bodies were murder victims, but he can't prove it.

Mal is getting more and more secretive. His friend Hector insists that the bruises happened when he ran into a door. Daniel is fighting unseen enemies without any of the information he needs.

And then there's Mal's family who want to pretend Daniel doesn't exist.

4: A Man

An early morning run. An abandoned child. A dead family.

Did John Edwards slaughter his wife and daughters, then kill himself? Why did the little boy survive the massacre? What are the hippies next door hiding?

DI Daniel Owen needs to be on top form for this one, but his last case won't leave him alone. His boyfriend's past won't leave either of them alone. Daniel and Mal need to talk, because not talking will tear them apart.

Then they find the next body.

. . .

5: Too Many Fires

Daniel Owen is barely holding things together when an old flame crashes into his life, with a dead body and enough emotional baggage to sink a ship.

Then the fires start.

Who is Jonathan Cole, and why is he living at a run down holiday park? Did he kill the park's owner? Daniel wants to believe Jonathan is innocent, and Jonathan wants to seduce Daniel. Mal, now Superintendent Kent, wants to come home. His undercover officer has disappeared from the same holiday park, and that can't be a coincidence, can it?

No matter where they look, Jonathan's past is engulfing them all in flames.

Manufactured by Amazon.ca
Bolton, ON